PRAISE FOR CATCH AND RELEASE

This was so spicy that I needed to find a bathroom afterward.

— JON (VANESSA'S HUSBAND)

Welp. That's a lot of sex.

— PAPA (VANESSA'S GRANDFATHER)

There's a lot of licking and fucking. When are they going to *make love*?

— NANA (VANESSA'S GRANDMOTHER)

D1522037

CATCH AND RELEASE

A SMALL TOWN NEIGHBORS-TO-LOVERS
ROMANCE

BEACH BABES SERIES
BOOK 1

VANESSA WILDER

For anyone who ever believed in me.
Thank you for not letting me give up on writing.

CONTENT WARNING

Dear reader,

While this book is a light-hearted, steamy contemporary romance, it also contains sensitive subjects that may be triggering to some readers.

The female main character in this book explores how cheating exes have shaped her. None of the cheating is on-page—not even as flashbacks—but the content may be upsetting to some readers.

Your mental health matters—check in with yourself before reading.

Here is a full list of triggers:

- Cheating (referenced, off page, she catches an ex at dinner with another woman)
- Death of parents (referenced, off page)
- Death of grandparents (referenced, off page)
- Explicit sex scenes between consenting adults (intended for readers 18+)
- Foul language
- Alcohol consumption

Take care of yourself. Not every book is for everyone.

XO,
   Vanessa Wilder

PLAYLIST

Vigilante Shit by Taylor Swift
Truth Hurts by Lizzo
Soak Up the Sun by Sheryl Crow
Catch And Release by The Wild Reeds
Island in the Sun by Weezer
Heartache on the Dance Floor by Jon Pardi
Partition by Beyonce
Sex With Me by Rihanna
Summer Girl by HAIM
Turn Me On by Norah Jones
Sex on Fire by Kings of Leon
Neon Moon - with Kacey Musgraves by Brooks & Dunn
Give In to Me by Garrett Hedland and Leighton Meester
I Wish I Was by The Avett Brothers

PROLOGUE

Willa was surprisingly calm when she found out her boyfriend of two years had a wife and child.

Oh, she was pissed.

She was fucking furious.

But she'd always had the gift of level-headedness in stressful situations. And besides, she wasn't going to make a scene at her favorite brunch place, and especially not in front of his daughter.

No, Willa would leave the responsibility of this particular childhood trauma to Leo. He was already off to such a smashing start.

But that didn't mean she'd let him continue with a perfectly pleasant Sunday morning.

Fuck, no.

Her day was ruined.

Scratch that. Her *year* was ruined.

Not to mention, she'd never be able to come back to her favorite restaurant again without thinking about his cheating ass. All she'd wanted were some eggs benedict and bottomless mimosas with her roommate, Charlie. Now, she was going to go home, throw up, and try to figure out how she found herself in this embarrassing, horrifying, and heartbreaking situation.

Again.

But not until she made sure he knew that she knew.

That motherfucker.

God, what an absolute *ass*. He *knew* this was her favorite brunch spot. He deserved to get caught, that cheating bastard. She stood across the street from Chadwick's and took a deep breath.

In for four counts, out for eight counts.

In four.

Out eight.

Again. And again.

As she performed this breathing exercise, Willa observed Leo and his family from afar. His daughter clung to his wife, her blonde pigtails bouncing as she played peek-aboo with people at a nearby table. Willa guessed she was about two years old, which meant Leo likely started dating her right around the time his daughter was born.

How did she let herself fall in love with such a *fucking jerk?*

AGAIN???

She sighed and soaked in the view of his gorgeous wife. She had fair skin and cascading blond hair that looked like it had been professionally blown out that morning. She was tall and thin, and she wore a long white dress that ruffled in the wind. Her lips were coated with a simple pink color, and she donned large, black sunglasses. Leo leaned across the table and kissed her softly on the lips. She gently caressed his cheek with her left hand, and a ginormous diamond sparkled off her ring finger, visible even from across the street.

Any doubts Willa had about them being married were gone now. The futile hope that maybe she was a sister Leo hadn't told Willa about slowly dissipated. And then his wife beamed at him, and Willa sighed.

She was happy. Beautiful. The mother of his child.

And Leo had cheated on her with *Willa*?

Sure, Willa knew she was attractive.

She'd been told often that she had great boobs, though she thought they were a little small. She had red hair, but she could somehow still get a tan. Throw in cerulean eyes and long legs, and she was bound to benefit from pretty privilege—and she knew it. She'd gotten into dozens of clubs without paying a cover, always gotten free drinks when she went out, and had been able to sweet talk her way into almost anything since she hit puberty.

So she knew that the only reason Leo would cheat on his perfectly lovely wife with her was simply because he could.

Because men just had that much audacity.

And, well, Willa couldn't stand for that level of entitlement.

"Willa?" Charlie tentatively asked. "You ok?"

Willa had forgotten she was there.

"I'm okay," she responded, her voice hard. "I'll be right back."

Willa strode across the street. As she approached the outdoor hostess stand, she took a deep breath and thanked the universe that Becky was working.

"Is that...?" Becky trailed off as Willa approached.

Willa was a regular at Chadwick's. Most of the staff knew her. Her apartment was right across the street, and she loved to have brunch here on the weekends or read a book here on weekday afternoons. So of course she'd brought her boyfriend a few times. Not all the wait staff knew him, but a few of them did. One of them was Becky.

"Yes, it is," Willa responded, and Becky's face went white. "Can I deliver some waters or something to their table?"

Becky bit her lip.

"I'm all for payback, but are you sure that's the best idea?"

"I'm not going to make a scene," Willa said. "Not in front of his daughter. But I'm also not going to let him get away with this. He just needs to know that I know."

Becky nodded and flagged a waiter named José over.

"Willa, is that Leo?" José asked.

Willa nodded, shaking with rage.

God, Leo was playing with fire. Why had he come here? Sure, she usually slept in on Sundays when she didn't have to teach a yoga class, so it was a fair guess that she wouldn't see him here. But he was practically begging to get caught.

"Get her waters to take to their table," Becky said, shortly after nudging him and giving him a pointed look.

José raised his eyebrows but said nothing. He reappeared a couple of minutes later with a tray of water glasses. Willa took it from him steadily, even though she'd never waited tables, and weaved through chairs until she reached Leo and his family. She started to place the drinks down in front of them, but neither of them looked up at her.

"What a lovely family you all are," Willa said cheerfully.

Leo stiffened immediately. His eyes darted to her. His lips formed an "oh," and then he slammed his mouth shut in an instant.

His eyes widened.

He cleared his throat.

"Thank you," his wife said kindly, without noticing her husband's odd behavior.

"Celebrating anything special today?" Willa asked.

"It's our daughter's birthday," she said, turning to her daughter. "How old are you, Ella?"

Ella scrunched up her face like she was thinking very hard, then she showed Willa two fingers.

"Two!" Ella shrieked.

Willa was right.

That motherfucker.

"Aww, well happy birthday, sweet Ella!" Willa said, her eyes burning with unshed tears of anger and sadness for this innocent little girl. And for herself. "Two years! That's a very long time to do *anything*, let alone grace the world with your lovely presence. And look how big you are! I would've guessed you were three."

Leo shifted uncomfortably in his seat. Willa smirked at him, then turned her attention back to his wife. She really couldn't leave well enough alone; she had to know for sure what she'd gotten herself into.

"You are such a beautiful couple," Willa plastered on a big smile, willing herself not to gag on the words. "How long have you been together?"

"Oh, thank you!" his wife said sincerely, turning to Leo. "How long's it been, darling? Ten... no, eleven years together total, nine years married."

Eleven years together.

Nine years married.

Willa was itching to grab her phone and block him in every way possible, but she forced herself to continue giving her best smile as she shifted her eyes to Leo.

"Nine years married to this gorgeous woman!" Willa

said, knowing she was being reckless now. "You must feel so lucky."

Leo gazed between Willa and his wife, who was looking at him with a lazy, expectant grin. He cleared his throat.

"I do," he practically grunted. "I feel very lucky."

He attempted to smile, but he looked like he'd swallowed something sour. His wife's brows began to furrow, and Willa took that as her cue to back off.

"I'll let the rest of the staff know you're celebrating a birthday," Willa told them with a wink.

"Thank you," his wife gave her a dazzling smile.

Willa turned on her heel and walked back to the hostess stand, where José and Becky were watching her with wide eyes. She handed José the tray.

"Thank you guys," Willa said, her voice wavering for the first time.

"You gonna be okay?" Becky asked, her brows furrowing.

Willa closed her eyes and shook her head.

"I don't know."

She swallowed a lump in her throat and opened her eyes back up. José and Becky were staring at her with wide eyes, and she took a deep breath.

"I'll be okay," she finally said. "I'll bounce back. I always do."

The concern in their faces didn't waver, but they nodded.

"I'll tell the cooks to spit in his food," Becky said, her lips quirking in a slight grin.

Willa let out a half-laugh, half-sob.

"Thanks, Becky," she said. "Oh, and it's their daughter's birthday. I told them I'd let you know. In case you can do anything special."

Becky's face looked torn between fury and compassion.

She opened her mouth as if to say something, but closed it and simply nodded.

Willa gave her a weak smile. Then she took a deep breath, and without turning back for a final glance at Leo, she left.

1

TWO WEEKS LATER

Willa had forgotten about humidity.

Well, not *forgotten* about it, but she just never really thought much about humidity living in the temperate state of California. But it was hot, and so fucking humid. She felt damp with sweat ever since her plane landed in Pensacola. She'd rolled down the windows in her Uber, but it did little to help.

After getting over the initial shock of the Leo incident—and releasing throaty sobs into her pillow for what felt like hours—Willa came up with a plan.

She was going to get a fresh start somewhere familiar: her childhood home on Perdido Bay.

She'd spent a few days replaying every moment of her time with Leo—the good and the bad. Enough to realize that she'd never be able to escape the memories of him in California.

Once she promised Charlie she'd find a good therapist, her best friend helped her get out the door. The next week was a blur, which was how Willa liked it.

Between figuring out someone to sublease the room in

her apartment with Charlie (luckily, a new instructor at their yoga studio jumped at the opportunity), packing up all her stuff (all of it fit into two suitcases and eleven boxes), figuring out what to get rid of and what to ship to her new address (a shockingly involved process on both fronts), resigning from her job at the yoga studio (they were, unsurprisingly, very zen about the whole thing), and planning her travel out to Alabama (a first class, one way ticket), she barely had time to wallow in her heartbreak and shame.

Until she found herself sitting in seat 2A, drinking a bloody mary and staring out the window, overthinking every moment of their relationship in her head. The six-and-a-half hour trip felt endless, and no amount of movies could make her stop thinking about it.

How she was played a fool.

How he broke her heart.

How much she hated herself for it.

Even now, with the car window open and the salty sea air wafting through her hair, she was replaying a recent conversation she'd had with Leo.

It was their two year anniversary, and he'd scheduled them a sunset dinner cruise. He'd gifted her a gold necklace with a ginormous ruby in the center. She'd gifted him a Giants sweatshirt he'd been eyeballing—and some expensive and complex lingerie she showed off later that night.

"Can you believe it's been two years since you fell on your ass after attempting to do a headstand?" Willa joked, her eyes crinkling with restrained laughter as she recalled how they first met.

"Hey, I can do a handstand just fine, so I really thought I'd be able to do it," Leo grimaced. "Clearly, I was very wrong, but it worked out for me, didn't it?"

She bit her lip.

"It worked out for both of us," she replied.

He grabbed her hand and gently kissed it.

This was it. The moment Willa had been waiting for to broach a topic that made her... well, jittery as hell. She considered herself a pretty self-assured, confident person. Being nervous? It made her uneasy. It made her feel like she didn't know herself.

"So, I've been thinking," she started.

Leo looked at her expectantly.

"Yes?" he grinned wickedly at her.

"Two years."

"We've established that," he continued smirking.

"That's a long time."

"Indeed."

"So I think it's time that we take a step forward. A big one. A good one."

He raised his eyebrows, a smile still playing on his lips as he left room for her to complete her thought.

"Do you want to move in together?" she asked.

Willa held her breath as his smile dropped. At the time, she just thought he was caught off guard. She was slightly annoyed that he seemed so shocked by the turn of the conversation because, like she'd prefaced, they'd been together for *two years*. She wasn't trying to get married and have babies anytime soon.

So why was he so surprised that she would want to move in together? She thought maybe it was just a guy thing, maybe he was just a little dense.

Of course, hindsight is 20/20.

She knew now that he was trying to figure out how to keep the relationship going without doing anything serious. His apartment—the one they usually stayed at—must've been a secret one his wife didn't know about.

"Move in together?" Leo repeated after a few moments of silence.

"I mean, don't you think that's the natural next step?" Willa said. "Then we'd get to spend more time together, and it wouldn't be so hard with you traveling for work all the time."

Leo ran his fingers through his hair and sighed. Wheels were turning in his brain, and he looked like he'd just worked an 18-hour day.

"I guess...," Leo exhaled. "Yeah, you're right. That is the natural next step."

Willa beamed. As she reflected, though, she realized Leo never enthusiastically agreed to move in with her. He just admitted that that was where the relationship ought to go.

"So, you're in?" she asked.

He gave her a too-big smile, one that she thought was overcompensating for his original response at the time, but now knew he was just trying to figure out his next move.

"I'm in."

Willa squealed, leaned across the table, and kissed him on the cheek.

"Soooo," she drew out the word. "Wanna start apartment hunting next week?"

"You sure are anxious to get this show on the road," Leo quipped.

She smirked at him.

"Of course I am," she said, running a finger down his muscular forearm.

"Apartment hunting next week sounds great," he said.

They never got around to apartment hunting, though. It was only a few days later that she saw him at Chadwick's, and she hadn't heard from him since. She blocked his number and his email, and he hadn't bothered to show up at her apartment.

Part of her was a little disappointed that he hadn't tried harder to get an audience with her and explain himself, but then she just got mad at herself for even wanting anything from him anymore.

She shook her head, as if that could get Leo off her brain.

Distractions—that's what she needed.

But this humidity? She could do without that distraction.

She thanked every god she could think of as the car pulled into the driveway.

"Thank you," Willa said to her driver as he put the car in park.

"No problem," he grunted, getting out of the car and unloading her luggage before she'd even fully opened the door.

She grabbed the handles of both of her rolling suitcases and pulled them up the front staircase. The humidity made her hands slick, and she accidentally dropped one.

"Well," she huffed, speaking to nobody in particular, "I guess I'll come back for that one."

She pulled the other suitcase up the porch stairs, then looked under one of the potted plants for the key. She unlocked the door and let herself in, breathing in the A/C and the smell of her family home.

It had been a few years since she'd been back. This was the place where she'd grown up. She learned everything here: how to walk, how to ride a bike, how to read, how to cook, and of course, how to fish. Willa would bet that she learned how to fish before doing anything else. There were pictures of her from old photo albums where she was holding training fishing rods when she was still in diapers.

Sometimes, Willa thought her upbringing on the water was what drew her to yoga. The steady ebb and flow of the waves was like a vinyasa yoga practice, and the self-reliance to fish for her own lunch made her respect what her body was capable of.

Her grandparents died several years ago, giving her fewer reasons to come back. This was their home, the one she came to on most weekends, the one she visited for Thanksgivings and Christmases. They left it to the family, and she and her cousins and aunts and uncles all shared it. Nobody had stayed in it for at least six months, but a cleaning crew came regularly to make sure everything was taken care of.

Willa had emailed them all last week to see if they'd all be okay with her moving in. None of them had any issue with it; after all, the house had ten bedrooms. If they wanted to come visit, they could still do that, and they could avoid Willa if they really wanted to, given the size of the house.

She left the respite of the A/C for a moment to bring in her other suitcase, then dropped them in the room that was always hers. It was simple: just a four-poster bed, a small armchair, a dresser, and a closet filled with trinkets from her grandparents' travels. She'd unpack and settle in later.

Right now, all she wanted was to breathe in the sea air. She stepped out on the back porch and closed her eyes, salty ocean wind kissing her cheeks, bits of sunlight peeking through the trees, and grinned.

This was the right decision. Coming home, reconnecting to her roots, getting away from all the things that constantly reminded her of Leo. She slipped off her shoes and walked barefoot along the grassy backyard and onto the wharf that had been rebuilt after the most recent hurricane. She took in the view of the hazel bay, the freshwater-saltwater mix, and felt warmth enclose her heart.

Suddenly, she saw a few fish jump playfully over the waves.

Mullet.

She smiled to herself, a decision made. She set off to check for supplies, then to head to the bait shop in the old Jeep Wrangler her family always kept here.

Willa was going fishing tonight.

2

S hawn resisted the urge to roll his eyes as a redhead dressed in a smocked, maxi-length sundress and ginormous sunglasses walked into his shop. She was tan, somehow, despite the red hair, and her dress was seafoam green, with straps that left her upper back on display.

Fucking tourists. Did she know she was at a bait shop?

Spotting the tourists was easy for Shawn. They were dressed to the nines for activities that required little more than a swimsuit and a ratty t-shirt. This chick looked like she walked straight out of a magazine. *Vogue* or whatever the hell. She looked like a fucking model. And for what? To buy a fishing rod?

As annoyed as he was by her unnecessary attire, Shawn had to admit just how gorgeous she was. Lean and fit, with boobs perky and round like plums, long and slender legs peeking out through the slit of her dress. She had a beautiful neck, long and delicate and feminine. When she lifted her sunglasses, he couldn't help but notice that her eyes were blue like the Gulf, like the sea that he took his boat out to explore every weekend, with depths just as mysterious. She had a soft tan, but her cheeks were rosy. And her lips— *God, her lips.* Plump and red, ripe for kissing, perfect—

What the fuck?

Why was he thinking about *the lips* of this overdressed Valley Girl?

Tourists were fun to fuck when he was 20, but the novelty of it wore off in his 30s. He knew he'd just be a notch on their belt, a vacation fling they pursued with a grimy fisherman to convince themselves they were reckless and adventurous when they went back to their strict routines and boring, suburban lives.

He hadn't fucked a tourist in a while. Wasn't interested in meaningless sex anymore. Gave up on one-night-stands after his best friend, Tucker, fell in love and became blissfully married and made Shawn realize that's what he wanted, too.

Shawn eyeballed the redhead as she perused fishing rods, and decided it was time for him to jump in and save her from embarrassing herself.

"Can I help you with anything, ma'am?" he drawled.

His heart stuttered as she turned to face him, those aquamarine eyes piercing his soul. His breath hitched as her lips quirked slightly upward, a rosy flush from the heat coloring her olive skin.

"I need some shrimp," she responded in an accent that betrayed no particular location.

Okay, he wasn't expecting that.

Most tourists who were going fishing without a guide stuck to fishing lures rather than live bait. Lures were easier to store and made for nice souvenirs.

"Shrimp?" Shawn responded dumbly.

"Yes, those small crustaceans you've got over there," she

smirked, pointing at the tank.

He cleared his throat.

"Sure, of course, ma'am," Shawn said briskly, busying himself at the tank.

"Not too many, a dozen or two should be fine," she continued. "And I'll just go ahead and buy this."

She swung an insulated bait bucket on top of the tank, then turned around to continue browsing. Shawn stopped what he was doing and crinkled his brows.

"Uh, ma'am?" Shawn said. "As much as I appreciate the extra business, there's no need to purchase a $60 bait bucket for a short trip down here. Tourists typically just take their shrimp in a bag."

She turned around and narrowed her eyes at him.

"Do they now?" she asked, a slight edge in her voice.

Shawn began to sweat a little. Had he offended her? He was just trying to save her some money.

"Yes, ma'am," he said.

"Well, I appreciate you trying to save me the money, but I think I'll buy it anyway."

That was... odd. But Shawn wouldn't fight her on it.

An extra $60? He'd take that any day. She went back to perusing and stopped at the small section of cast nets. She ran her fingers over a few of them, and Shawn caught himself watching her and got back to the task at hand.

As he finished putting shrimp in the bucket, she approached the cashier stand with a box of hooks, a few bobbers, some fishing line, and one of the smaller nets.

"Cast net, huh?" he asked.

She pressed her lips together as she looked at him.

"Yep."

"Going on a tour?"

"Nope."

Why she was dropping $150 on something she probably didn't know how to use, Shawn didn't know. But he'd learned his lesson with the bait bucket. He wouldn't comment on the net. He closed the bait bucket and grabbed a spare hook nearby.

"If you'd like, I can show you how to put the shrimp on your hook," Shawn said.

It was the least he could do, since she was spending so much money at his shop.

She glared at him.

"No, thanks," she responded curtly.

"You sure? It seems simple, but it's easy to lose all your bait if you do it the wrong way."

She put the cast net on the checkout desk and stalked over to him. She grabbed the bait bucket from the floor and fished a shrimp out with a bare hand, then snatched the hook from his hand. Her long, delicate fingers perfectly hooked the shrimp, and she glanced at him expectantly.

Well, shit.

She knew exactly what she was doing.

Probably thought he was a condescending dick.

"Seems like you know what you're doing," Shawn said tightly after a beat of silence.

She pursed her lips.

"Indeed."

She unhooked the shrimp and tossed it back in the bucket before handing him the hook. Then she walked back to the cashier stand and crossed her arms. Her auburn waves flashed in the bit of sunlight that was peeking through the windows of the store, and Shawn ran his fingers through his hair nervously as he tried to figure out what the fuck just happened. She cleared her throat and he startled, realizing she was waiting on him to check out.

He stumbled over to the cashier's stand and started scanning her items, wondering if he should apologize. Would that be weird? What would he even say? *Sorry for assuming you didn't know how to hook your shrimp?*

"That'll be $223.63."

Shawn's voice sounded smaller than normal. He scanned her credit card and he bagged the smaller items.

"Need help carrying anything to your car?" Shawn asked, hoping it would make up for earlier.

"I think I can manage," she smirked.

The door jingled as she walked out.

SHAWN'S PHONE buzzed as he locked up the bait shop. He pulled it out, saw it was Tucker, and sighed.

"Hey, Tuck," Shawn answered the phone, forcing his tone to sound chipper.

"Hey, Shawn. Wanna come over for dinner tonight?"

Shawn unlocked his truck and got in the car. Of course, Tucker had timed this call right when he knew Shawn would be heading home for the day.

Before he could answer, Tucker added, "I'm making those crab cakes you like. And Hanna's dying to see you. We miss you."

Guilt panged through Shawn's chest. He knew he was being a bad friend, but he couldn't find it in him to say yes.

"Promised Grams I'd help her with some stuff tonight," Shawn lied. "Rain check?"

He heard Tucker exhale through the phone.

"You sure she won't let us steal you for one night?" Tucker asked, then joked, "We'll have you home before curfew."

"Sorry, man. I can't tonight. But thanks for calling."

They said their goodbyes, and Shawn leaned his head forward against the steering wheel.

He was a shitty friend.

He wasn't denying it.

But *fuck.*

It had gotten hard to be around Tucker and Hanna.

Shawn took a deep breath and started his car, letting his thoughts run amok.

He loved them both—they were like family to him, even though he hadn't seen them in months. He and his best friend used to be attached at the hip—used to go to the club every weekend and crash at each other's places after a wild night out. They'd grown up together. Shawn was the one who had encouraged Tucker to go to culinary school—he even offered to help pay for it when it looked like Tucker might not be able to. And he was there at the opening night of Tucker's restaurant, Fish Food.

But then, Tucker met Hanna.

Hanna—a kindergarten teacher with tiny tattoos all over her fair-skinned arms, dark brown hair, and a penchant for ending up in awkward situations. Hanna had immediately fit into their little group. She and Shawn hit it off instantly, even though back when he met her, he was an unapologetic playboy and didn't bother to hide it. Hanna, of course, saw right through Shawn in a way that unnerved him, but also made him immediately respect her. The three of them were inseparable—a dynamic trio of sorts.

Shawn was their best man and only witness at the quick, courthouse wedding they had a couple of years ago. But since then, it just felt like there wasn't enough room in Tucker's life for Shawn—at least, not the way there used to be.

Shawn didn't begrudge Tucker for it—or Hanna, for that

matter.

He knew it was more than that.

Knew that, at the root of it, he was jealous.

He'd grown up in the years since they got married. Stopped sleeping with tourists. Started trying to date.

Problem was, the dating pool was tough. His grandmother had set him up on enough terrible first dates that he was about ready to throw in the towel.

His mind drifted to the pretty redhead who put him in his place earlier. That was the kind of girl he wanted—strong and stubborn and sexy to boot.

He shook his head.

Stupid.

It was stupid to think he'd ever see her again after today, and even more stupid to daydream about someone he didn't even know.

His heart ached with longing.

Shawn felt stuck. He loved his best friends. He wanted to spend time with them. The truth was, he missed them as much as they missed him. But it was hard as fuck to sit with them through dinner and watch them hold hands and not feel overwhelmed with the ache of loneliness. And he didn't know how to say it—how to tell them how jealous he was, how sad he was, how desperately he wanted what they had.

Because even though he was man enough not to lie to himself, it was unimaginable to say something like that out loud to the people he loved most in the world.

He pulled into his driveway, shaking away the self pity he'd started feeling on the drive home.

The smell of chocolate wafted through the foyer as Shawn walked in the door.

"Grams?" he shouted, tossing his keys on the front table.

"Kitchen."

His grandmother was arranging brownies onto a paper plate, donning black leggings and a red flannel shirt. Her hair was unruly; she'd clearly been out on the wharf earlier that day, where she liked to go to pray or watch the sunrise. He looked out at the waterfront from the kitchen window. The sun still shone brightly out above the water, and there were white caps on the waves. Maybe he'd try to go wind-surfing before dinner, if he could muster up the energy.

Shawn grinned, his mouth watering at her special, homemade brownies. As he reached from behind her to grab one, she smacked his hand.

"Hey!" he tugged his hand back.

"Not for you, Scooby," she said sternly.

Shawn sighed. He'd never escape the nickname he earned as a 5-year-old when he dressed up as Scooby Doo for Halloween. It probably wouldn't have stuck, but he refused to take off the costume for two weeks, and Grams called him Scooby ever since.

"Can't I just have one?" he asked. "They'll never know."

She turned around to face him, placing one manicured hand on her hip and raising her eyebrows.

"You don't even know who these are for," Grams said.

"The ladies at church?" he guessed.

"Hmph."

She turned back around, covering the brownies with tin foil.

"C'mon, Grams," Shawn continued. "It doesn't matter, anyway. Nobody will know if one brownie is missing."

"I'll know."

Shawn sighed.

"They're not for the church ladies, anyway," Grams continued. "They're for our new neighbor."

"New neighbor?"

That was news to him. No houses on their street had been put up for sale recently, and everyone knew each other well enough to know if anyone was considering it. Most people who lived in their neighborhood had retired here. When they died, most of them passed the property onto someone else in their family—their kids or grandkids.

"One of the Greene girls moved in."

Interesting. Shawn didn't know the Greenes all that well.

The grandparents had died several years back, within a few months of each other. He tried to recall their names... Robert and Betty, perhaps? Robert died of a heart attack, and Betty died of heartbreak a few weeks later. They'd left the house to their kids and grandkids, split equally among them with a trust to pay the bills.

Nobody lived there full-time, but people were always staying there for weekends and holidays. Since they were never here for long—and since Robert and Betty died long before he moved in with Grams—he never got the chance to get to know the family.

"Moved in?" Shawn asked.

"You heard me," Grams said, crossing her arms. "I don't know the whole story, but Barb told me this morning. I think it was pretty sudden. So I thought you could welcome her to the neighborhood with some of my famous brownies."

"So she's here for good? That's unusual for the Greene house."

"That's what I'm told. Either way, no harm in being neighborly. Her grandparents were good people. I want to look out for her."

Shawn sighed. Of course, she did.

Grams knew everyone, and she was beloved. Because, of course, she did stuff like this. Looked out for people. Took them under her wing. Spent an afternoon making them homemade brownies.

She also had the tendency to say every thought that entered her head. That lack of filter often got her into trouble, but people loved her sass. So did Shawn.

Most of the time.

"Wait," he said, replaying her words in his head. "Did you say you thought that *I* could welcome her to the neighborhood?"

She winked.

"Grams, please tell me you're not matchmaking again," Shawn said, stifling a groan.

A blooper reel of terrible first dates Grams set up for him played in his head. One of them was extremely shy and barely spoke the whole time. Another wore Lily Pulitzer everything and asked him to escort her to an upcoming ball in Mobile, which he politely declined after a few minutes of being rendered speechless. And another belittled him for running a bait shop.

"I've learned my lesson," she said. "I won't set you up on a date. But I will make you take her those brownies. She's very pretty, from what I hear. I knew her back when she was a little girl. She was a sweet, curious little thing. And oh my, she had a mouth on her. Of course, her family moved away from Mobile when she was barely a teenager, and I don't think I've seen her since."

Shawn pressed his lips together. He loved his grandmother dearly. He would do anything for her, and had. After his grandfather died last year, he moved in with her after one phone call where she confided in him that she was terrified to live alone for the first time in her life.

Naturally, she put up a small fight about it. The woman was stubborn, and loved him more than anything in the world. She told him she didn't want to hold him back. But he insisted. They'd always been close, he and Grams, so he knew she was thrilled when he decided to move in with her. She never would've asked it of him, but he was more than happy to do it. He loved living with her, even if it meant that bringing girls home was out of the question. He didn't know how many years he'd have with Grams, and he knew their time together was precious. But her habit of meddling was getting on his nerves.

"Grams, please."

"Shawn Porter Gray, you will do this for me," she said, her voice stern.

Shawn bit his lip, frustration rising.

Damn, she could be so pushy.

"Fine," he said, and Grams beamed. "I'll do it on one condition."

She narrowed her eyes and looked at him expectantly.

"After this, no more setups, no more introductions to your jazzercise friends' granddaughters, no more girls casually dropping by for dinner, and no more taking brownies to new neighbors. I love you, Grams, and I appreciate what you're doing, but it's not working. Alright?"

She studied him for a moment and blew out a breath.

"Fine, Scoob. You win."

He grinned at her.

"Can you say that again and let me record you?" he asked her.

She glared at him, but was clearly holding back a laugh.

"Leftovers for dinner?" Shawn asked.

"Yes," Grams said. "And then you're taking those brownies to our new neighbor."

"Right. And what's her name?"

"Willa."

3

All of Willa's new fishing supplies were messily sprawled out on the kitchen table, along with some old fishing rods and the tool box she'd found in the garage closet. Her brow was furrowed in concentration as she considered where to begin. She grabbed her cell phone and connected it to her bluetooth speaker before turning on some music.

As she sat at the kitchen table and began to reline and hook the rods, she thought back to her visit to the bait shop. She was used to people taking one look at her and assuming she was a ditz. Being conventionally attractive came with that price, and most of the time, she didn't mind it. She'd used it to her advantage more times than she could count, hustling men at bars when they challenged her to a game of pool.

But Willa grew up on Perdido Bay.

She knew the telltale signs that a storm was coming before any weatherman could predict it, she knew the best fishing spots to find flounder or trout or redfish, and she grew up catching mullet by the dozens in her castnet and cooking them for lunch. She spent most of her childhood at this very kitchen table with her grandparents, talking about the different wildlife they could spot through binoculars and arguing with her cousins about who got to bait the crab traps. Her grandfather made sure she knew how to throw a cast net and cast a fishing rod when she was barely out of toddlerhood, and he'd taught her everything he could about the flora and fauna of the Bay.

She knew she didn't look like a fisherwoman. At face value, she probably did look more like a tourist than a local.

But it hurt her more than she wanted to admit to herself that the guy at the bait shop assumed she was an airhead, that she was biting off more than she could chew.

His polite yet emotionless demeanor didn't soften the blow, and as much as she wanted to put it out of her head, she couldn't forget the way he looked at her—like she was a toddler trying to get behind the steering wheel of a car.

Cute until they start honking the horn.

Willa couldn't help feeling like this place was quintessential to who she was, but perhaps the Bay didn't need her nearly as much as she needed it.

Perhaps that was what was so alluring about it.

After hooking and relining all the rods, she quickly changed into her favorite navy bikini and threw on some light-wash jean shorts. It took her two trips to take the fishing rods, the bait, and the rest of her tools out on the wharf. By the time she finished, the sun was hanging low over the sepia waves, littering the sky with pink and orange clouds. She turned on the fishing light at the end of the wharf, praying that it would attract some trout within a few hours after nightfall, and trudged back to the kitchen, where she grabbed her newly purchased cast net and a bucket from the garage.

She cast the net a few times, reactivating old muscles she hadn't used in the years since her grandparents died. Once she got the hang of it, she started biding her time until she saw a mullet jump. Then she cast the net over the school of fish she saw, and dragged in her loot. After about 30 minutes, it was starting to get dark and she'd caught about a dozen mullet that were sizable enough for her to eat. They were clamoring around in the bucket she'd brought out to the wharf, and she wiped a sheen of sweat off her forehead as she admired her handiwork.

"What are you going to do with them?"

A deep voice carried over the sound of the waves crashing the shore, startling Willa enough that her heart hammered as she gasped.

She turned around, her right hand clinging to her chest as she let out a curse. When she locked eyes with the source of the question, she recognized the guy from the bait shop. He had sandy blonde hair pulled into a bun and a slightly scruffy, tan face, with a jawline sharp enough to cut her fishing line. Her stomach dropped in annoyance.

"You scared the shit out of me," she said, releasing a heavy breath.

He reached his hand behind his head, seeming a bit self-conscious. Willa couldn't help but notice his perfectly displayed biceps, toned from what she imagined were many mornings spent reeling in fish.

"Sorry about that," he said gruffly.

Willa was still trying to regain control of her breath as she said, "You work at the bait shop."

"I *own* the bait shop," he responded with a small smirk. "I'm Shawn, by the way. I live a couple houses down."

Cocky bastard, Willa thought, resisting the urge to roll her eyes.

"Seems like we both underestimated each other today," she responded, pressing her lips in a thin line.

Shawn grimaced.

"Sorry about that," he said. "You clearly know your way around a cast net, Greene."

She flushed at his casual use of her last name. He must've remembered it from her credit card, and she couldn't help the rush of pleasure she felt. "Among other things."

Did she imagine the way his eyes darkened when she said that, before quickly skirting over her body? He looked away too quickly for her to be certain.

"So what can I do for you, Shawn?"

"My grandmother made you brownies. To welcome you to the neighborhood."

Willa pointedly looked at his empty hands.

"And where are these brownies?" she asked, lifting an eyebrow.

"I left them on the table up there," he all but grunted, pointing to the deck in the backyard.

"Oh," Willa responded. "Well, thanks. That was nice of her. Your grandmother."

"Ida."

The name rang a bell. Willa squinted her eyes together, searching her memory. Suddenly, a sunny, summer afternoon from her childhood flashed in her head. She was young, maybe 7 or 8. She had spent the entire day building sandcastles with her cousins. She'd come inside for a snack, and her grandmother had been visiting with a friend. *Ida*. They were eating a treat that Ida had brought over, and they offered some to Willa. In fact, Willa was pretty sure they'd been eating...

"Brownies," she breathed. "Ida. I remember her."

If memory served her correctly, those were some of the best brownies she'd ever had. A special family recipe, in fact.

Ida and her grandmother often spent Sunday afternoons visiting after they got home from church. They walked together during the weekdays, gossiping about townies and their latest exploits. Once, not all that long before she died, her grandmother had called her hungover after a night of drinking sangria on the wharf with Ida.

Willa was overwhelmed with the sudden memories of someone who had meant so much to her grandmother— someone who had been thoughtful enough to make her brownies to welcome her to the neighborhood. For a split second, Willa wondered how Ida even knew she'd moved in, but then again, word traveled fast on the Bay.

"I'd love to see her," Willa said suddenly, bringing herself out of her reverie. "Ida, I mean. Can I drop by some-time to say hello?"

Shawn was quiet for a moment, his eyes boring into Willa's.

"She's only gone on Tuesday and Thursday afternoons for bridge, Friday nights for Bingo, and Sundays for church," he finally said.

"Alright, then," Willa nodded.

Putting pieces together, Willa suddenly realized that Shawn must live with his grandmother.

"How long have you lived with her?" she asked him.

His jaw tightened.

"Since my grandfather died, about a year ago."

"I'm sorry," she said quietly. "I'm sure she's grateful not to be alone."

A beat of silence passed between them, and then Willa noticed that it was almost completely dark.

"Well, I'd better get these inside," she said.

"I'll help," Shawn responded, grabbing her bucket of mullet before she could protest.

She sighed, dropping the cast net on the wharf and following behind him. Shawn was wearing the same thing he had on at the bait shop: gray shorts, a white t-shirt, and some well-loved sneakers. He was effortlessly strong, and she was sure that unlike the men in California who worked out to keep a certain appearance, Shawn's muscle came from frequent fishing. She could see the ripples of his back through the white shirt he wore, and couldn't help but admire the way his calves flexed as he walked up the hill toward her house.

Once they got to the back porch, she directed him to a cooler she'd gotten out to put the fish in.

"You're going to eat these?" he asked, sounding a bit incredulous.

"Of course," she said.

He grunted in response.

She rolled her eyes as he dumped the fish into the cooler. She was losing patience for this guy and his damn assumptions. She picked up the bucket and began to carry it into the garage.

"What is it this time?" she huffed.

He wrung his hands. "I can carry that for y—"

"No, thanks."

He followed her into the garage.

"I'm not—" he cut himself off. "It's just that most people don't eat mullet."

He really didn't know how to shut up.

She sighed. She knew she was short-tempered right now, knew her trauma and heartache were making her abrasive and rash and unkind, what with everything she was processing. But every time he opened his mouth, he just became more punchable. Where was her zen when she needed it?

"They think they're bottom feeders or whatever," he added.

She smirked. "They *are* bottom feeders."

Shawn crossed his arms.

"I grew up catching mullet in the morning and eating them for lunch," Willa's said, her eyes narrowing.

She dropped the cooler and turned around, heading back toward the wharf. When she came around to the back of the house, she found the brownies where he said they'd be. She pulled the tin foil back and smiled at the full plate—too many for her to finish tonight. But she grabbed one and took a bite. She groaned. It was the best brownie she'd ever had.

She turned around, licking her lips. His gaze dropped to her mouth, and she knew she didn't imagine it this time when his eyes blackened with desire. She raised her eyebrows and smirked at him, before he looked away.

"Want one?" she responded. "It's just me. There's no way I can finish them all."

He eyed the plate.

"Grams wouldn't be happy with me," he said solemnly. "She told me I couldn't have one."

Willa stifled a giggle, both exasperated and amused.

"It can be our secret," she said conspiratorially.

Shawn narrowed his eyes.

"You don't understand," he said, frowning. "She'd *know*. The woman always knows."

Willa couldn't hold back a full-blown laugh this time.

He barely showed any emotion since he'd come over, but was shaking in his boots at the thought of his grandmother scolding him for eating a brownie.

She turned on her heel, shoving the rest of the brownie in her mouth, and walked out toward the wharf.

4

Shawn gaped after her as she swung her hips, walking back on the wharf, where he could vaguely see a fishing light shining at the end of it.

He couldn't believe his fucking luck. The redhead from earlier—*Willa*—lived right next door to him.

When he first left his house, he could see her casting the net from his backyard in that tiny little bikini. Her tits were perky and supple, and as he'd gotten closer to her backyard, he nearly drooled over the way they bounced slightly every time she tossed that fucking net in the water.

He observed her for longer than he'd like to admit as she cast that net before finally making himself known. And he hadn't lied when he said she knew her way around a cast net. She was far better at it than he was, a fact he wasn't too proud to admit to himself. Each of her casts spread the net open wide, a perfect circle. She methodically searched for schools of mullet before sending it to the water, and she caught at least a few fish with each cast, often tossing the ones she judged too small back into the water.

And *that laugh.*

He thought a smirk or belittling glare was all she was capable of, but when she laughed at him, her eyes lit up, showing warmth he hadn't seen before.

She was gorgeous, but when she laughed—*God*, she was absolutely stunning.

Shawn watched her walk away for all of ten seconds before grabbing a brownie, shoving the entire thing in his mouth, and chasing after her. He was ten steps behind her when she picked up the cast net from where she'd left it and continued walking.

"If you're going to join me, you could be a little quieter," she quipped. "I'd rather not scare all the fish away before I even toss a line in the water."

He slowed his pace, feeling like a chided schoolboy. Then he grinned to himself.

He had a *crush*.

Fuck, he hadn't had butterflies like this since he was a teenager.

And he was fumbling the bag so badly every time he opened his mouth.

Willa breathed in deeply, inhaling the ocean air with her eyes closed, a slight smile curling her lips upward. She looked so natural out here, the moonlight reflecting off her auburn hair. When she opened her eyes, she glanced over to him and bit her lip as she noticed him gawking at her.

"Not much fish tonight, huh?" she gestured to the water.

Shawn whipped his head toward the spotlight shining on small bait fish swimming underneath it. A few saltwater catfish swam in and out of view, on the periphery of the light.

"I figure I'll need to keep the light on every night for a few weeks before the fish I want start showing up," Willa continued.

Shawn grunted in response, then felt an overwhelming desire to face-palm.

He was a self-proclaimed ladies' man for most of his life, but one little crush had him at a loss for words.

God, how embarrassing.

"But in the meantime," she said, turning around and grabbing a couple of fishing rods and the bucket of shrimp she'd bought from him earlier, "there's no harm in a little catch and release."

She offered him a rod, which he accepted, before she baited her fishing line and tossed it into the water. He followed suit. They cast their fishing poles in companionable silence for ten minutes or so, replacing bait that got taken by the catfish occasionally, before his curiosity got the better of him.

"My grandmother heard that you moved here," Shawn said. "For good."

Willa hummed in agreement as she methodically reeled in her line, and damn it if Shawn couldn't help but wonder what it would be like for her to hum like that with her lips around his cock. He shifted as his pants suddenly felt tight at the thought. Why couldn't he keep his mind out of the gutter today? He'd been around hot girls in bikinis his whole life. Taken them fishing on his boat. Considered himself all but immune to the wiles of women in bikinis holding a fishing rod.

But he wasn't standing behind Willa, teaching her how to bait a hook and cast the line. She was doing it all on her own. She didn't need direction or help from him; in fact, if he tried to offer it, Shawn was pretty sure she'd put him in his place with that smart mouth of hers. He held back a smile at the thought.

"Why?" Shawn followed up, hoping to get more in response this time.

Willa sighed, and she frowned.

"Bad breakup," she finally said, her knuckles white as they clenched onto the fishing pole.

Shawn's head ran wild wondering what kind of bad breakup she'd been through. Was she dumped, or did she do the dumping? Was it someone she'd been with for a while? It had to have been, for her to have that look on her face. Did he break her heart? His curiosity begged him to ask her for details, but he couldn't bring himself to pry.

"That sucks," he said.

She let out a humorless laugh.

"Yeah, well. Let's just say I've sworn off men for a while."

A pang of disappointment ricocheted through him.

"So you thought the best place to escape them would be here?" he asked.

"I thought the best place to escape everything would be here," she responded quietly.

Her ex must've been the one to call it off. That had to be the reason she looked so broken-hearted. Shawn wondered what kind of guy would let go of a girl like her.

He suddenly felt like shit for underestimating her earlier. God, what a dick move.

"Look, I feel like I need to apologize," he said, and she looked at him with a bemused expression. "For earlier."

Willa set her fishing rod on the chair near her and crossed her arms, looking at him expectantly.

Okay, so she wasn't going to make this easy for him at all.

"I shouldn't have assumed you were clueless at the bait shop," he said. "I'm a fucking feminist, and I acted like a dick. Sorry."

She bit her lip, clearly trying to hold back a laugh.

"It's just that you don't look much like an experienced fisher," Shawn said, trying to bring himself back to the conversation at hand.

He immediately knew he'd said the wrong thing. Her smile dropped slightly and her eyes narrowed.

"Yeah, well," she said, quickly reeling in her line. "You don't look much like a feminist. So."

Shit.

Shit.

What he meant to say was, *You were just so gorgeous with your flowing hair and your piercing eyes and your delectable tits that I thought, surely a creature this perfect can't also fish like she was born to do it?*

And instead, he'd said... *that.*

Once her line was all the way in, she withdrew the left-over bait from her hook and tossed it in the water. She put her fishing rod in a holder mounted on the wharf before facing him.

"I'm heading inside. Just put your rod away whenever you're done."

As she walked back to the house, she unceremoniously dumped the cast net into a dock box. Shawn watched her walk away until he could barely see her silhouette through the flashlight she was using to navigate back to the house. He sighed, reeling in his rod and disposing of his bait like she did, before hanging it on one of the holders they'd mounted on the wall.

As he walked back to his house, he checked the time and noticed over an hour had passed since he left to bring her the brownies. She operated on the water with the comfort of a local, fished like she'd been doing it since she was a baby —which, Shawn realized, she probably had. He wanted to make sense of her.

But she dressed like a Valley Girl and was as forth-coming as a barnacle.

And his stupid little crush meant he desperately wanted her to like him, which she clearly didn't. He'd spent years doing nothing but flash a pleasing smile to tourists before teaching them how to fish, laying his accent on thick because he knew the effect it had on people, getting easy approval and trust from strangers.

Not to mention, he was a people-pleasing Southerner. He'd become the town's go-to handyman over the past several years, ever since he took over the bait shop and his grandmother started giving out his phone number like it was the peppermint candy she carried in her purse. He'd fixed people's docks after tropical storms, taught his elderly neighbors how to use Netflix, and mowed lawns for his grandmother's friends while they were out of town. He knew the best fishing spots and took a group of elderly men fishing every month, before bringing them home to filet and cook their fish for them.

Everybody liked Shawn. He'd never had a problem charming women and he always knew what to say when someone was going through a rough time. He was reliable and steadfast and never hesitated to help someone out.

He didn't know what to make of the fact that Willa tongue-tied him so much that everything out of his mouth seemed to offend or annoy her. Most of the time, it seemed better to just keep his mouth shut. And he wished to God, more than anything, that he didn't care as much as he did.

Because even though he had butterflies again, he kept replaying what she'd told him.

Let's just say I've sworn off men for a while.

A single lamp was lit in the living room. His grandmother was curled up under her favorite blanket knitting, and he grinned as he pushed open the back door.

"Can't believe you're still awake, Grams," he drawled as he took his shoes off and sat across from her.

"You sure have been gone a long time, Scoob," she said, lips pressed together and eyebrows lifted expectantly.

Shawn groaned, dragging a hand over his face.

"So that's why you're still awake," he muttered.

"She's pretty, isn't she?"

"I thought you said you hadn't seen her since she was a kid?"

"I've got binoculars for a reason, Scooby," Grams said.

"Lord, have mercy, Grams. Don't tell people that."

"I'm 78 years old. I'll do what I want."

Shawn was torn between wanting to laugh and wanting to hide her binoculars. Instead, he got up and started heading to bed.

"Excuse me, I wasn't done talking," Grams pouted as he walked away.

"I was."

"Just answer my question."

Shawn turned around with the enthusiasm of a teenager being forced to tell a parent how school was. He glared at her.

"Don't you think she's pretty?"

Pretty didn't even begin to cover it. But he wasn't going to tell Grams that.

"I have eyes, don't I?"

5

Willa was ready to cry into her large iced vanilla latte with whipped cream.

Overconfident idiot, she told herself.

She sat down at a corner table in the coffee shop she'd stumbled upon, folded her arms on the table, and dropped her head as an upbeat Taylor Swift song played over the speakers. It took everything in her not to audibly groan in frustration, but she was in public, and this wasn't San Francisco.

"Rough day?" a soft southern drawl had Willa lifting her head up.

A woman with curly, raven-colored hair that starkly contrasted her pale face gave her a concerned smile.

"You have no idea." Something about this stranger's presence was comforting, so Willa asked, "What about you?"

"Oh, same old, same old for me. It's my break at work right now, and I like to come here sometimes for a quick coffee."

Willa winced. "Sorry to bother you with my self-pity."

"Don't be," she smiled, sipping her coffee. "Why are you having a bad day? If you don't mind me asking."

Willa sighed as she leaned back into her seat, defeat coursing through her. "I need a job. Just moved here from San Francisco, where I taught yoga at one of the best studios in the country. So I thought getting a job would be easy. But none of the gyms want me, and the closest yoga studio to my house isn't hiring right now. And have I mentioned I've barely driven a car in the past decade? I never needed one in SF, and now I feel like a teenager again, trying to re-learn how to operate a vehicle. You'd think it'd be like riding a bike and I'd pick it back up no problem, but no. I drove past, like, four stop signs. Accidentally, of course. But still. I'm an unemployed menace to society."

"Here," The raven-haired woman extended a plastic-wrapped chocolate chip cookie to her. "You need this more than I do."

"Oh my god, yes." Willa grabbed the cookie, opened it up, and took a bite. "I guess I should've been more ladylike and pretended to turn down your cookie offer, but I didn't have it in me."

Her companion laughed. "Don't worry about it."

Willa grinned. "I feel like I should know your name, unless you want me to call you the Cookie Fairy."

A small laugh trinkled from her. "I'm Layla."

"I'm Willa." She took another bite of the cookie. "So, Layla, do you know of anywhere hiring yoga instructors?"

"Hmm." Layla pinched her lips together in thought. Her eyes widened, lips quirking up for a moment, before she frowned again.

"What?" Willa couldn't help herself.

"Well," Layla bit her lip. "I'm the hotel manager at The Beachside Inn."

Willa furrowed her eyebrows together in consideration. Then she got it. "Oh. *Oh.*"

"We're a boutique hotel. We only offer the best of the best, but for activities, we contract with a lot of external vendors. Not a lot of in-house options." Layla's hands twiddled nervously around her coffee cup. "But I've been pushing our General Manager to try to branch out and incorporate a few in-house, luxury activities for a while now. Like yoga."

"What are you thinking?" Willa asked breathlessly.

"You tell me. If you were me, what would you pitch?"

Willa couldn't help it. She started getting excited as she considered the possibilities. The idea of building out a yoga program at a hotel was too thrilling for her to pass up.

"Sunset yoga, a few days a week. That one's always a winner. And a sunrise class on Saturdays. And then we can expand, if people like it."

Layla nodded thoughtfully, a grin growing. "We'd have to do a trial basis, of course."

"Of course. And I can help think through where we should do the classes. And the marketing."

"And we'd have to get my General Manager's approval." Layla frowned.

"Will that be hard?"

Layla sighed. "It's not that. It's just..."

Willa felt her energy shift.

"Look, I appreciate that you're trying to help me out, but the last thing I want to do is create trouble for you, Layla." Willa smiled. "Even the fact that you'd want to help me means a lot."

Layla shifted in her chair. "No, no. It's okay. You know how managers can be."

Willa frowned. "What do you mean?"

"He's just..." Layla blew out a breath, fidgeting. "Blake can be difficult."

"Difficult how?" Willa asked, feeling concerned for her new friend slash Cookie Fairy.

Layla gave her a smile—one that Willa felt was a bit forced. "Let me worry about that." She checked her watch. "I have to head to the hotel. Drop by at the end of the day and we can finalize everything. Yeah?"

Willa bit her lip, recognizing that she shouldn't push her new friend. She felt a bit uneasy, but responded, "I'll be there."

"WHAT DID YOU COOK TODAY, GRAMS?" Shawn asked, crossing his arms and leaning against the doorway into the kitchen, sweet aromas basking over him.

Her white hair was windswept, like she'd spent the morning sitting out on the wharf before coming inside, putting on her "Queen of Damn Near Everything" apron, and cooking what looked to be an assortment of pies.

"It's for the church bake sale, Scooby," she said swiftly, not even turning around to look at him. "It's on Wednesday and we're raising money to install a ramp in the entrance. Lord knows, us old people can't use stairs the way we used to."

It had been a slow day at the bait shop, which had given Shawn enough time to agonize over how he'd put his foot in his mouth in front of Willa. He kept replaying their encounter last night in grave detail, trying and failing not to think too much about what it'd feel like to stuff her smart mouth with his cock. He felt like a creep for fantasizing about her when she clearly hated him. She brought something out of him—something idiotic and primal.

"Willa really liked those brownies last night, by the way," Shawn said, attempting to seem casual.

He was anything but casual when it came to the groan she released as she licked her fingers clean of that brownie last night. Even the memory of it surged through him like she was right there, and his cock twitched uncomfortably in his pants as he thought about her sinful tongue. He couldn't ever remember being this gone for a woman—let alone one he barely knew. He didn't like it one bit, especially since she'd all but confessed there was no way she'd ever go out with anyone anytime soon after her breakup.

"Is that so?" Grams turned around, eyebrow lifted, both hands on her hips.

Shawn ducked his head, knowing he was caught.

"She remembered you," Shawn said. "I think she'll drop by at some point to say hello."

"Well I'm not sure how anybody could forget me." She grinned like a cat, expectation thick in the air. A few beats of silence passed. "Out with it, Scoob."

He sighed. There was no hiding anything from her, so he might as well milk it.

"Any chance you could spare one of those pies?" he asked gruffly. "You know. For Willa."

Grams pinched her lips together in poorly concealed amusement.

"I suppose you could take one of the pecan pies," she conceded. "But it'll cost you."

He groaned internally.

God, he was pathetic. Using his grandmother's award-winning cooking as a reason to talk to a pretty girl. He'd wooed dozens of tourists over the years, but this one woman put him on his knees with a simple glare. And he needed everything in his arsenal to get back in her good graces. Of course his grandmother would exploit that. She was little and white-haired, but she was clever.

"Of course it will. Well?"

"You have to accompany me to Bingo this Friday night."

Shawn narrowed his eyes.

"That's it?" he asked, waiting for the other shoe to drop.

"For now."

She turned back to her cooking, as if he hadn't even walked into the kitchen, so before she could change her mind, he snagged the pecan pie and scurried out the back door. As soon as he stepped outside, the sea breeze calmed him, and he made his way to Willa. He could see her immediately, at the edge of the water, doing yoga. Her auburn hair was in a big clump on top of her head, and the sunset made it burn brighter.

God, she was beautiful. And he had the burning desire to tell her so, but he had some making up to do first.

As he approached her, he noticed that every few minutes, she grabbed her phone. It looked like she was either sending a text or writing down some notes. But after a few moments, she'd put the phone back down and get back into her flow, picking right up where she left off. Once he was only about twenty feet away, she'd settled into a position that perched her ass in the air, and he could see up close how perfect it was.

He forced himself to clear his throat before he started drooling, startling her out of her flow.

She turned to face him, her face pleasantly relaxed but guarded.

"Grams made you a pie," he offered by way of introduction.

"Another one?" She looked puzzled.

"What do you mean?"

"She dropped one off earlier."

Well, shit. Grams had played him like a fiddle.

"I think she accidentally made a few extras," he said quickly. "For the bake sale. At the church. Now she's trying to get rid of them. You know how she is. Old. Forgetful."

God, he sounded like an idiot.

Willa narrowed her eyes at him, lips twitching in amusement.

"She seemed pretty put together to me, but whatever you say," she said, trudging toward the house. "Let's take it inside."

He followed after her and sure enough, sitting on the counter in her kitchen, was the pecan pie Grams must've dropped by earlier. He set the one in his hands next to it and stuffed his hands in his pockets.

"Look, I feel like every time I'm around you, I put my foot in my mouth. I'm sorry for what I said last night. And I just want to make sure we're... cool."

He felt so stupid as he looked at her, and her ocean blue eyes twinkled at him. She chuckled, and he marveled at how good it felt to be the reason for her smile.

"I'm sorry, too," she said. "For being so... curt. I'm not in a great headspace right now. It's making me a little more... combative than usual. Obviously. But yeah, we're cool."

"Cool. Good. Yeah. Okay. Great."

She bit her lip, clearly trying not to laugh at him, and he crossed his arms.

"So. Yoga?"

Maybe changing the subject would help him figure out how to talk to the stunning creature in front of him without sounding like he just got whacked over the head with a baseball bat.

"Yes, yoga," she smirked at him. "I was an instructor back in California. I just got a gig at one of the local hotels teaching a few classes a week for their guests, and I start tomorrow. So I was just trying to prep."

"Which hotel?"

"The Beachside Inn."

"Oh, that new one? Well, they're lucky to have you."

She smiled.

"Thanks."

"I've never done yoga before. Maybe I should come to one of your classes."

"Maybe you should," she said.

He licked his lips, and noticed her gaze drop to his mouth for a split second before returning to his eyes. He had about a hundred different fantasies playing in his head right now, all starting with devouring her mouth and ending with taking her right on top of the kitchen table.

But she'd sworn off men.

And he'd sworn off women who only wanted to spend a night with him.

"Well, listen, I'll get out of your hair," he said, trying not to kick himself for sounding exactly like his grandmother. "But good luck with your yoga class tomorrow, Greene. And I hope you like the pie."

"Thanks, Shawn," she said, peeking up at him through long lashes, and dammit if his heart didn't skip a beat as he heard his name leave her mouth.

6

Shawn loved the smell of fresh cut grass. It was partly why he took no issue with mowing lawns for the elderly folks in the neighborhood when they asked —and for Amos, a good family friend, he was always willing to help out.

His phone vibrated, so he cut the lawn mower, wiped the sweat from his brow, and answered.

"Hello?"

"Shawn Porter Gray, I'd almost forgotten what your voice sounded like," Hanna's stern tone—the one she undoubtedly used with her kindergartners when they were up to no good—came through the line.

Shawn held his breath, then sighed. He should've known that when Tucker was unsuccessful, Hanna would step in.

"Hey, Han," Shawn said.

"Hey? That's it?"

He grimaced, bringing a hand to the back of his neck. "Uh, well, I—"

"Why are you avoiding us?" She cut him off.

"I'm not avoiding you." *Liar.* "It's just been a busy summer, that's all."

"Hmm," Hanna said, sounding an awful lot like Grams. "So busy you can't come over for dinner tonight?"

"I have a sunset cruise booked." At least he didn't have to come up with a lie to get out of it. "Rain check?"

He heard Hanna release a disappointed sigh. "We miss you," she said quietly.

"I miss you guys, too." The truth, even if he was the reason for the distance between them. "Some other time soon?"

Silence passed over the line.

"Is everything okay, Shawn?" His eyes burned, but he didn't respond. "You know you can talk to us about anything, right?"

Not this. It was on the tip of his tongue.

"I know, Han."

"We love you," she added.

"I love y'all, too." *Even if I'm not acting like it.*

"Shawn—" As Hanna began to say more, Amos walked out of the front door of his house and eyed the lawn.

"Shawn, thank you!" he boomed.

"Anytime, Amos," Shawn forced a smile as he heard another sigh from Hanna over the line.

"You're busy," she said flatly.

He searched for words as Amos approached him, but none came.

"I'll let you run, Shawny. Call me when you're ready to talk. Love you." Hanna cut the line.

Shawn pocketed his phone, frustration with himself coursing through his body.

"You need a ride home?" Amos asked, not seeing Shawn's truck anywhere.

"No worries," Shawn said. "I jogged here. I'll jog home, too."

It was only a mile home, and he needed to pound out the confusing mess of emotions he was facing—and figure out how to get over himself and talk to his best friends.

"You sure?"

"Positive."

WILLA GRINNED to herself as she walked down the beach toward Ida's house. When Ida dropped by yesterday with the pie in hand, she'd been in a rush to get back to her kitchen and keep cooking, so Willa promised she'd drop by this morning for a visit.

Of course, when Shawn showed up with another pie barely an hour later, she'd seen right through him. He must've asked Ida for a pie to bring her in apology, and it was refreshing for a man to try so hard to get into her good graces.

Unlike Leo, who wouldn't be caught dead saying the words "I'm sorry."

She sighed, realizing the bar was on the fucking floor.

Shame surfaced as she thought back to how she overlooked some of Leo's more obvious red flags.

And when she met Blake after dropping by the hotel, she couldn't help but notice similarities between the Beachside Inn's General Manager and Leo. For one, he talked to her boobs, not her. Not to mention, he kept hinting at her giving him "private lessons" since he mostly lifts—as if that was supposed to impress her. Willa was thankful for the gig, but was not looking forward to the regular one-on-one meetings he insisted on having to stay updated on the progress of the new yoga program.

At least she had Layla.

Shaking herself out of her stupor, she raised a hand to knock on the door when it swung open.

"Right on time," Ida said, clad in joggers, a Smash the Patriarchy t-shirt, and sneakers. "Let's go on a walk."

Willa chuckled in spite of herself. Ida was a spitfire, that was for certain. She took no shit from anybody, and she got right down to business. Willa hadn't known the older woman wanted to be accompanied on a walk, but she was grateful for the excuse to get a bit of movement in.

"Good morning to you, too, Ida," Willa said with a smile.

"Oh, honey, now listen," Ida said, positioning a visor on her head, white hair spilling out onto her fair-skinned, wrinkled face. "I'd love it if you called me Grams."

"Grams?"

"I'd never try to replace your grandmother, God rest her sweet soul, but anyone in cahoots with my grandson gets to call me Grams. If you're comfortable with it, that is."

"Cahoots? Ida, listen, I—"

Ida cleared her throat and gave her a pointed look.

"Grams," Willa corrected herself, trying to bite back a bemused grin. "I wouldn't say I'm in 'cahoots' with your grandson."

She used air quotes around the word "cahoots."

"But I'd love to call you Grams."

"Well that's settled then," Ida said, brisk and business-like, but with a smile on her face.

They started walking toward the Bayou, the marshy

stream that fed into the Bay—the place where Willa went when she was looking for the occasional appearance of an alligator or heron.

"I usually try to walk to the Bayou and back every morning. It's just over a mile and helps me get my steps in."

"Well if you go around this time every morning, I'd love to join you," Willa said.

"I'd love that, sweetie," Ida responded. "Now, tell me. How are you settling in?"

Willa relished the way it felt to have Ida look after her. She was raised mostly by her grandparents and her nannies while her parents were off jet-setting, and since both her grandparents died, she hadn't felt this looked after in a while. It was a bittersweet feeling, knowing Ida cared about her. It made her ache with a warmth she hadn't felt in years.

"It's fine," she said. "The house is exactly like I remember it. I got a job teaching yoga classes at The Beachside Inn. I start tonight. So that should be good."

"Good for you," Ida said. "But tell me, how are you *really* doing?"

Willa wanted to cry. She couldn't remember the last time someone asked her that and genuinely wanted to know the answer.

"I'm alright," she said, her voice breaking a bit.

"Oh, honey," Ida came to a stop and drew her into a tight hug. Shawn's grandmother was a few inches shorter, but Willa still felt engulfed. Her eyes burned with tears that slowly began falling, and she buried her head in Ida's shoulder for a moment before pulling back.

"I'm sorry," Willa said.

"Nothing to be sorry for, dear," Ida said. "We can turn around if you want. I can make a pot of tea."

"No, I'm okay. Let's keep walking."

They continued in a comfortable silence for a few moments. Willa felt a strange connection to Ida—this woman she vaguely remembered from childhood, who was friends with her grandmother, and who would probably bring her another homemade treat this week. Before she knew it, Willa was spilling everything.

Her sordid dating history.

How she found out about Leo.

How she felt like she needed a break from men for a while.

How she'd never felt more alone.

How sometimes, she thought the anxiety of it all would swallow her whole.

By the time she finished talking, her tears were dry and they were almost back to Ida's house. Ida ushered her inside, and true to her word, she made a pot of tea. Even though it was hot and humid, it still felt comforting for Willa to take a sip of the tea and warm up her insides.

"Listen, hon," Ida said. "I wish I could bottle up this pain you're feeling and take it from you. All I can say is, most men in this life are trash, but some of 'em are worth holding onto. But you know what matters more than any of that?"

Ida took a sip of her tea.

"You. You matter, sweetie. And I'm proud of you for kicking ol' Leo to the curb and making him shake in his boots while you were at it. Now you've gotta learn how to trust yourself again, and that can be tricky business. But I'm here for you, alright? You come over and see me anytime."

Willa smiled at Ida, warmth flowing through her.

"Thanks, Grams."

"And listen, sweetie, I want you to meet my friends," Ida

clapped her hands together. "Oh, they'll love you! Would you join me for Bingo this Friday night?"

Right as Willa nodded in agreement, the door flung open and a shirtless, sweat-covered Shawn walked in.

"Hi," she squeaked.

Well, that was new.

She'd never squeaked in front of a man before.

Usually her confidence threw them off, but she hadn't realized just how hot Shawn was—or maybe, she hadn't wanted to realize it. But standing before her, there was no ignoring the strong curve of his arms, the way his six-pack glistened under his sweat, how that little V pointed down, down, down...

She was looking at his crotch. She couldn't tear her eyes away, though, because below that were his legs, and fuck. She'd never considered herself much of an appreciator of men's legs, but with Shawn, she could make an exception. They looked like they were sculpted, as rigid and muscled as Michelangelo's David.

Heat pooled in her core, and she cursed herself for suddenly feeling horny.

Horny and boyfriendless for the first time in years.

Not to mention, she'd sworn off men and had yet to unpack her favorite vibrator.

"Are you okay?" Shawn's breathless voice interrupted her rapt perusal of his body.

He'd taken out an Airpod and was looking at her with so much concern that she wanted to start crying again.

Had Leo ever looked at her like that?

Had anyone?

And suddenly, she realized how she must look—red-faced and blotchy and puffy, like she'd just cried. Which she had. She stood so abruptly she almost knocked over her tea.

"I'm fine," Willa said. "Thanks, Grams. For everything."

"Anytime, hon. See you tomorrow."

Willa walked past Shawn and their shoulders brushed, enough to send a zap of need coursing through her.

First order of business when she got back to the house: find her vibrators.

7

"**D**on't beat yourself up, Willa," Charlie said.

Willa had her on speakerphone as she laced up her sneakers to go over to Ida's for another walk. She'd had two of her yoga classes that week, and only a few people showed up to both. Of course, Layla came to both of them, but Blake showed up, too. Presumably, he was there to keep an eye on things and gauge the success of their program.

"I just feel like there should be more people showing up, but maybe I'm not doing enough to help them spread the word," Willa said.

"Okay, so make a flier," Charlie said. "Ask them to mention it to guests when they're checking in. Woo the bartender into telling everyone about it."

"Making a flier isn't a half bad idea."

"See? Everything starts out small. A few people is still a few people. And you get paid either way."

Charlie was right about that, but Willa didn't want low attendance to cause her to lose the job. She'd never worried about this before. Back in San Francisco, she'd had her regulars. Her classes were always well-attended, and even when they weren't, she was able to brush it off. As much as she wanted to pretend like she was unbothered by Leo's betrayal, she knew her deepest insecurities were surfacing since finding out he cheated on her.

Or rather, he cheated on his wife.

With her.

Willa sighed. She felt like she couldn't trust herself. Didn't know who she was anymore. She'd been with a married man for two years without knowing. She thought she was smarter than that. She thought she would see through a guy like him.

She thought a lot of things, and she didn't know what was true anymore.

"Willa? You there?" Charlie said.

"I'm here."

"Look, babe. I know you're going through it right now. Who wouldn't be reeling after everything that's happened to you? God, it's only been a few weeks since you found out about him." Charlie knew better than to say Leo's name. "I say this with all the love in the world: You need to go to therapy. It's not good for you to just sit with all these feelings and let them fester. I'm here to lend an ear whenever. You know that. But I really think talking to a licensed professional would go a long way. And you promised me you'd find a therapist after you moved."

"I know," Willa said. She'd been in and out of therapy for a lot of her life. She believed in the value of it, but just never found a therapist who stuck. "You're right. I'll look into it this week."

Charlie sighed, clearly relieved.

"Good. I'm going to check in and make sure you actually do it. Getting started is the hardest part."

Willa grinned. "Thanks, Charlie."

"So...," Charlie cleared her throat. "How's it going with your sexy neighbor?"

Willa gasped. "I never said he was sexy!"

"Didn't have to," Charlie said, clearly holding back a laugh. "I could tell. He's getting under your skin."

"Look, I'm friends with his grandma and he brought me a pie. It's not that big of a deal."

"So you know how big his deal is? Interesting."

"Charlie."

"Alright, alright. I'll shut up."

Never mind that Willa had gone through a few boxes before digging out her favorite vibrator and masturbated to the image of a sweaty Shawn fucking her like there was no tomorrow. No, she wasn't going to think about the fact that she'd had a sex dream about him that same night that made her wake up in a cold sweat wondering how talented he was with his tongue. And she definitely wasn't going to mention that she'd never felt hornier in her life.

"Did I lose you?" Charlie asked, a smile sneaking through in her voice.

"Maybe I should have a one-night stand."

A beat of silence passed.

"With your sexy neighbor?"

"No, Charlie. With... someone. Like. At a bar?"

Charlie laughed.

"You don't do one-night stands. You do boyfriends."

"Right, but you do. So teach me."

"It's not that hard, Willa. Just go to a bar. Dance with a guy. Ask him to come back to your place. Tell him what to do to you. Kick him out before you go to bed. The end."

Willa's stomach dropped at the idea of it.

She didn't love the idea of having sex with a total

stranger and kicking them to the curb. Shouldn't there be an inherent trust with a sexual partner, even if there's nothing long-term there?

Then again, she'd trusted Leo, and look where that landed her.

Maybe she could just go the friends-with-benefits route. Have casual sex with someone she knew and trusted, but stick to her plan of staying away from men. Shawn popped into her head for a brief moment. She felt heat creep up her cheeks as she allowed herself to imagine it, but almost instantly threw the idea away. There was no way she could casually sleep with Ida's grandson and then face her every morning for their walk.

"I can hear you overthinking this," Charlie said.

"Okay. Ugh. I'll figure it out."

"Yes, you will. Now I have to run to work, but text me later, okay?"

They hung up and Willa walked over to Ida's. She knocked on the door, but nobody answered. She tried again, but again no answer. She pulled out her phone to check the time—it was five minutes after their usual walking time. Ida was not usually late, but maybe something came up today that she'd forgotten to tell Willa about.

"You looking for Grams?"

She jumped, dropping her phone as a voice startled her out of her confusion. She knew before turning around that it would be Shawn, but she didn't expect him to be shirtless and sweaty.

Again.

She could feel her face turning red, and her gaze fell to his abs.

Fuck, a man had never affected her like this before—not even Leo. Hot men were a dime a dozen in San Francisco, especially in the yoga community. And she looked her fill. But never had she had such a volcanic reaction to someone just by looking at them. The way his brown eyes pierced hers made her feel like she would melt into a puddle, and she had the sudden urge to lick the sweat off his neck.

"Willa? You okay?"

Was that the first time he'd ever said her name? Or would it always sound like the first time, the way he said it? The way his husky, deep voice hit her had Willa clenching her thighs.

God, she was horny.

She cleared her throat and tried to pull herself out of the sex spiral she was falling into.

"We usually walk at 10," she told him.

Willa checked her phone again. It was 10:07 a.m. Shawn's brow furrowed in concern, and she wanted to run her index finger along his forehead and smooth it over.

"I'm sure she just forgot," Willa offered.

"No, she didn't," Shawn said, moving past her and opening the front door slowly. "She was about to go get dressed for your walk when I left for my run."

Willa tentatively followed him inside.

"Grams?" Shawn said. Then louder, "GRAMS?"

Willa heard a small whimper down the hall, and Shawn booked it toward where the sound came from. She followed behind him, and when she entered what she assumed was Ida's room, she saw her laying uncomfortably on the floor. She was dressed in her regular walking attire—joggers and a t-shirt—and one sock was half on.

"Grams," Shawn whispered, his voice strained as he kneeled next to his grandmother. "What happened?"

"Fell," she said, her weak voice cracking Willa's heart. "Lost my balance putting my socks on. Stupid."

"Let me help," Willa said, kneeling on the other side of her. She pushed Ida's hair out of her face and rearranged her limbs, which were skewed uncomfortably about her. "I was worried you stood me up."

Willa smiled weakly at her, hoping her attempt to lighten the mood wasn't poorly received. She was rewarded with a smirk and a wink from Ida.

"I'd never forget about our walks, hon," she said thinly.

Shawn left the room briefly and came back, tugging a shirt over his head.

"Grams, I'm going to pick you up and put you in bed," Shawn said, his eyes never leaving Willa.

"Alright, Scooby."

Before Willa could process the odd nickname, Shawn effortlessly picked up Grams and gently—so gently, it made her want to cry—set her in her bed. Willa grabbed an extra pillow from her bed and put it under her feet before draping a blanket over her.

"Do you want me to get you some water? Tea?" Willa asked, desperate to help Ida feel better.

"Shawn can get me some tea," Ida responded. "He knows how I like it. You can sit here and tell me how your yoga class went last night."

Willa held Shawn's gaze for a split second before he nodded and left the room. She grabbed an armchair from the corner and brought it to the edge of Ida's bed before sitting down and launching into how yet again, her class was not well-attended.

She told Ida about her plan to make a flier and try to work with the staff to better market her class, and then she dove into her plans for the sunrise class on Saturday. Ida, ever the patient listener, asked a few clarifying questions, but mostly let Willa speak uninterrupted. And Willa, hoping to take her mind off whatever pain she might be feeling, rambled for as long as she could.

"Well, honey, it sounds like you've thought this through," Ida said.

"Thanks, Grams," Willa said, before asking, "Are you in any pain? I can help you with some stretches that might make it better.

"What kind of stretches?" Ida asked, looking concerned.

"Nothing crazy," Willa said with a smile. "But I used to teach a few yoga classes for seniors back in San Francisco. I even helped a few of them work through pain and stiffness after falls like yours. You can lay down the whole time."

"Alright, then. Might as well try it."

Willa stood up and gently pulled Ida's legs forward, straightening them as much as she could. Then she folded them in and turned them to the right side, then the left side. She never pushed, and a few times she paused at the sound of a slight intake of breath from Ida. But Ida never told her to stop, so she repeated the motion over and over until Ida loosened up a bit more.

Then she folded the right leg, while keeping the left extended, and swapped them. Over and over she did these simple movements, trying to help loosen the stiffness in Ida's body. After a few rounds of that, she pulled the folded right leg over, twisting the spine and intensifying the stretch, before doing it on the other side. Willa repeated these movements, hoping to provide additional mobility to Ida and help her work through residual pain.

"What's going on here?"

Willa had just moved onto Ida's upper body, circling her wrists and adding slight pressure to forearms, when Shawn walked in glaring at her. Still sweaty from his run, hair tousled, he was carrying a teapot and a saucer for Grams.

"Sheesh, Scoob, who peed in your cheerios?" Ida said. "She's stretching me out, and it's making my limbs feel looser than they have in years, so put that scowl away and bring me my tea."

A muscle twitched in Shawn's jaw as he approached his grandmother's bed and set the tea on her bedside table.

"Are you sure you should be doing that?" Shawn asked, his glare only slightly softer as he looked at Willa.

God, she was going to get whiplash from him.

The way he stared at her with sweetness one minute and like a landlord evicting her from his house the next was enough to make her dizzy. Anger surged in her at the thought that he'd believe she would ever do something that would hurt Ida, but as she caught his eyes, she saw something beneath the cold glare: fear. She knew what it was like to love your grandparents dearly and worry about them constantly.

"I used to teach yoga for seniors," Willa said, maintaining eye contact with him. "I know what I'm doing."

With a tight nod, he turned around and left the room, leaving Willa both irritated and flustered.

"He worries about me," Ida said, startling Willa out of her stupor. "It was hard for him when his grandfather died. Lord knows, I won't be around forever, either. But Shawn will do everything in his power to make sure I'm around as long as I can be."

Willa took a deep breath, squaring her shoulders and continuing with the stretches.

"I understand. I would have done the same for my grandparents."

"Oh sweetie," Ida grabbed her hand. "They loved you. So much."

"I know," Willa said, her eyes burning.

If she'd known moving back to her family home would be this emotional, she might have avoided the hassle of it all. But then again, she was emotionally raw when she got here in the first place, so that wasn't helping matters.

"You should probably be stretching every day, Grams," Willa said, shoving aside thoughts of the grandparents she missed so much it ached. "I can help you when we get back from our walks every day."

"If you say so, dear," Ida said. "And you're still coming with me to Bingo tomorrow night, right?"

"Wouldn't miss it."

8

I t had been a long day at the bait shop.

Tourist season was always equal parts fantastic and nightmarish. The money Shawn earned in the summer months was at least five times the amount he earned during the months in the off-season. But some days, he wished he never had to interact with tourists. He'd become an expert in tourist personas, and he had them perfectly categorized.

First, there was The Overconfident Tourist. This was usually a man in his 40s or 50s who went fishing once and suddenly thought he knew how to line a rod or which bait worked best for redfish. When Shawn tried to help him with his selection, this man adopted the most condescending tone he could to explain to Shawn that he didn't need any help. Shawn rarely saw these guys again—probably because they didn't want to have to face him after squandering their time and money for a fishing trip that wasn't successful.

Then, there was The Flirty Tourist. He didn't mind the flirty men: they were nice and funny, and usually they had a pleasant conversation that led to them making a sizable purchase so they could do a photoshoot pretending to fish off their pontoon boat. But the women? They were sharks. They came in all ages, and they ruthlessly flirted, often touching Shawn's forearm or pointedly checking him out or even leaving their number on the receipt. A few years ago, Shawn took advantage of every last one of them. No strings attached sex? Yes, please. But it got old, and boring, and, most of all, lonely. Now, it was just uncomfortable when women shamelessly hit on him, not picking up on his signals that he definitely was not interested. It was worse because he couldn't ask them to stop without offending them and losing business. He'd tried.

And who could forget The Drunk Tourist? The ones who went on vacation so they had an excuse to start drinking the moment they woke up and chug their last beer before going to bed. Shawn loved a good time as much as the next guy, but those were the ones he worried about. They showed up with beer on their breath, looking for Shawn to take them on a booze cruise disguised as a chartered fishing trip, and how could he say no? They paid well, tipped even better, and he barely had to do any work besides babysit them to make sure nobody fell overboard.

His favorite customers—aside from locals, the regulars his grandfather had provided with shrimp and fishing line and lures before he took over the shop—were the families. He loved helping little kids find fishing rods they could use and watching them marvel over the shrimp tank and talking to the parents about best places to take their little ones.

But most of all, he loved taking the families on chartered fishing trips. Sure, he occasionally got big family groups—reunions, cousins getting together, and impromptu gatherings—wherein there'd be an undesirable tourist.

Maybe an uncle would be The Overconfident Tourist or

an aunt would be The Flirty Tourist or some college-aged cousins would be The Drunk Tourists. But even when that happened, he always felt the happiest after those excursions. The fullest. Like what he did made a real difference. Like he was bringing people joy and helping kids create memories they'd never forget.

But today? Today, he exclusively worked with The Flirty Tourists. And they came in with a vengeance. He felt dirty and used—the way they drew their long fingernails up his arms without his consent making him want to shower. It was nonstop all day long, and he'd even let a Bachelorette Party rope him into taking them on a chartered fishing trip tomorrow. He'd charged twice his usual rate for it, but he was still dreading it with every fiber of his being.

As he parked his truck in the driveway, he leaned over the steering wheel and banged his head on top of it. He still had a long night ahead of him.

He'd promised Grams he'd go with her to Bingo, and he wouldn't go back on his word. But the idea of spending his evening with a bunch of old ladies fawning over him wasn't exactly how he'd like to wind down after a long day.

Tap, tap.

He lifted his head and looked out the window of his truck to find Willa staring at him with a curious and hesitant smile. The air was knocked out of Shawn as he took her in. Her hair was pulled back into a loose bun with curls framing her face, and she was wearing a white sundress that tied together in the front, giving him just enough of a view of her tits that his mouth started to water.

As if he needed another reason to look at her lips, they were painted pink, and her tan and freckles shone brighter than normal, as if she'd spent the entirety of her time outside since she'd arrived.

The butterflies were back.

He tried to steady his thrumming heart.

Willa smirked and tapped her finger on the window again, and he realized she was waiting for him to respond. He opened the door of his car and stepped out, gruffly asking, "What are you doing here?"

He immediately kicked himself for his curt tone. Every time he was around her, everything came out his mouth like he was a caveman. He'd be apologizing to this woman for the rest of his life, but before he could say anything else, she responded.

"I'm here to go to Bingo with Ida," she said. "If her keeper will let her out for the night, that is."

"Nobody can tell Grams what to do. Not even me. Not even my grandfather."

"A woman after my own heart."

He grunted and started walking toward the house. Of course, Grams roped both of them into going to Bingo tonight. Of course, she just *forgot* to mention it to Shawn. Of course, Willa had to show up looking like that. If he could get through the night without getting a hard-on, it would be a freaking miracle.

"We'll probably leave in a minute or two," Shawn said without facing her.

"...we?" Willa asked, her voice coming out breathless.

So Grams hadn't told Willa about their group outing, either.

Because of course she hadn't.

Right as he was about to open the front door, Grams walked out wearing black pants and a white button down shirt, her purse in hand.

"Perfect timing, both of you," she said. "Shawn, you're driving."

And without a second glance, she headed toward his truck and opened the back door.

"Ida," Willa said, but a stern look from the woman in question had her backtracking. "Grams, I can sit in the back. You sit in the front with Shawn."

"Nonsense," Grams said, and Shawn hurried to help her climb into the back. "The front seat makes me dizzy anyway."

Shawn bit his lip, trying to hold back laughter. His best friend, Tucker, got carsick easily and always sat in the front to combat it. He knew Grams was full of shit, but she clearly still had bright ideas about matchmaking, and he wasn't about to try and call her out on her BS. He'd done that before and it never ended well for him.

Plus, he wasn't opposed to Willa sitting up front with him.

The idea gave him butterflies.

Stupid butterflies. Again.

"The front seat makes you dizzy," Willa deadpanned, crossing her arms.

"Yes, dear, that's what I just said."

"Grams, that makes no sense."

Grams raised an eyebrow at Willa and gave her a look that still made Shawn feel like he was about to be grounded or have his phone taken away. It harkened back to the time he'd prank called the neighbors and Grams had sent him to bed without getting dessert.

"Are you calling me a liar, Willa Mae Greene?"

"Am I calling you a—" Willa paused and scrunched her nose. "Wait, how do you know my middle name?"

"I know a lot of things, missy," Grams said sternly. "And I also know you shouldn't disrespect your elders."

"Disrespect? Grams, I'm just asking a question."

"Here's a question: Why are you about to make us late for Bingo?"

Willa sighed and turned her head toward the sky, as if asking God for mercy. Shawn couldn't remember the last time he'd been this entertained, and he wasn't anxious to end this interaction between Willa and Grams, but he knew better than to encourage this when being late to Bingo was on the line.

"C'mon," Shawn whispered to Willa. "It's not even a 10-minute drive to the church. You don't have to sit next to me for long, Greene."

Pink crept into Willa's cheeks, and Shawn was thrilled to have caused it.

"I—it wasn't—I don't—" she spluttered, and Shawn guided her to the passenger seat and opened the door for her.

"Don't worry about it," he said with a wink.

COULD you orgasm just from seeing a man wink? Because Willa thought she just might.

She'd done everything she could to put Shawn out of her mind. Behind all the grunting and saying the wrong things at the wrong time, he was a nice guy. She could tell. And he was also sexy as fuck, which was the problem.

Ida clearly had grand plans to bring them together. Willa had started to suspect the older woman during their walk this morning, when she waxed poetic for all of thirty minutes about how Shawn took such good care of her, how he was so kind and caring, how he had always been a good man. But her blatant attempt to make them sit next to each other in the car was clear proof that Ida harbored a hope that Shawn and Willa would get together.

Which couldn't happen.

Because Willa promised herself that she was taking a break from men.

At least, from boyfriends. She didn't trust herself not to fall for a man who'd do her dirty, just like they all had before. And even with Ida's ringing endorsement of Shawn, she still felt uneasy. Plus, she wanted casual sex. A one-night stand. Or better yet, a fuck buddy. And she couldn't do that with Shawn.

Could she?

"So, Ida, how was your day?" Willa asked, desperate to focus on something other than the man sitting so close to her that there was no avoiding his intoxicating scent—like a mixture of the salty air and some sort of aftershave.

"Can't hear you from back here, sweetie," Ida responded. "We can visit once we get there."

Willa looked back at Ida with an incredulous expression on her face. Ida shrugged and looked out the window. Willa faced forward and sighed, rolling her eyes in irritation.

"Sorry about her," Shawn said quietly. "She gets tunnel vision once she puts her mind to something."

"Clearly," Willa smirked. "So. How was your day?"

Shawn grimaced, and glanced over at Willa. He sighed.

"Tourist season is always interesting," he said, then paused in thought. "It's busy, and I have a few local kids help me out at the shop so I can keep up with everything. But some of the customers can be... challenging for me to work with."

"What, like Karens?" Willa asked.

"Sometimes," Shawn said.

A beat of silence passed, and Willa looked over at him,

brows drawing together. Where was the guy who winked at her a few minutes ago? The guy who sheepishly apologized for his grandmother's not-so-subtle matchmaking? Something happened at work—that much was clear, based on his awkward silence and his white knuckles and the way she found him earlier, with his head on the steering wheel.

"But not today," Willa said.

Shawn released a breath and glanced over at her. "Not today."

He pinched his lips together as if in thought, then it all came bumbling out.

"I feel like this is going to make me sound like a cocky bastard, but—"

"Language!" Grams shouted from the back.

"Thought you couldn't hear us, Grams?" Shawn said, eyeing her through the rearview mirror with a bemused grin. "Anyway. I know this'll make me sound like... well, like the word I said before. And you already probably think I'm a di—a jerk."

Willa bit her lip at his attempt to watch his language.

"But sometimes, women come into the shop. Tourists. And they... well, they flirt with me. Pretty hard. And it's just... I don't love it. It makes me uncomfortable. I just want to sell them bait and take them on fishing trips, but the way they touch me makes me feel dirty. Used. Like all I'll ever be seen as is a good time."

Her heart ached for him—because she knew exactly how he felt. How many times had she made up a fake boyfriend to get a sleazy, disgustingly persistent man to leave her the fuck alone?

"There were a couple of girls who..." Shawn trailed off, as if deciding how much he should share. "Well, I thought it was the real thing with them. Thought they'd want to stick it out with me—make it work. Turns out I was just being stupid. They ghosted me the day they left. There was one who I later found out was here for her bachelorette party. I was her last hurrah before getting married. Made me feel like a piece of shi—"

He cut himself off and checked the rearview mirror to see if Grams was paying attention. He smirked, then added, "Anyway, after that, I decided I was done with tourists. Unfortunately, tourists have not decided they're done with me. And on days like this, it really sucks."

So maybe this guy was not the emotionally unintelligent caveman she'd made him out to be when they'd first met. Maybe he was kind and caring and in touch with his feelings and dealt with some of the same bullshit she did. Maybe he wasn't just nice. Maybe he was actually a good guy.

Fuck.

She was in trouble.

"This is the part where you say that I'm being stupid and if I were a normal guy, I'd just flirt back and give them what they're after," Shawn said.

"I would never say that," Willa said, equal parts annoyed that he assumed she'd respond that way and empathetic that he clearly felt so insecure sharing this with her. So she threw him a bone—a peace offering, of sorts. "I know what it's like to get unwanted attention from people like that. To be shamelessly flirted with and not know how to get it to stop. To be reduced to nothing but your body."

Shawn looked over at her, surprise lighting up his eyes at her admission.

"I can imagine," he said.

"And what is that supposed to mean?" Willa asked, crossing her arms and biting back a grin.

"Fuck, nothing, I just—"

"Watch your language, Scooby. I won't ask again."

Shawn rolled his eyes.

"Grams, you either can hear us or you can't. You don't get to have it both ways."

"Hmph," was all she said in response.

Shawn sighed and muttered under his breath. Something about "eccentric old woman" and "give me a conniption."

"Willa, look," Shawn said. "I... fu—I mean, crap. I always say the wrong things around you, don't I? All I meant was that... God, you'd have to be blind not to see how pretty you are. So I can imagine that it leads to unwanted attention, is all."

She could feel him looking at her, but she stared out the passenger window digesting what he'd said. Her stomach fluttered in pleasure, which was stupid, because guys called her pretty all the time. But the way Shawn said it was like he'd combust if he didn't tell her. And it made her feel things she didn't want to feel.

"Well, for the record, I was just messing with you," Willa said quietly. "But thanks. You're not bad, yourself."

Out of the corner of her eye, she saw his lips quirk up in a half smile as he pulled into the church parking lot.

"Next time it happens, tell them you have a girlfriend who teaches yoga," Willa heard herself say as Shawn's lips parted. "They don't have to know it's not true. But use me as an excuse anytime you want. It's how I get men to leave me alone. Making up a fake boyfriend."

After staring at her for a second too long, Shawn nodded and put the car in park.

9

W illa never thought she'd describe Bingo as a bloodbath.

But sitting in the cafeteria of Ida's church with a few dozen other people—mostly seniors—Willa was both amused and terrified. Apparently, the church had been hosting Bingo nights every Friday during the summertime for years now. It was a popular weekend activity among older locals, and with a suggested participation fee of $10, it served as a decent fundraiser for the church. Local businesses donated the prizes people won, but people mostly cared about the bragging rights.

Clearly, because Ida's best friend, Barb—a petite Black woman with short, curly hair—was currently sticking her tongue out at the rest of the table after having won the first round. She got a $5 gift card to a local coffee shop, and as the moderator brought it up to her, she grabbed it from him and started shaking her hips in a victory dance.

"Sit down, old lady!" Ida shouted.

"I'm younger than you!" Barb shouted back.

"So listen to your elders, then!"

"Oh, don't get your panties in a wad because you lost!"

Ida harrumphed and crossed her arms.

The rest of the older women at the table laughed at their exchange as the moderator came over the speaker and announced the start of the second round.

This time, you could win one of two ways: By getting an X or getting a row of five. The two winners would get a pie from the pastry shop. As Barb sat back in her chair, Ida pointedly ignored her and put her glasses on in solemnity.

"They do know this is mostly a game of chance, right?" Willa asked Shawn quietly out of the side of her mouth.

He looked up in alarm, then glanced around the table before looking back at Willa.

"Whatever you do, do *not* say that to them, Greene," he said. "Grams gave me the silent treatment for two days last time I insulted the very strategic and intellectually complex game of Bingo."

"You're kidding," Willa giggled.

"I wish I were," Shawn said, then leaned in to whisper in her ear. "They take their Bingo very seriously, in case you haven't picked up on that. And whatever you do, don't mention Nancy Siders."

She tried not to shiver at the way it felt for his hot breath to cascade over her ear.

"Who's Nancy Siders?" Willa asked breathlessly.

Ida gasped, and Shawn dragged a hand across his face.

"We don't say that name around here," Ida said, looking disgruntled. "It's bad luck."

Willa raised her eyebrows and looked at Shawn with a curious glance. His eyes widened and he gave a slight shake of his head, causing Willa to chuckle.

"It's not a laughing matter, young lady," Barb chimed in. "That woman is in cahoots with the devil."

The moderator called out the first letter and number combo, and the two women went silent and focused on their Bingo cards, leaving Willa wondering what she'd just witnessed. She turned to look at Shawn, who was checking his card to see if he could put a chip down, and had an adorable look of concentration on his face.

"So... who is She-Who-Must-Not-Be-Named?" Willa whispered.

He looked up at her with a grin, his long hair falling into his face.

"The reigning champ of Bingo," he whispered back. "Bit of a sore winner, too. That's why they hate her."

"Ahh. So, what? She made a deal with the devil that she'd win small town Bingo every Friday? Who even keeps track of how many times someone wins?"

"The regulars do. They all pool in $50 each and whoever has the most all-time wins at the end of the summer gets the pot."

"You're fucking kidding me."

He chortled.

"How did I never know this existed? Did my grand-mother do this?" Willa asked.

"I didn't know Betty very well," Shawn responded softly. "I did see her here a few times, though. She wasn't as intense as Grams."

"Thank God for that. I don't know if the world needs anymore of them."

He grinned at her, and she realized this was the most pleasant interaction she'd had with him.

Okay, so she couldn't ignore the fact that he was mouth-wateringly hot, but maybe she could still be friends with him. It'd be nice to have a friend her age. She and Layla chatted a few times when she was at the hotel, but she seemed a little timid. Maybe with Shawn, she could actually start to put down roots here.

"So are you two dating or what?" Barb broke the silence.

Shawn groaned, his cheeks reddening as he dragged a hand over his face.

"No, we're not dating," Willa said. "Just because two people are roughly the same age doesn't mean they're dating."

"That's not why I asked," Barb responded. "I asked because this round just wrapped up and neither of you have put a single chip on your card because you've been whispering in each other's ears."

"We haven't been—" Willa cut herself off, rolling her eyes. "Look, we're not dating. 'Kay?"

"Well, that's a shame," Shirley, another woman at the table, cut in. "You make such a pretty pair."

"But if you're available, Willa, then I can set you up with my grandson," one of the other ladies cut in. Willa was pretty sure her name was Mary. "He's a doctor."

Mary waggled her eyebrows.

"Um, thanks, but I'm taking a break from dating for a while," Willa said. "Bad breakup."

"Oh, you poor thing," Shirley chimed in. "Well, what about you, Shawn? My granddaughter is going to be in town next weekend. Maybe you can take her out on the boat."

Willa's insides clenched at the thought of Shawn taking a girl out who wasn't her. Which was silly, she reminded herself. Stupid. Idiotic, even. They weren't dating. They were barely even friends. And she wasn't going to date him, anyway. She couldn't—not without breaking her promise to herself that she'd stay single for a while. She noticed her fists were clenched at her sides and tried to relax them, avoiding looking at Shawn with everything she had.

He cleared his throat.

"Thanks, Miss Shirley," he said, ever the Southern gentleman. "But I'm going to have to take a rain check this time around. I'm booked solid next weekend."

Shirley looked disappointed but didn't press the issue.

A few more rounds of Bingo passed, and Willa and Shawn didn't talk as much after that. Willa felt like she might explode from the tension, but just focused on trying to get through the night so she could go home and not be under the scrutiny of half a dozen older women.

"Alright, this is the last round for the night," the moderator came over the speaker to say. "This time, there's only one winner. The catch? You have to be the first to have a blackout."

A hush of anticipation came over the crowd.

"The winner of this round will get our most coveted prize: a free, chartered fishing trip with our very own Shawn Gray! You can bring up to five people with you, and he'll take you on a two-hour boat ride on the Bay to fish in the best spots."

Excited chatter buzzed throughout the cafeteria and Willa looked up at Shawn quizzically. He caught her eyes for a moment and then looked away. God, was he... bashful? Why was that the most adorable thing that had ever happened in the history of men? And why was she grinning like an idiot?

"Alright, let's get started. B-45!"

"Dang it, don't have that one," Barb said.

"Me either," Ida responded, grinding her teeth.

"Grams, he's your grandson," Willa said, placing a chip on her card.

"A win is a win, missy. And I wouldn't mind a little extra time with my grandson."

Willa bit her lip as the announcer read out five more letter and number combos, all of which Willa had on her card.

"Watch out, folks, the newbie might win this one," Shirley said teasingly.

"We've still got a long way to go," Willa responded.

But the moderator kept calling out spaces she had on her card.

N-6.

G-57.

G-2.

I-33.

B-1.

O-12.

On and on it went, and Shawn grinned at her as she filled in the second to last piece on her board.

Suddenly, Willa was nervous. The stakes weren't high. Logically, she knew that. She didn't care much about a chartered fishing trip with Shawn. She had her own boat. Never mind that it'd be romantic as hell to watch his steady arms steer the boat. Maybe he'd help her reel in fish, coming in behind her and holding the rod for her while she reeled. Maybe she'd bring along a six pack of beer and some sandwiches for a picnic.

She shook her head. What was she thinking? She didn't care about winning.

"B-34."

Willa released a sigh as she realized that wasn't the one she needed. Frantically, she looked around the cafeteria to see if that had been the winning call for someone else. When silence followed for a few moments, she breathed easily for a second. Shawn looked at her with a lifted brow, as if he was saying, *You can pretend all you want, but I know you're dying to win.*

She bit her lip.

"O-7."

Willa sighed in relief as she put her final chip down.

"We have a winner over here, Amos!" Ida shouted at the moderator, fluttering her eyes in his direction.

Did Grams have a crush? Willa's eyes darted to Shawn, who was watching Ida ogle Amos with bemusement. Willa bit back a grin as Amos made his way to their table and reviewed her card to confirm she won.

"Let's all give a round of applause to this evening's big winner!" Amos said.

The cafeteria began clapping, and even Barb and Ida looked pleased that she'd won, even though she was sure they'd be sore losers. Amos put an envelope on the table in front of her. She assumed it was her certificate for the boat ride with Shawn. She dared a glance over to him, and he was grinning at her, clapping along with the rest of them.

10

The waves gently crashed onto the shore and Willa breathed in the salty air.

It was going to be a good day. She could feel it.

After she got home from Bingo last night, she shoved the certificate she won into her bedside table and spent some quality time with her vibrator, trying not to think about how she felt when Shawn winked at her or whispered in her ear.

Saturday morning classes were always her favorite. They tended to bring in people who were trying yoga for the first time or who couldn't make it during the week, always leading to a fun atmosphere. She was only bummed because she couldn't walk with Ida on Saturdays since it conflicted with the time of her class.

She'd run into Blake this morning, but to her surprise, he was perfectly pleasant. He let her know that there was a coffee bar she was welcome to, if she wanted. Willa wondered if she'd judged him too harshly at first, or if Layla's concerns colored her first impression.

Sure, Blake was attractive in the same way Leo was, and there were a few similarities in the way they dressed and carried themselves. But perhaps she had been too quick to group them together, and she decided she'd make a conscious effort to give him another chance.

She laid out her mat as people started making their way toward her. Usually, she taught yoga classes in one of the conference rooms on the first floor. She'd been bringing incense and her bluetooth speaker to improve the ambience, but she wasn't sure it was helping much. So she'd posted a sign in the conference room today that she'd be doing yoga on the beach, hoping that it'd be a better location for people to connect with themselves.

As people showed up—some with yoga mats the hotel had on hand, others with beach towels—she started playing music and encouraged them to get settled and begin stretching however they saw fit. She was happy to see that Layla had joined today, along with one of the hotel bartenders, a blue-haired woman she hadn't met yet. All in all, about ten people had showed up which was a promising development for her.

"Alright everyone, let's get started," Willa said.

She guided everyone through warm-up stretches and a simple sequence, offering modifications for those who were new to yoga. She demonstrated some poses, helping some people adjust the position if they got the footing wrong.

"And remember, yogis, it's okay to skip the bind," Willa said as she demonstrated how to go from warrior two into a bind, where her arms wrapped behind her back and looped between her legs.

A few people toppled over as they attempted the bind, and she went over to help them assume the correct position.

"Now, yogis, it's time for one of my favorite parts of yoga —going upside down," she said. "I'm going to show you a few ways you can do this. For my beginners, spread your legs out and forward fold. Grab your ankles if it feels comfortable, pulling yourself deeper into the stretch. For more advanced yogis, put your hands down on either side of your head, and pull yourself into a headstand."

She pointed her toes and pushed her feet into the air, taking deep breaths before bringing her feet back to earth. While in the pose, she reminded students to protect their necks and listen to their bodies, offering tips on the healthiest ways to get into their headstand.

"Feel free to spend a few minutes in that pose or challenge yourself to do something you haven't tried before. I'll come around and see how everyone's doing, and then we'll wrap up in a moment. So this is your last chance to really push yourself today. And remember, it's okay to mess up! That just means you tried."

She went around and spotted a few people attempting a headstand. A few students, like the hotel bartender she had yet to meet, were clearly practiced yogis who could pull off a headstand effortlessly. Most of them fell over or stayed in the forward fold.

A few moments later, she wrapped up the class with gentle stretches and an extended shavasana. Willa said goodbye to everyone else, encouraging them to come back next week if they'd still be in town, before visiting with Layla.

"This is Amanda," Layla said, gesturing to her alabaster-toned companion.

"I recognize you from the bar," Willa said, extending her hand. "It's nice to meet you. Thanks for coming today."

"I loved your class," Amanda said, her blue hair blowing in the breeze. "So you can definitely expect me to be one of your regulars."

"Thanks," Willa said.

"We typically go out on Friday nights," Amanda said. "Girl's night and all that. Want to join us next week? We get drinks and vent about work. You're one of us now. Come hang."

Willa grinned. "I'd love that. Thanks for inviting me."

After exchanging numbers and promising that she'd join them next weekend, they said goodbye and she headed back home. The drive back to her house was one of her favorites—ocean views on every side of her, and a steady exit from tourists galore back into her locals-only haven.

It'd only been a few weeks, but she was starting to feel like herself again. Willa thought she'd miss San Francisco more—the walkable city, the infinite amount of restaurants, the hustle and bustle. But she was beginning to realize she was more suited for a slower pace of life—one offered by her home on the Bay.

As she came up on Shawn's bait shop, she decided to pull in and get some shrimp for that evening.

Maybe she'd even invite him to do some off-the-wharf fishing with her.

As friends.

For fun.

SHAWN HAD NEVER HAD two back-to-back days filled with tourists that made him feel like he'd rather be taking a nap in the middle of the highway, but here he was. Dealing with one of the same groups of women from yesterday. Trying to explain to them—again—that he was booked solid for the next week and couldn't take them on a ride. Pretending to ignore their alcohol-stained breath.

"C'mon," said the ringleader of the group, a busty

blonde who batted her eyelashes as she laid a hand on his forearm. "Can't you make an exception, just this once?"

Shawn heard the door jangle as someone came in, but was too busy trying to calm himself down enough to deal with this woman, when a voice he recognized pierced the silence.

"Hey, babe."

Shawn's heart pounded as he looked at Willa.

Holy fuck, she was *actually* following through. When she'd said he could use her as an excuse—as his fake girl-friend—to keep the tourists away, he didn't think she'd show up at his bait shop and help him with the ruse.

"Hi," he said, breathlessly.

She smiled at him.

God, being on the receiving end of that smile felt like catching a 40-pound grouper—like he was the luckiest son of a bitch on the Gulf. He felt the edges of his lips curve up in response until she pouted.

"Aren't you going to kiss me?"

A temptation too hard to resist.

He barely registered pushing past the blonde who had cornered him and grabbed Willa's hip with one hand and her cheek with the other before claiming her mouth. She tasted better than he imagined. Like strawberries and sunshine and salt.

He'd daydreamed about these lips—about what it'd be like to suck and nibble and bite them, and so he did. He tugged her closer and she fisted her hands on his chest before digging her fingers into his hair. He couldn't hold back a groan when she thrust her tongue into his mouth, and he consumed her. He wanted to taste every inch of her, wanted to get lost in this moment, this kiss—

Suddenly, she was gone.

Someone had cleared their throat behind him.

Willa looked over his shoulder, still panting from the kiss.

The kiss he wouldn't have stopped if she hadn't pulled away.

He rested his forehead against hers.

"Hi," he whispered.

"Hi," she responded, her eyes drifting to his mouth again.

"So is this your girlfriend?" the busty blonde asked.

"The one and only," Willa said, pushing past him and crossing her arms as she studied the tourist. "Maybe you shouldn't touch men unless you know they want you to."

"He certainly didn't seem to mind it."

"Not what it looked like to me."

"How would you know?"

"Trust me," Willa said, her voice thick with meaning as she rested a sultry gaze on Shawn, bringing a hand to his cheek and rubbing her thumb across his lips. "I know."

Shawn's heart thumped.

He was still recovering from that kiss. If someone had told him the world stopped spinning while his lips were locked with Willa's, he might have just believed them.

His little crush was getting out of control.

He didn't question it when she asked for a kiss. He'd thought about it enough since last night. Since the pure joy on her face when she won Bingo. Since the way she looked at him after he dropped her off. He'd jacked off this morning, thinking about those plump lips around his cock, those delicate fingers dragging him into her mouth.

"Look," he said, feeling light-headed from the kiss he'd never stop thinking about. "Like I said, I can't take you on a ride this week. Happy to help you find some rods or lures, if you want some. But I'm booked solid for anything else."

The blonde stared at him for a split second before responding.

"Time to go, girls."

As the door jangled on their way out, he turned back to look at Willa, who was staring at him with square shoulders and a lifted chin.

"Sorry if I went too far," she said. "I just walked in and saw her touching you, and I thought about what you told me yesterday. And I wanted to make her stop. I didn't think..."

She didn't think he'd kiss her.

Those were the unspoken words hanging in the air. She must've thought he would just peck her on the cheek to keep up the charade.

He tried not to look disappointed. Did that mean she hadn't felt as affected by the kiss as he had? That she hadn't felt like the world stopped for a moment, and all that existed was the two of them? That she hadn't wanted to keep going?

"Thank you," he said honestly, knowing that if she hadn't come in when she did, he'd still be trying to get away from that woman. "I'm sorry if I—"

"No," she said, cutting him off. "No, it's fine."

She bit her lip and crossed her legs, eyes darting to his lips again. A spark of hope coursed through him.

So she was affected, after all.

"Maybe I should use you as my fake girlfriend more often, Greene," he murmured as he walked closer to her.

"Do fake girlfriends get discounts? Because if so, I'm in."

"I'll have to take it up with management." He paused. "Management says you get 20 percent off every purchase."

She giggled.

"Why'd you come in today, anyway?" he asked.

"I was on my way home from yoga and thought I'd get some shrimp. I was thinking of fishing off the wharf tonight. I was going to invite you to join me, actually," she sucked a deep breath in. "But I'm just now realizing I don't have my bucket."

"I can bring some home for you," he jumped in. "At the end of my day. I have a bunch of buckets out back I use to bring bait home or on the chartered trips."

"I don't want to be a hassle."

"Not a hassle at all."

She hesitated, then nodded.

"Should I go ahead and pay for them now?"

"This one's on the house."

"Shawn, you don't have to—"

"Please, it's the least I can do for my fake girlfriend," he smirked.

She grinned at him. "9 o'clock. My wharf."

"I'll be there."

11

S hawn wasn't sure why he was nervous. There was no reason to be.

The insulated bucket he carried sloshed a bit, though it was covered. He filled it with upwards of thirty shrimp—more than she asked for, but he told himself he threw in some extra as a thank you for being such a great companion to Grams. Ever since her fall, Willa had been insisting that Grams stretch every day, and she even walked her through stretches and exercises to do after their walks.

He tried not to acknowledge the fact that if they had more bait, they could stay out on the wharf and fish for longer.

That definitely wasn't the reason he gave her extra shrimp.

For sure.

He loved the Bay at night. The way the water went nearly still, the gentle breeze making the humidity bearable, the way the stars shined bright. In the distance, he could see the main highway along Orange Beach—the brightness of the hotels and beachside bars making it easy to pick them out. The rest of the Bay was sleepy—quiet.

His phone buzzed, and he set down the bucket to check. It was a text from Tucker. Shawn's stomach sank.

Hey, man. Want to come over for dinner soon? We miss you.

Shawn had been a shitty friend and he knew it.

He'd been ignoring Tucker's calls for months, and he was running out of excuses. It was hard watching his best friend so blissfully happy and in love when Shawn desperately wanted the same for himself.

Shawn texted back.

Maybe next month. Booked solid for tourist season. Tell Hanna I say hi.

He felt bad writing his friend off like that, but he and Tucker had known each other since they were in diapers. Shawn knew he'd understand. But one of these days, he'd have to actually come clean and explain why he'd been so distant lately. Guilt churned inside him, but he tried to brush it off as he put his phone away and picked the bucket back up, continuing on his way to the Greene's place.

As he approached Willa's house, he noticed the kitchen light was off but the light on the end of the wharf was on. He could just barely make out the outline of her figure at the end, and he headed her way quietly. He heard little splashes as he approached the edge of the wharf. It was a good sign —meant the fish were active tonight. They'd likely get some bites—maybe even catch a few big ones.

She didn't hear him approach, her nose buried in her kindle, the light from it shining on her sea-blue eyes and freckled face. Her brows furrowed in concentration, and she was wearing loose fitting shorts and an oversized t-shirt, her hair thrown in a messy bun. It was the most casual he'd ever seen her, and it felt intimate to see her like this with the full moon above them.

He cleared his throat and she looked up, then grinned at him.

"Got the goods?"

He lifted the bucket in response and set it on the table next to her. She went to the edge of the wharf, where the LED light was beaming into the water, and grabbed two fishing rods from the holders she set them in.

"Should be a good night for fishing," she said as she handed him one of the rods. "There's been activity under the light all night, and I keep hearing them jump."

Then, just as she did on the day they met, she reached into the bucket with her bare hand and pulled out a shrimp before expertly baiting it onto the hook. Its legs twitched, and she released the line before smoothly casting it into the water. Her line landed several meters beyond where the LED light shone, and she slowly began reeling.

He could watch her like this for hours. Days, probably. So at ease with a fishing rod underneath the moonlight that she looked like she was conjured out of thin air by some celestial being.

"Aren't you going to join me?" she smirked at him over her shoulder, her hands still gripping the rod firmly.

It was then that Shawn realized he not only had yet to say a word to her, but he'd been gaping at her like an idiot since he'd put the bucket down.

And this, he realized, was why he'd been so nervous. It was like he forgot to function like a regular human around her.

She was so goddamn beautiful, and she knew her way around a fishing rod like a pro. Willa moved like life was a dance—smooth and easy, unhurried and precise. He didn't want to tear his eyes away from her for a second, not when he could watch the way her delicate fingers reeled in her line or the way her hips swayed gently as she stood at the edge of the wharf or the way that smart mouth curved when she teased him.

And of course, he knew what that mouth tasted like now.

How could he forget the way her lips felt on his, the way his cock immediately responded to her, the way it felt for her fingers brush his mouth?

He never would. Now that he knew what it felt like to kiss her, Shawn was desperate to do it again. But she'd made it clear that wasn't going to happen.

He was supremely fucked.

"Was just enjoying the view," Shawn said, immediately regretting his poor attempt to flirt. "But yes, I'll join you now. Thanks again for inviting me."

She chuckled and shook her head at him, and his eyes lit up as he caught her gaze briefly before she turned back around.

He quickly attached bait to his rod and joined her. He cast his line out, careful to avoid the area hers was in so they wouldn't get tangled. Then he set his fishing rod in the holder and grabbed a couple of chairs for them to sit in.

"Thank you," she said softly.

They sat in companionable silence for a few minutes before she'd reeled her line in completely only to find that her bait had been eaten.

"Damn," Willa said. "I felt some nibbles, but wasn't sure."

"Hate it when that happens," he said. "Don't worry, though. I brought some extra bait."

"Knew I'd be losing my bait so easily, did you?"

He laughed—quietly, though, so he didn't scare off the fish.

"Nah, just thought I'd do my best to earn brownie points with my fake girlfriend."

Yeah, he was going to milk the fake girlfriend thing for all it was worth.

Maybe he could convince her to drop by more often and scare the tourists away.

Maybe she'd want to be his real girlfriend.

He shook away the thought and brought his attention back to his rod. Back to Willa. She cast her line back into the water again after baiting it, and slowly started reeling.

"So," Willa said.

Shawn grinned. "So."

"Scooby?" she asked.

He chuckled. "Yeah, I'll never get out of that nickname."

"Why does Grams call you that?"

He bit back a smile. "When I was 5, I was obsessed with Scooby Doo. Had the lunchbox. Watched the cartoons every Saturday morning. And I dressed up as Scooby for Halloween."

Willa laughed. "That's cute."

He wondered if his pounding heart would give away how much he loved her laugh—if she could hear it over the gentle crashing of the waves.

"You'd think," he responded, feeling his cheeks redden. "But I went a bit overboard with it. Made my family call me Scooby and treat me like a dog, did tricks for Scooby Snacks, did the voice—the whole nine."

"You didn't," she giggled.

"I did. And then, I refused to take the costume off for two weeks. I imagine that was not a fun experience for anyone involved, but I loved it. And Grams has called me Scooby ever since."

Willa fell into a fit of laughter, clutching her stomach and wiping her eyes.

"Oh my god, that might be my favorite story ever," she said.

He couldn't hold back the grin that stretched across his face as he watched her laugh, trying to memorize the unadulterated glee she was exuding. Once her laughter died down, she stole a glance at him, and he could've sworn he saw her cheeks flush as he held her gaze.

"Did she raise you?" Willa asked softly.

Shawn stiffened. "Her and my grandfather."

Willa looked back to her rod, giving him space. It was vulnerable—raw. He wanted to tell her this part of his story, but it never got easier to talk about.

"My parents died when I was two," Shawn continued. "Car accident on I-98. I barely remember them, but Grams and Pop... They helped me. To remember them. To grieve. To navigate life without them. They put me in therapy pretty early on. I'm grateful for that."

She gave him a grim smile. "I'm sorry."

It was all she could say. "Thanks." He reeled in his line and cast it back out. "I know my parents were good people. That they loved me. And being raised by Grams and Pop was... well, it could've been a lot worse. I had a really good childhood, and I know how lucky I am."

He loved his grandparents dearly. Missed Pop every day. Savored every moment with Grams, even when she made him want to rip his hair out. And he knew he was lucky to have grandparents who loved and supported him—who knew therapy was what he needed, who refused to let the stigma around it keep their grandchild from getting the care he needed.

Shawn tipped his head to the side. "What about your parents?"

Willa sighed, her lips curling up. "They live in London these days. Dad is the high-powered career type. Mom's a socialite."

The pieces of Willa started falling into place. He gave her the space she gave him—let her sit in silence, deciding what she wanted to share.

"They've always been jet-setters, and sometimes I think they don't know what to do with me," Willa added with a chuckle. "We're so different. But I know they love me, and I love them—even if our relationship looks different than most parents and kids. They have never once made me feel lesser than for pursuing a yoga career rather than some big-wig corporate job. They're extremely supportive. They're just a little... absent. It's something I made peace with a long time ago."

She brought her legs up to her chest as she reeled her line.

Shawn decided to throw her a bone. A few moments of silence passed before he asked her, "How's yoga going at the hotel?"

"It's alright," she responded, perking up a bit at the subject change. "Had more than ten people there today, so that's an improvement."

"How'd you get into yoga anyway?"

She was quiet for a moment.

"I wanted to be a ballerina. I know it sounds dumb. What little girl doesn't want to be a ballerina when she grows up? Usually people grow out of that. But I was—well, at the risk of sounding extremely full of myself—I was really good."

She sighed.

"I started doing yoga in college at the suggestion of one of my instructors. My body was basically falling apart. Being a dancer can be brutal. The pressure is... intense. I've never experienced anything like it. I would dance for eight hours a day and barely eat enough to make up for all the calories I was burning. It didn't help that the boyfriend I had at the time encouraged that sort of behavior. He commented on my weight, my body, every chance he got. My self esteem wasn't great. Ballet is competitive, you know? At the time, I was willing to do whatever it took to make it. And I've never been great at picking boyfriends. Obviously."

Shawn's jaw ticked, anger coursing through him stronger than he knew he was capable of.

"I'll never forget my first yoga class. The instructor said we could just lay in child's pose whenever we needed a break. And I laid in child's pose the whole time. That's when I realized how exhausted I was. Not tired, the way a long day makes you. Exhausted to my core. In my body, mind, and soul."

She reeled in her shrimp, saw that it was still there and intact, and cast it out again.

"I started going to yoga every day and... honestly, I know it sounds cliché, but it healed me. It helped me love my body again—not for what I could make it do, but for what it did for me. And so I decided to do the yoga teacher training just to deepen my practice, and about halfway through it, I realized ballet hadn't made me happy in a long time. So I dropped out of the program I was in, finished my yoga certification, became a yoga teacher, and tried to help other people find solace in yoga the way I did."

Shawn closed his eyes and took a deep breath. He didn't know where to begin.

This woman—this beautiful, strong, intelligent, fierce, compassionate woman—had just shared with him something so deeply personal that he was endeared to her even more. Anger and sadness coursed through him for her, for what she went through. But mostly, he felt gratitude that she shared with him something so raw and vulnerable. And he didn't know how to put that into words.

Suddenly, his fishing rod dipped down.

There was something on the end of it.

He grabbed it tightly and began reeling in. It was heavier than expected. Usually, fishing off the wharves in the Bay could yield decent-sized fish, but typically nothing over ten pounds.

You had to venture closer to the Gulf for that. He'd fished enough to be able to tell pretty quickly how large a catch would be—and his gut was telling him this was at least 15 pounds. Maybe more.

"Shit, this sucker is big," he grunted, and Willa set her rod in the stand and grabbed a net from where it was hanging.

"Well, this is exciting," Willa said with a breathless grin.

Suddenly, her rod bent forward dramatically from where it was in the stand.

"Shit," she said, dropping the net she'd grabbed to reel her own line in.

"Tug it back, then reel, Greene," he said.

"I know what I'm fucking doing," she snapped. "Focus on your own damn line."

He chuckled, losing himself in the steady rhythm of reeling the fish in. His got close to the wharf and he saw the outline of it before releasing an explative.

"Goddamn carp."

She laughed, still reeling in her own line.

"Sucks," she giggled.

Carp were generally not eaten around the Bay. They weren't all that populous, either, so Shawn couldn't help feeling a little jilted as he tugged it onto the dock. Carp were known to have a high tolerance for pollution, so people didn't typically eat them. But he couldn't help marveling at how big it was.

"Damn," he murmured to Willa as her line got closer to the wharf. "Gotta be 20 pounds, easy."

She glanced over at him and grinned.

"Still wouldn't be my biggest catch off this wharf," she quipped.

He jolted in surprise, but didn't press for more information as Willa grabbed a flashlight and expertly removed the hook from the fish's mouth. He heard her fish flop onto the deck, and he turned around to see what it was.

"Trout," she said. "Six or seven pounds, probably."

He grinned at her and moved the flashlight in her direction. She'd already removed the hook and asked him to bring the cooler over for her to stick it in.

"How does it feel to be bested by a girl?" she asked.

"Well, first of all, you're a woman, Greene," he said. "And honestly, it feels pretty damn humbling to be bested by you, but if you keep grinning like that, I might just let you beat me at everything."

Her cheeks turned a beautiful shade of scarlet before she looked away, busying herself by hooking another shrimp on her line.

"And second of all," he said, tossing the carp he'd caught back in the water, "there's no harm in a little catch and release."

W<small>ILLA BEGGED</small> her heartbeat to slow.

Shawn was *flirting* with her.

And quoting back to her what she'd said the night they met.

Either he'd learned how to use complete sentences or the caveman that was ruling his body up until tonight had taken some time off, because he'd not grunted once and he kept complimenting her.

Not to mention the way he kept staring at her mouth made her feel like he was silently begging to kiss her again.

And underneath the romantic moonlight and the way it shined over the Bay, she might just let herself kiss him again. She'd been doing everything she could to put that stupid kiss out of her mind all day.

Except for when she got home from the bait shop and spent some quality time with her vibrator.

But that was a momentary lapse of judgment, and she needed to stop thinking about the way it felt when his big, calloused hands wrapped around her hips and then grabbed her cheeks and pulled her closer to him. She was really trying to avoid remembering how the hardness of his erection pressed against her as she fisted her fingers against his chest and pressed her tongue into his mouth.

Because he was her neighbor.

Her *friend*.

And she might die from awkwardness if her cheeks kept flushing every time she was around him.

It would be a hell of a lot easier if he stopped saying things that made her want to crawl on his lap and beg him to say everything else he was thinking.

"So what's the biggest fish you've caught off this wharf,

Greene?" he asked her, his eyebrows raising expectantly in that cute way of his.

"My grandfather and I caught a 27-pound black drum out here once," she said, grinning at him. "We didn't keep it. Didn't look like it'd be any good. But we had a good time reeling it in."

He whistled. "Damn."

They fell into easy silence, grabbing a new shrimp as needed and reeling in a few more trout and one flounder. Not much more passed between them other than the occasional checking in or offering to help unhook a fish. Willa lost herself in thought—about the summers she spent here growing up, how her grandfather would spend late nights on the wharf fishing with her, how she felt like she could finally hear herself think in the quiet of the nights here.

And she thought about how she'd misjudged Shawn.

He said the wrong thing a few times, but he was quick to apologize and easy to be with. And as much as she wanted to try and forget the kiss, she knew she was lying to herself if she thought she could.

She just needed to get him out of her system, she decided.

A one night thing.

Scratch the itch, then move on.

Charlie did it all the time. She could do it, too. After all, it would be an understatement to say she was attracted to him—that much was certain. And she also trusted him. After seeing how he'd taken such great care of Ida, how all the old ladies at Bingo fussed over him, she realized he was clearly a standup guy.

So now it was just a matter of broaching it with him. She'd never done this before; usually, men propositioned her and she said no. She wasn't quite sure how to go about it, but she took a deep breath, squared her shoulders, and turned to Shawn.

"I can't stop thinking about our kiss from earlier," she said.

He looked up at her, his eyes darting to her mouth and darkening.

"Glad I'm not the only one," he rasped.

"I want to do it again."

"Then do it."

"I want to do a lot more than that actually."

His eyes widened for a moment and he shifted in his seat, opening his mouth as if he were going to respond but then quickly snapping it shut.

"I'm not looking for anything serious," Willa said, darting her eyes away from Shawn. "I already told you I just went through a bad breakup. I can't... I don't want a boyfriend. I just want something fun."

"Something fun," his voice was stony.

She looked up at him.

His jaw ticked, and she flinched, realizing she probably sounded like all the tourists who made him feel like he could never be more than sex. Like he was only worthwhile to her because of the orgasms he could give her.

"Shit," she said. "I wasn't thinking. About what you said the other night. I just... forget it."

She bit her lip.

Shawn groaned.

"Willa," he said. "You're not making this easy on me."

"Sorry," she whispered.

"Don't—" he sighed. "You don't have to apologize. Look. I told you I feel like people only see me as a good time."

"I know, and I didn't think," she responded. "Clearly. You opened up to me and I should've—"

"Wait, Willa."

He dragged a hand over his head and dropped his fishing rod in the stand.

"Look. For years, I fucked almost every tourist who propositioned me. But it got lonely. Isolating. And I started wanting more. I promised myself I wouldn't do that anymore. It wasn't... it wasn't good for me. I did a lot of therapy to realize that I'd been looking for fulfillment in all the wrong places because of a bunch of childhood shit I won't bore you with. But I can't. I can't just do casual sex anymore."

She sucked in a deep breath and closed her eyes, leaning back against her chair.

"I'm sorry."

"You don't—"

"I know you said I don't need to apologize, but I want to," Willa said. "You're a good guy, Shawn."

"Willa," Shawn said. "Look at me."

She opened her eyes and turned her head toward him. His eyes were dark, full of lust. She almost gasped at the way he devoured her with a simple look, the way it made her core pulse in desire.

"I can't stop thinking about that kiss either," he said, licking his lips. "And fuck if I haven't tried all afternoon. But if we want different things... maybe we're better off being just friends. Can we do that?"

She nodded.

"I'd like that," she said softly.

He grinned at her.

"Me too."

12

Willa felt like she had been crawling out of her skin ever since she asked Shawn if he wanted to sleep with her a few days ago.

It was mostly the guilt that was killing her—that she'd so thoughtlessly asked him to give her a good time barely 24 hours after he'd told her tourists used him so thoroughly that he no longer felt comfortable in his own store some days. But it was also the knowledge that it wasn't going to happen and she had to find some other outlet to get orgasms.

Oh, and the pesky little fact that she'd been rejected.

Not a fun feeling.

Not a feeling she was familiar with at all, actually.

And it was made worse by the fact that her vibrator wasn't cutting it. Especially since she and Shawn had fallen into a steady rhythm of fishing off the wharf together in the evenings and he always showed up looking delicious.

Like last night, when he wore gray sweatpants and a t-shirt that stretched perfectly over his shoulders. God, she wanted to lick his biceps. She wanted to lick a lot of things, especially now that she'd seen him in those sweatpants that left little to the imagination.

Willa shook her head.

Stop it, she told herself.

She was walking up and down the wharf with the cast net in hand, looking for schools of mullet to catch. When she'd woken up this morning and saw the sun shining, the waves falling at the perfect cadence, and fish jumping from the kitchen window, she knew it would be a great day to throw the net.

Plus, since she was a kid, the steady cadence of tossing it out and pulling it back in calmed her.

Out of the corner of her eye, she saw something in the water. It didn't look like a fish—it was stagnant, unmoving.

It wasn't uncommon to see odds and ends in the water on occasion. The hurricanes that rampaged this part of the world made sure of that. Sometimes wood from people's wharves across the Bay would wash up on their shore weeks later. Sometimes they found jewelry. And sometimes, more dangerous things washed up—scraps of metal or nails.

Typically, the community got together after hurricanes and did their best to clean up the water, but her grandparents had taught her to be cautious and keep her eye out.

Suddenly a big wave broke through and the dip of it left room for the item to sit out of the water for a moment—long enough for Willa to realize what it was: a metal chair. It was damaged and covered in barnacles, with shards of metal sticking out where the feet used to be.

A hazard if there ever was one. On days where the water wasn't clear, somebody could trip over that while swimming. The water was shallow here; even at the end of the wharf, the deepest it'd get was three or four feet. Plus, she didn't want her cast net catching on the remnants of that chair.

Willa dropped the net where it was and headed into the closet in the garage. It was where her grandfather had stored everything—fishing supplies, tools, buckets, and anything else one might need living on the water. She dug through a few boxes and found some gloves reserved for fishing.

She came back out to the wharf and shimmied out of her shorts. Down to just her bikini and the fishing gloves, she walked down the stairs to the beach and waded out to where she saw the chair.

Since she'd left the cast net where she was when she saw it, she used it as a marker to figure out how close she was to it. After a few minutes in the general area where she knew it was, she found it. Pushing her hands under water, she gave it a tug and felt very little movement.

She sighed, pushing her hair back, and correcting her stance so she could put more effort into pulling it. She reached into the water, grabbed the chair, and—

"What the hell are you doing, Greene?"

Startled, Willa lost her balance right as a wave crashed into her. Normally sure-footed in the water, she felt shock ripple through her as she toppled over, right into the rusted, pointy ends of the chair. She hissed, feeling it cut her legs, and she tried to wiggle her way out, reaching her feet for the ground to steady herself.

She heard a curse and a splash, and as she tried to stand back up in the water, she felt strong arms grab her and lift her out of the Bay.

"Fuck, I'm sorry for startling you," Shawn said, his eyes wild. "Are you okay?"

He started booking it to shore, careful to keep Willa above the water. Her head was spinning.

"I'm fine," she said. "You can put me down."

She kicked her legs a bit, and he gripped her tighter. Her arm rubbed up against his chest, and that's when she realized he was shirtless. She looked up at him, but his gaze was concentrated ahead. Though his eyes were still frantic, he was honed in on getting her to safety. She sighed in resignation as he carried her up the stairs and into her kitchen, where he gently set her down in a chair and inspected her legs.

She definitely didn't miss the feeling of his strong arms around her now that he set her down.

Definitely wasn't thinking about what it felt like for him to pick her up like she was nothing and carry her out of the water with almost alarming ease.

Definitely didn't wish he'd let her run her fingers along his muscled arms and abs.

Nope, not one bit.

"Not too deep, but these cuts need to be taken care of immediately," he looked up at her, and she remembered that she'd hurt herself on the rusty chair. "You up to date on your tetanus shot?"

She nodded.

Shawn grabbed another chair and propped her legs up on it.

Willa tried not to think about how his rough fingers felt on her calves,

"Got a first aid kit around here?" he asked.

She stood up to go get it, and he gently pushed her back down, eyes darkening.

"Stay put. Where is it?"

"I can—"

"Where. Is. It."

She rolled her eyes. "Above the sink."

He went into the kitchen and opened the cabinet, returning with some peroxide and cotton balls.

"Shawn, you don't have to do this," Willa said. "I'm fine."

He looked at her, his eyes hardening.

"Don't."

A single word never sounded so menacing.

She didn't say a word as he put peroxide on the cotton balls and dabbed them over the cuts that danced across her calves, her feet, and her thighs. It burned, but not enough for it to be uncomfortable for her. She'd gotten stung by jellyfish in this bay more times than she could count; her pain tolerance was high.

He went back into the kitchen and washed his hands. Then he returned with Neosporin and gently rubbed it over all her wounds. His calloused fingers were remarkably tender as he put it on the cuts on her feet.

Then he lifted her right leg and set her foot on his shoulder so he could better reach the cuts on her upper thigh.

Willa's breath hitched as he took care of her with such concentrated intent. She felt heat creep up her neck and into her cheeks. He didn't notice; he just finished her right leg, set the foot on the ground, and moved to her left leg, setting that foot on his shoulder again.

Willa's imagination ran wild as she imagined what it'd be like for her legs to be draped over his shoulders because of something else.

And then she released an embarrassing groan as he finished rubbing neosporin over one of the cuts high up on her thigh with his thumb.

Shawn looked up at her in confusion, then seemed to

realize the position he was in: kneeling between her legs, his hands drifting up her thighs. Heat flared in his eyes as he stood up.

"You should clean those cuts a few times a day," he said, his voice thick.

She nodded, and without another word, he left her kitchen.

WILLA SLID into a seat at the bar and waved at Amanda, who was taking the order of someone across the way. Attendance at her yoga classes had steadily increased, and the class tonight was fantastic. The group was engaged and fun, and people of all levels tried new things. Plus, the sunset was absolutely gorgeous over the water.

She thought she'd take the chance to get to know Amanda a bit before heading back home. It wasn't completely dark out yet, but she was dreading going home.

She knew Shawn would come over to fish off the wharf tonight—it had become an easy, unspoken agreement between them. He came over every night with shrimp—free of charge—and they sat together and caught fish. Sometimes they released them back into the water, but she kept a lot of them in her freezer so she could eat them in the coming weeks. She always offered some to him, but he never took them.

Willa's thighs clenched together as she thought back to how he'd tended to her earlier that day, the spark that jolted her as his fingers caressed her leg, how his hot breath felt on her.

And now she was trying to avoid going home, where she and Shawn would inevitably sit out on the wharf and try to pretend like there was no sexual tension between them.

"What can I get you?" Amanda said with a grin.

"A vodka soda with a lime."

"On it."

Amanda effortlessly mixed the drink in front of Willa and handed it to her.

"So how are you settling in?" Amanda asked, propping her chin on her hands.

"Good. I grew up coming here every summer, so honestly it just feels like coming home. It's nice being here. What about you? How long have you lived here?"

"Moved down here about a year ago after visiting with my mom," Amanda said. "She had cancer and wanted to see the beach one last time. So I brought her here, and when she died a few months later, I needed to get out of my hometown. So I moved here. I realized I could just wake up and be at the beach everyday and that could be my life. Best decision I ever made."

"Wow," Willa said softly, sipping her drink. "I'm so sorry about your mom."

"Thanks. It was pancreatic cancer. Basically a death sentence from the moment she was diagnosed. I miss her, but I know she'd be happy I moved here. I'll never forget the look on her face when I brought her here. She'd been here before, of course. But the time before she died? It was like she was seeing it for the first time. Like she was trying to memorize every last inch of this place."

"I supposed I'd want to see the beach one last time, too, if I were her."

A beat of silence passed before Amanda cleared her throat.

"Well, enough about me. What's your story?"

Willa released a half-hearted chuckle.

"Let's see. I found out my boyfriend of two years had a wife and child, so I blocked him on everything and moved here immediately. I have yet to get a therapist even though my best friend keeps nagging me about it and I know I should." Charlie had sent her three texts earlier that day checking in to see if she'd found a therapist yet. "So now I'm living in my dead grandparents' house, eating fish for every goddamn meal, and I barely have a job. Oh, and to top it all off, I'm dealing with this weird sexual tension with my disgustingly hot neighbor."

She sighed and polished off her drink.

Amanda gaped at her.

"Damn. I'd offer you a shot but I know you still have to drive home."

"Good thing we're going out tomorrow night," Willa responded with a smirk.

"Yeah, sounds like a girl's night is just what the doctor ordered," Amanda said.

"You have no idea."

Willa pulled out her wallet to pay but Amanda waved her off.

"On the house."

"Thanks," Willa grinned.

"See you tomorrow night."

"Wouldn't miss it."

13

W here. The. Fuck. Was. She.

Shawn's heart was thundering. They never had a set time they met, but usually it was shortly after the sun went down. She'd been a little later than usual last night, but he knew she taught sunset yoga classes on Thursday nights. Plus, she'd told him she'd grabbed a drink to get to know the bartender, a woman who'd attended her class last weekend.

But tonight? He didn't know where she was.

Thirty minutes after the sun went down, he started to get antsy. All the lights were off in the house and even though the LED light was on at the end of the wharf, she was nowhere to be seen.

Then thirty minutes turned into forty-five. That turned into fifty. And here he was now, an hour after sunset and she'd still shown no sign of turning up. His skin crawled with worry. He couldn't stop himself from imagining worst-case scenarios.

Maybe she got in a car accident on Highway 98. That road was notoriously dangerous during tourist season. He would know—it was the highway where his parents died in a car accident.

He felt stupid for never asking for her number. But then again, he'd never needed it.

Shawn roughly picked up his insulated bucket of shrimp and started jogging.

Back down the wharf.

Across her backyard.

To his backyard.

Into the back door.

"I need her number," he ground out.

Grams was reclined in her favorite chair. She had the news on a volume so loud that it should've been illegal, and in her hands was a knitting project she started a few days ago. She looked up at Shawn briefly, then went back to her knitting.

He growled. Picked up the remote. Turned off the TV. Looked at her.

"Watch it, Scoob," she said, a scowl on her face.

"Grams," he said, attempting and failing at patience. "I need Willa's number."

"What makes you think I have it?"

"She told me she texted you the other day when she ran out of eggs."

"Hmm," she said, squinting her eyes at him. "What makes you think I'll give it to you?"

Shawn's jaw ticked.

"Dammit, Grams," he said, pulling a hand across his face. "Usually we fish off the back of her wharf around this time every night. She never showed. I'm just worried that—"

He cut himself off and looked away. Grams sighed.

"I'm sure she's fine, Scooby," she said. "It's Friday night. She probably has plans and forgot to mention it."

He tried to ignore the pang of disappointment that coursed through him at the idea of her having plans that she didn't bother to mention to him.

And then the mortification hit—that he'd entertained worst-case scenarios before realizing it was Friday, and Grams was right.

She probably *did* have plans.

Plans that didn't involve him.

Shawn tried not to think about the idea that these plans might involve another guy. One who could give her what she wanted: no-strings-attached sex.

"Here," Grams harrumphed, handing her phone to him. She'd opened up Willa's contact information.

He sent it to himself, then saved her contact.

"Sorry, Grams," he said sheepishly.

"Turn my TV back on if you know what's good for you."

Shawn did as she said and went to his room. It was on the second floor of the house, and used to be a guest room. It still had the remnants of what it used to be—a decadent, white comforter, a trunk at the foot of the bed filled with extra blankets, a barely-used desk against the wall.

Since he'd moved in, Shawn had added little touches to make it feel more like his. Pictures of him and his grandparents. A taxidermied fish someone gave him as a thank you for a great tour. Fishing supplies, tools, and a few books were scattered across the desk he rarely used.

He sat on the edge of his bed, opened his phone, and started a new text. He stared at the blinking cursor for a few minutes, debating whether to text her. If nothing was wrong, he'd look like an idiot. But if she had plans and forgot to tell him, he was pretty sure she'd feel bad. And he didn't want to make her feel bad, even if it was her own damn fault.

His curiosity got the better of him. He had to know where she was. Why she didn't show up.

He started typing.

> Hey Willa, it's Shawn. Just checking in to make sure everything's alright since I didn't see you on the wharf tonight.

That was good, right? Casual. Didn't come off like he'd been waiting for her like a lovesick fool for over an hour. Which he had. But she didn't need to know that.

He sent it before he could overthink anything.

A few agonizing minutes passed before she responded to him with several texts in rapid succession.

> Shit!!!

> OMG I suck. I'm so sorry!!

> Out with some girls from work

> I forgot to mention it last night

> I'm really sorry!!!!!!

He sighed in relief. She was fine.

He was not going to lie to himself and pretend like he wasn't equally relieved that she wasn't on a date, she was just having a girl's night. His phone buzzed again. She'd sent a selfie of her and her friends, each of them with a large margarita in their hands. God, she was gorgeous. Wearing a low cut, white dress and bright pink lipstick. Her eyes sparkled with mischief.

Probably the tequila.

No worries

But there were, in fact, worries.

Did she have a designated driver? Catching an Uber in this area was laughable. It got touristy, sure, but never touristy enough that finding a ride back to their rural paradise was easy late at night. There were only a handful of Uber drivers in the area.

Looks like y'all are having fun. Call me if you need a ride home tonight.

She responded with a thumbs-up and a heart emoji. He laid back in his bed and stared up at the ceiling, unsure of what to do with the time on his hands when all he could do was think about Willa.

≈

WILLA LAID her head on the table and groaned.

She was officially the worst.

Layla had offered to pick her up for their night out. It was a little out of her way, but she said Willa could drive next time. They'd been at the Mexican restaurant gossiping and eating their weight in chips and salsa for a couple of hours.

When she got ready earlier this evening, she gave herself a pep talk. She wasn't going to think about Shawn, or the way he looked at her like she was something to be consumed, or the sexual tension that she felt when she was within a 100-yard radius of him. Last night, they'd fished together for only 30 minutes before she told him she was tired and went inside to hang out with her vibrator.

But today was a new day. She was going out with girlfriends and since Layla was DD'ing, Willa was ready to get her buzz on.

Which she had.

Thoroughly.

The margarita she ordered was the size of her head, and it was delicious. But now, she thought she must've done *too* good of a job putting Shawn out of her mind. Or attempting to. Because she hadn't even had the decency to tell him she would be out tonight, and therefore unavailable to fish off her wharf with him like they usually do.

She didn't even have the decency to leave him a goddamn note.

Willa groaned again.

"Tequila getting to you, babe?" Amanda asked.

Willa sat up and rested her head in her hands.

"Remember that hot neighbor I told you about?" Willa asked.

She nodded.

"Apparently she's got some weird sexual tension with her sexy neighbor but they refuse to bang it out," Amanda said to Layla, who looked confused.

"Well," Willa covered her face with her hands and groaned again. "Fuck."

"Let it out," Amanda said. "Want us to order you a shot?"

Willa let out a humorless laugh.

"No," she said. "I don't deserve it."

"And why is that?"

"For the past few weeks, my hot neighbor and I fish off my wharf after the sun goes down. It's never been, like, a thing we talk about. It just started kind of organically. But I forgot to tell him I had plans tonight and he just texted me worried that I didn't show up." Willa eyed her phone. "That means he probably waited on me for an hour!"

Amanda and Layla shared a look, then turned back to Willa.

"So wait, am I missing something?" Layla asked. "Why do y'all refuse to—as Amanda so delicately put it—bang it out?"

"Yes, do tell," Amanda said before sipping the straw of her margarita.

Willa sighed and took a big gulp of her own marg.

"Because," she said, swirling her finger around the edge of the ginormous glass. "He doesn't do casual, and that's all I'm looking for."

"Explain." Amanda commanded.

"After everything with my ex," she'd already filled them both in on the gory details surrounding her awful breakup with Leo, "I just don't want anything serious for a while. I really don't want any sort of relationship with a man, but honestly? I'm dying here. This is the longest I've gone without sex since I was a teenager."

Layla blushed, choked on her drink, and started coughing. Amanda studied Willa steadily.

"And how long has it been?" Amanda said.

"A little over a month."

"A month?! Girl, that's not even a real dry spell."

"Okay, well it is for me. And Shawn..." Willa sighed, rubbing her temples with her forefingers. "He's just had some bad experiences with women. Tourists who use him and lose him, basically. He doesn't do casual anymore. We talked about it, realized we want different things, and decided to stay friends."

"And how's that working out?" Amanda asked, a knowing glint in her eye.

Willa deadpanned, "The other day, he saw me hurt myself and fireman-carried me out of the water before tending to my wounds. I had to take, like, ten cold showers afterward."

Amanda laughed, then looked at Layla.

"You know where we should go?"

Layla's eyes widened, then she closed them and tipped her head back.

"Please don't say what I think you're going to say."

Amanda's devilish smile grew.

"Flora-Bama," she said.

Layla groaned.

"The club?" Willa asked, crinkling her brows. "The tourist spot? Why?"

"You need casual sex."

"I don't know how I feel about a one-night stand," Willa said. "I've never done that before. That's why I wanted to try it with Shawn. I know him. I trust him."

"Okay, well maybe you can dance up on some hot tourists and make out with one to scratch the itch."

Willa wasn't sure if that would help or make things worse, but she figured she'd give it a try.

"Alright, let's do it," she said.

Amanda smirked.

"Let's get you some sex."

14

Bras hung from the ceiling and tourists were packed tightly into the beach-front club of Flora-Bama. Willa had been here before. In college, she and a few girlfriends came down for Spring Break and spent most of their days here—and a few godforsaken nights. But that was years ago.

Fortunately, she didn't feel out of place. There were people of all ages at the club—one group was celebrating a twenty-first birthday, another celebrating a bachelorette party, and another group of women that had to be in their fifties. When they'd arrived, Amanda immediately ordered the three of them Bushwackers, a dangerous drink made with five different types of alcohol and chocolate ice cream, even though it only tasted like a chocolate milkshake if you'd had enough to drink. Willa sipped on hers and took in the view around her. The bass thumped loudly—some pop song she vaguely recognized—and people were swaying to the tune of the music.

"So what now?" Willa shouted over the music to Amanda.

"Pick one."

"What?"

"Pick a guy you want to hook up with."

Willa bit her lip, then turned back toward the dance floor, scanning through the crowd of people. Finally, her eyes landed on a guy that didn't remind her of Leo or Shawn. He was about 5'10", if she had to guess, and had a buzz cut, a sharp jawline, and tattoos all over his arms. He was wearing shorts and an unbuttoned Hawaian shirt, showcasing his abs.

"Nice," Amanda said, following her eyes. "Solid choice. He's definitely a tourist. Won't be calling you tomorrow trying to take you home to mom."

Willa chuckled. "Okay, so what's next, O Wise One?"

"Careful. I might just get used to that nickname," Amanda grinned. "Now, look at him."

"I'm looking."

"Just wait. He'll feel your gaze in a second."

Willa felt like an idiot.

"This is dumb."

"Trust the process."

Willa continued staring at him, feeling herself wonder why Amanda didn't tell her to just go over there and say hello. Her eyes started to water, and she felt the desire to look away. The guy was good-looking, but she didn't want to study him the way she wanted to study Shawn.

"Much better, keep that smolder going," Amanda said. "You looked like you wanted to murder him for a second there. Now you look like you're thinking about sex."

Well, fuck. Of course she had fuck-me eyes when she was thinking about Shawn. Suddenly, Buzz Cut turned to face her.

"Smile at him," Amanda whispered out of her mouth,

then amended what she said after Willa gave him a toothy grin. "Damn girl, take it back a notch. I meant a soft smile. Like a come hither look. It's a good thing you have great tits because you're shit at this."

Willa softened her smile and resisted the urge to roll her eyes at Amanda. Buzz Cut smirked at her and said a few words to the people he was with before making his way toward Willa.

"Hey, Red," he said. "Wanna dance?"

God, she hated when people came up with unoriginal nicknames for her. Especially Red. She was teased for her red hair when she was little. She'd been called everything in the book, and of course, disgusting men loved to ask if the carpet matched the drapes. Willa loved her red hair, but people's fixation on it tended to air on the weird side.

But this guy was hot, and the goal was to dance and maybe make out with a stranger. So she nodded, and as he turned around, she whispered to Amanda, "Is it always this easy?"

"Everyone's easy at this place," Amanda said with the sage wisdom of a practiced seductress.

Willa followed after Buzz Cut, and as they got to the center of the dance floor, they started swaying to the rhythm of the music. She had to admit, he was a good dancer. He knew what he was doing, which was nice for her, because as a yoga instructor and former ballerina, she did, too.

After the first song ended, he came behind her and started grinding. Even though it made her feel like a horny teenager, she had to admit, it was honestly kind of fun. She continued sipping her drink and grinding with him. She closed her eyes to the music and lifted her arms in the air, feeling her buzz get stronger. Several songs passed, and he got more bold: putting his hands on her hips, running them along her sides, burying his face in her neck. It felt nice to be touched by a man, even if his fingers were too soft for her to pretend like it was Shawn touching her.

A few songs passed and she looked at Amanda, raising her brows in question. Amanda only smirked back at her—extremely unhelpful. So she excused herself and told Buzz Cut she needed to run to the restroom, realizing she still didn't know his name.

Willa tossed a beckoning look toward Amanda and felt her and Layla follow as she headed to the bathroom. There were a few other women in there—some waiting in line for the bathroom, a couple touching up their makeup, and one girl who was running her hair under the sink.

"Someone spilled their bushwhacker all over my head," she said miserably as Willa gave her an inquisitive glance.

"Damn, that sucks," Willa said, then turned toward the rest of her trio. "So what now? Are you two just going to watch me all night?"

"I don't do dancing with strangers," Layla said, her cheeks reddening. "Not since college, anyway. I'm perfectly happy to watch you."

"And I'm afraid if I don't supervise, you're going to overthink it like you are now and not get what you need tonight," Amanda said. "Look, are you having fun?"

"Honestly?" Willa thought about it for a minute. "Yeah. I am."

"Do you feel safe?"

"Yes."

"Do you want to go back out there?"

"Yes, I just—"

"Have you stopped thinking about your hot neighbor?"

Willa pressed her lips together. "Mostly."

"I'll take that as a win." Amanda sighed. "Listen, just go

back out there and keep dancing with him. Let him make the moves. He'll probably initiate kissing you or ask you to go back to his place. The ball is in your court, Willa. Turn him down if you're not feeling it. But you deserve to have some fun."

Layla nodded.

"I know it's none of my business," said the girl washing her hair in the sink, "but your friend is right. Plus, you're like, stupid hot and you have a killer rack."

God, Willa loved women's restrooms at clubs.

"Okay. I can do this."

"You can do this," Amanda confirmed.

"Well, now that I'm here, I actually *do* have to go to the bathroom."

Amanda and Layla left, and Willa got in line for the toilets. She absentmindedly pulled her phone out and noticed Shawn had sent her a few more texts. The first was about an hour ago.

> Grams wanted me to tell you that she says hi.

He'd included a picture of Grams sitting in front of the TV with knitting in hand, grinning like Shawn had just told her a good joke.

Then 30 minutes later:

> She somehow roped me into watching Mamma Mia with her. It's actually pretty good.

And just a few minutes ago:

> At the risk of sounding overbearing, I just wanted to check in and make sure you have a designated driver.

Rather than text him back, Willa decided she wanted to call him. It was possibly the buzz she had going that made her feel that way. It rang twice before he picked up.

"Willa?"

"How's Mamma Mia?" she asked.

"One of the older ladies is singing a song right now," he said. "The fancy one."

"'Does Your Mother Know?'" Willa responded, grinning. "Classic."

"How are you?"

"I was dancing with a guy at Flora-Bama," she said. "But now I'm in the bathroom."

Was she trying to make him jealous? Willa knew she was. She was buzzed and slightly bolder than usual and wanted to see how he'd react. The line went silent.

"Anyway, don't worry about me," she continued when he said nothing. "I have a ride home."

She was now next to go in line for the bathroom, and Shawn still hadn't responded to her.

"Are you there?" she asked.

Willa was beginning to get frustrated, and she only had herself to blame for pushing. She wasn't playing fair and she knew it.

A bathroom opened up, and she decided to put him out of his misery.

"Well, it's my turn to go to the bathroom," she said. "And by the way, it's not overbearing. Thanks for checking in. I... honestly, I like that you're looking after me."

Then, before she could say anything else she'd regret, she hung up and went to the bathroom.

SHAWN STOOD FROZEN on the back porch, trying to digest everything he'd heard. She'd been dancing with another guy, and he had no right to feel the jealousy coursing through him. She wasn't his. She wasn't even his fuck buddy, though she'd basically offered herself on a silver platter for him. She was just his neighbor. His friend. He didn't have any claim to her.

But also.

I like that you're looking after me.

Fuck, those words were almost enough to melt the ice-cold jealousy she'd pierced him with earlier in the conversation.

Before he knew what he was doing, he barged back inside with such force that he startled Grams enough for her to pause the movie.

"Where's the fire, Scooby?"

"Willa needs a ride," he called over his shoulder.

He heard Grams chuckle and turn the movie back on before he grabbed his keys and bolted to his truck. On a busy night, it would be about a 40-minute drive. He was ready to push traffic laws to get there in 30. And every single one of those 30 minutes was agonizingly slow. He didn't really know what he was doing, just that he needed to see her. Needed to be near her. Needed to make sure she got home safe.

He got to Flora-Bama shortly after 11 p.m., and it was crowded and rowdy. He forgot how many damn rooms there were in this godforsaken place. He started out in one of the smaller rooms, scanning the tipsy crowd for red hair. When he didn't see any, he moved on. Scanned the next room. Nothing.

He was considering going to check the outdoor areas or head upstairs when he entered the room with the bras on the ceiling. Her red hair shined bright under the neon flashing lights, and her arms were up in the air as she swayed to the music. His heart stuttered at the sight of her, and the tips of his mouth turned up in the beginnings of a smile.

Until he saw the man behind her. Grinding with her. Hands roaming. Face buried in her hair.

It was like he'd jumped into a bucket of ice. Why had he come here? What delusions did he have about showing up? Did he think she'd just throw herself at him, melt in his arms?

He couldn't look away from her, though. Her body swayed with so much grace, he could tell she'd been an incredible ballerina. Suddenly she looked in his direction and her mouth opened in an O shape as their eyes met. He saw her lips mouth his name, and she stopped dancing for a brief moment.

The guy she was dancing with apparently took that as an invitation, because he tipped her chin toward him and claimed her mouth.

Shawn's feet carried him over to them before he could register what was happening.

"Get off her," he growled.

"Woah man," the guy Willa locked lips with responded, raising his hands, palms forward. "I didn't know she had a boyfriend."

"I don't," Willa said, looking at Shawn in equal parts confusion and dismay.

"Whatever," the guy said, looking annoyed. "You're hot and I had fun dancing with you, but I don't want to get in the middle of whatever this is."

Willa crossed her arms and looked at Shawn.

"What are you doing here?" she hissed.

"You want to dance with a guy?" Shawn said. "Dance with me."

He grabbed Willa's hips and spun her so her backside was against his crotch. She yelped at the sudden movement and he clenched her hips, swinging to the beat of the music. She was stiff for a moment before she slowly started moving again, and a minute or two later, she was dancing the way she had been when he arrived.

And Shawn was overwhelmed with lust. It was a struggle to keep his hands in one place. He desperately wanted to run them up and down her sides, to palm her tits, to run a hand through her hair.

But he kept them firmly on her hips, instead focusing on the sensation of her perfect ass riding up against his dick. He was getting hard and he knew she could feel it; she started leaning against him even more, tipping her head back and closing her eyes, hands raised in bliss.

"Were you trying to make me jealous, Greene?" Shawn whispered in her ear, succumbing to the urge to let his hands wander. He reached up and dragged a finger along her cheek before nipping at her earlobe. "Because you succeeded. I'm sporting a hard-on in this fucking club because you made me so damn jealous, and I can't stop thinking about your ass cheeks hugging my dick."

She bit her lip, and he felt her thighs clench.

"Is this what you wanted to happen?" Shawn asked, continuing as desire coursed through him. He pressed a kiss to her neck, and she shivered. "Did you want to make me so fucking pissed with jealousy that I drove down here to hold you like this and kiss that perfect neck?"

He ran his tongue up to her ear and grazed his teeth along it.

"You're a fucking fantasy, Greene. All I want to do is pull this damn dress down and suck on your tits and tongue your pussy 'til you come all over my face. Want to taste every last inch of you. Want to feel you clench around my dick."

Willa turned around, wrapped her arms around his neck, and tugged him down for a kiss. Shawn was startled for only a moment, then grabbed her lower back with his left hand and her cheek with his right, loving the sensation of her messy, needy kisses.

The thrum of the bass and the people dancing around them disappeared. All that was left was Willa.

Her perfect lips.

The feel of her body rubbing against his.

Her fingers tugging through his hair, pulling him closer.

She was warm and wet and perfect.

And he was going to come in his pants if she kept going like this, but he didn't care. Willa pulled out of the kiss and, panting, looked at him through half-lidded eyes.

"Take me home," she said.

15

W illa felt Shawn trailing close behind her as she sought out Amanda and Layla. They eyed her curiously as she approached. Amanda was buzzing with anticipation, no doubt wanting the scoop on what exactly just went down on the dance floor.

And Willa wished she knew.

Nobody had ever talked to her like that—the way Shawn did. It made every guy before him look like a poor excuse for a dirty talker.

And God, she was soaked. She needed him. Desperately. Didn't know how she'd make it the entire drive home before pouncing on him again, losing herself in the sensation of his calloused fingers running along her delicate skin.

"Please, for the love of God, tell me that is your hot neighbor," Amanda demanded.

Willa grinned and bit her lip, then turned around. Shawn quirked a brow at her, clearly having heard Amanda's question.

"That's him," Willa said. "And we're leaving."

Both of her friends were studying Shawn. Layla looked

at him with curiosity, like a puzzle she wanted to solve. Amanda, on the other hand, was caught between looking amused by his sudden appearance and like she'd devour him if given the chance.

Willa understood the feeling. Her knees still felt weak from kissing him, and she was counting the seconds until she could do it again.

Amanda smirked, then leaned in to whisper, "I want all the details tomorrow."

Willa rolled her eyes, then turned to Shawn, grabbed his hand, and headed out the way she came in. Once they got outside, he guided her wordlessly to where he'd parked his car. He lifted her into the passenger seat, his hands lingering on the curve of her hip. His thumb traced her lip reverently before rounding the car and climbing into the driver's seat.

He put the keys in the ignition and looked over at her. Bit his lip. Dropped his eyes to her mouth. Then her tits.

She couldn't take it anymore. She crawled across the bench seat, straddled him, and pressed her lips against his. Fuck, it felt so good. His hands rested on her ass, roughly pulling her into him. She moaned as he tugged her closer, and he kissed her harder, tugging her tongue into his mouth, nipping at her lips, using a hand to pull her mouth deeper into his.

God, she'd never been so turned on in her life.

It was like the last several weeks with Shawn had been nonstop foreplay, and she was finally getting what she wanted.

Needed.

Every inch of her body was hot with desire, and she grinded on his erection, coaxing a moan from him.

"Fuck, Willa," he said, pushing his hands up her thighs

and tugging at her panties. "How much have you had to drink?"

"I'm buzzed," she replied breathlessly, kissing along his jaw. "Not drunk. You're not taking advantage."

"How many drinks?" he asked again, his fingers halting.

"One marg at dinner, one bushwhacker at the club."

When he still didn't move, Willa sat back and grabbed his face in her hands, forcing him to make eye contact with her.

"Are you going to make me beg for your dick, Shawn?" she asked. "I've never done it before, but I might if you keep holding out on me."

"I'm not fucking you right now."

"But I told you, I'm not drun—"

"I'm not fucking you in this car, in a busy parking lot, Greene," Shawn said, his voice rough and steely. "The first time I sink inside you, the first time you take my cock, it will not be where I have no space to spread you out and see you. And it certainly won't be where others could see us. See you."

Willa stopped breathing for a moment, caught up in the vigor and passion of his words. Then she looked around the parking lot. There were a few people, several cars away, but nobody near them. It wasn't crowded. Most people probably wouldn't leave for at least another hour.

"There's barely anyone here, Shawn. Please."

"Willa," he said, an edge to his voice.

"Shawn, my fucking vibrator won't cut it anymore. I swear to God, all I can think about is you making me come, and if you don't do it in the next minute, I think I might pass out."

His eyes darkened.

"What do you think about when you use your vibrator, Greene?"

Willa bit her lip.

She'd said too much.

Stupid alcohol.

"Henry Cavill," she said, and he smirked. "Idris Elba. Harry Styles."

"Liar."

"Don't make me say it."

He stared at her expectantly.

"You," she whispered. "I think about you and your rock hard abs and your stupid jawline and the way it felt when you freaking fireman carried me out of the water the other day and—"

He cut her off with a kiss.

His mouth captured hers with such intensity she thought she'd elevated to another plane. She ran her fingers down through his hair, along his neck, to his arms. She gripped the muscles she'd been obsessing over since she met him, letting her fingers explore the ridges of his biceps and triceps.

Then he ripped her panties off.

She gasped, and he claimed the sound with his mouth.

"You want to come," he whispered against her lips, rubbing his thumb along her bead of nerves. "I'll make you come."

She whimpered, and he growled in satisfaction at the sound.

"How long have you been this wet?" Shawn said. "Since I started dancing with you back there? Since I grabbed your hips and pulled that perfect ass into me? Since you kissed me on that dance floor?"

Too much.

The feeling of him—after all this time, after fantasizing about him—it was too much. His fingers, the ones he used to tend to her wounds just a couple days prior, felt so good against her sex.

"Or did you get wet for that other asshole?" he asked, pressing his thumb harder against her clit.

"Shawn," she gasped.

He leaned down and whispered in her ear.

"We both know he couldn't touch you like I can," Shawn said. "Isn't that right, Greene?"

She bit her lip and nodded as he nipped her ear, kissed her cheek, claimed her mouth—all while continuing to circle her clit with his thumb.

"Do you like this, baby?" he asked, and she nodded, groaning. "Like the way you make me bend to your will? Like the way you make me lose my goddamn mind? God, you're so fucking beautiful. Your pussy feels so good, baby. Can't wait to feel you around my cock."

Willa was delirious with pleasure. Then he pressed two fingers into her core, hitting her so perfectly that she cried out.

"Shawn, please."

"That's right, baby. Say my name. Remember who makes you come."

He continued to rub her clit while massaging her G-spot, his fingers falling into a steady rhythm as he kissed her, sucking and licking her lips. She couldn't take it anymore, it was too much. Whimpering, she buried her face in his neck as he continued fingering her, a climax steadily building within her.

"Lost my mind when I saw that other guy kiss you. Fuck, I want those lips to myself. Want this pussy to myself. Feels so warm and wet, baby."

"I'm going to come," Willa breathed against his neck. "Shawn, please."

He grabbed her face with his free hand and kissed her, thrusting his fingers deeper into her as she clenched around them, her moan as she finished muffled against his lips. Pleasure coursed through her, so intense that she started trembling, making sounds she didn't know she was capable of. He pushed her over the edge, and she threw her head back, riding out the waves of bliss.

Then he pulled his fingers out from inside her, and locking eye contact with her, he brought them to his lips and sucked the remnants of her off of them. Grinning wolfishly, he kissed her deeply, letting her taste her own arousal on his lips.

"Shawn," she whispered. "Fuck."

"That's the idea," he smirked, leaning his forehead against hers. "Let me take you home now, Willa. Please."

She kissed him softly on the mouth, then settled into the passenger seat and clicked her seatbelt in as he started moving. Still reeling from the heady sensation of how he made her come, Willa took a deep breath and turned to look at him when the car stopped at a red light. Her eyes dipped lower, and she noticed his erection was still bulging out of his jeans.

Reaching over to him, she started to unzip his pants when he grabbed her wrist.

"What are you doing?" he asked.

"I want to make you feel good."

"You don't have to. We'll be home soon enough anyway."

"No, we won't. It's, like, 45 minutes away."

She finished unzipping him, his hand looser around her wrist now. She gulped at the size of him. Even through his boxer briefs, he was breathtaking.

"I want to," she whispered. "That's got to be painful. Let me make it better."

He released her wrist, and their eyes met for a brief moment before he gave her a curt nod. She tugged his boxer briefs down and gripped the base of his cock with her hand, flicking a thumb over the head of it.

"Fuck, Willa," he said, his jaw ticking.

She salivated at the sight of him, at the sound of him so turned on, at how his body reacted so strongly to hers. Then, she leaned forward.

"What are you do—ooooohhhh, fuck," Shawn said as Willa bent over and clasped her lips around his cock, taking him as deep as she could.

Willa had never enjoyed giving men head that much before.

She did it occasionally, if she was feeling particularly generous or excited. But it had never felt so good for her, so innately hot. God, she'd never even had semi-public sex before. All of her other sexual encounters had happened behind the safety of closed doors. Preferably, in her apartment. In her bed.

Never in a car. Never in a parking lot. And definitely not in the middle of the busiest highway in South Alabama.

She could barely think past her lust-dazed state, so caught up in post-orgasmic bliss. All she could think about was sucking his cock so he would feel as good as she felt. And fuck if she wasn't having fun in the process, savoring his taste, the way his body trembled as she licked every last inch of him.

She sucked him deep, and he groaned.

Willa felt pure, unadulterated lust and power—to make this man putty in her hands, to make him want her so badly, to hear his breathless reactions to her mouth.

"Willa," he panted, bringing a hand down to rest in her hair, his thumb gently caressing her neck.

Out of the corner of her eye, she could see reflections of headlights and traffic lights outside the car. His knees shifted slightly as he switched between the gas and the brake, continuing to drive them home. She felt his cock swell inside her mouth, and she hummed around him.

"Willa, fuck," Shawn grunted. "I'm about to come. You need to get up."

But Willa sucked him harder, her tongue swishing around his cock as it swelled even more.

"Dammit, baby, unless you want me spilling down your throat, get the fuck up," he said.

She giggled around his cock—a delirious, potent feeling overtaking her as she kept sucking at the tempo she'd kept the last few moments.

He roared, his cock pulsing and spewing down her throat. She sucked it in, making sure to swallow everything he gave her, the warm, salty liquid easily falling down her throat. She took one last suck, licking the tip of his cock, then sat up and wiped her mouth.

Shawn beheld her with admiration and barely-sated lust, his thumb coming up to rub her lips. She licked it playfully and he shuddered, bringing his hand back to the steering wheel and eyes back to the road as she situated herself in her seat.

"Well, I've never done that before," she said, leaning against his side, her head resting gently against his shoulder.

"Bullshit."

"I mean, I've given blow jobs before," she clarified, her voice going soft as exhaustion began to take over. "Never road head, though. And definitely never swallowed before."

"Could've fooled me. That was the best fucking blow job of my life."

Willa chuckled sleepily, her stomach fluttering at his praise.

"I'm glad you came tonight," Willa confessed, pliant and open after everything they'd shared tonight.

She yawned, and her eyes blinked shut. As she drifted off, she thought she heard him mutter, "Lord help me."

As SHAWN PULLED his truck into their neighborhood, he glanced down at Willa's head, still resting against his shoulder as she slept. She'd been that way since moments after she sucked him off so well that he thought he might wreck the car because he was seeing stars after the way she finished him.

He'd never felt so satisfied after a sexual encounter, which blew his mind because he hadn't even properly fucked her yet. But God, the way she came on his fingers, the way her pussy felt as it clenched around him, the way she screamed as he gave her pleasure—he'd never forget it.

God, help him. He didn't even want to try.

And then she unflinchingly swallowed everything as he spewed into her mouth. Seeing her swollen lips after she finished him off was easily the sexiest, most erotic thing of his life. And now she slept on his shoulder, so sweetly, so peacefully.

Even though she said she just wanted sex.

Even though he said he wanted more.

They'd have to talk about this tomorrow. What it meant, where to go from here. But for now, he was trying to enjoy this quiet moment, where he could watch her sleep. There were more layers to Willa than he thought, and he wanted to peel back each of them, learn everything he could about her. Her red hair hung loosely over her shoulders, cascading over the deep cut of her dress that made her tits look so delectable he thought he'd sprout an erection again on the spot.

He pulled into her driveway and turned off the car. She didn't move at all, her breath falling heavy with signs of deep sleep. Gently, he leaned over and unbuckled her, then himself. He opened the car door, then pulled her out and gently cradled her in his arms. She stirred slightly, her eyes blinking slowly.

"You can stay asleep, Greene," he whispered. "I'll bring you inside. Just tell me where the keys are."

"Back door's unlocked," she murmured sleepily, turning her face into his chest and sighing happily.

If she kept doing things like that, his heart might just splinter into a million pieces. Her scent was stronger now— something sweet and calming, some smell he couldn't recognize but wanted to bottle up and keep forever.

He walked around to the back door and let himself in, then paused, unsure where her room was. He'd vaguely known her grandparents, but had only moved in with Grams recently, so he'd only ever spent time at the house with Willa. And now, he realized he'd never been past the kitchen.

"First door past living room," she yawned softly into his chest, as if his pause made her realize that he probably had no clue where to go from here.

He started heading in that direction and into her bedroom. It had a four-poster bed and a soft, white comforter. Family pictures were scattered across the wall, and he noticed a few touches Willa must've put on the place.

A salt rock lamp. What looked like incense on the dresser. A stack of books on the bedside table. Some of her clothes piled in an armchair in the corner.

He walked to the side of the bed that looked like she frequented most and set her in it. He tugged her shoes off and set them on the floor by the bed, then pulled a spare blanket over her. Eyes still closed, she rolled to her side and released a contented sigh.

He needed to leave. He knew he needed to leave. But he couldn't stop staring at her, at the way her hair formed a halo around her head, the way her lips almost puckered in sleep, the way her nose scrunched every moment or two as if she were having some sort of dream. He kissed her softly on the forehead.

"Goodnight, Willa," he murmured against her forehead.

Then he turned around and left, stealing a final glance at her sleeping figure when he got to the doorway before heading home.

16

When Willa's alarm went off the next morning, two thoughts immediately entered her head.

First, she'd come on Shawn's fingers last night because his calloused hands fucked her better than any cock ever had before.

And second, she'd repaid the favor in kind by giving him road head and then having the gall to swallow.

And she didn't hate it.

"Shit," she muttered, covering her face in her hands as the events of the night came back to her in a haze.

Dancing with the stranger.

The way Shawn came in right as he kissed her.

How pissed he got.

How they danced and he whispered things into her ear that still made her toes curl, even a day later.

Every single moment in the car.

The way she rode his fingers like her life depended on it.

How good he tasted in her mouth.

What it felt like to fall asleep on his shoulder.

And then her blurriest memories reminding her how

she somehow ended up in her bed—that he carried her inside so gently that she barely stirred.

She bit her lip and groaned, but tried to put him out of her mind as she woke up and did her regular morning routine. She lit some incense and meditated for longer than usual in an attempt to soothe her racing heart. She pulled on her favorite yoga outfit, washed her face, ate a clementine and drank a cup of coffee, then headed to her car.

Willa knew she needed to talk to Shawn. And before that, she needed to put some serious thought to what she was going to say.

But first, she had to teach her Saturday morning yoga class.

She turned on one of her favorite podcasts during her commute to take her mind off of Shawn, and before she knew it, she was pulling into the hotel. Standing outside with iced coffees in hand were Layla and Amanda, and Willa would bet her freezer full of fish they were waiting to hear all the juicy details from last night.

Her suspicions were confirmed a few moments later when Amanda saw her and grinned like a cat. She extended an iced coffee in her direction.

"Thought you might need this," Amanda said. "A little sustenance while you tell us what happened last night."

"We're dying to know," Layla chimed in, her cheeks reddening. "Your neighbor looked like he was about to rip the head off the guy you were dancing with, then a few minutes later, you were hot and bothered and leaving with him."

"Please tell me he didn't just take you home," Amanda added. "Please tell me things took an R-rated turn."

Willa took a large gulp of her coffee and heaved a sigh.

"I'm really trying to compartmentalize so I can get through this yoga class," she said.

"We have thirty minutes til the class starts," Amanda insisted. "Give us the reader's digest version of what happened. Please. I'm begging you. I brought you coffee and everything."

Willa chuckled.

"Okay, fine," she said, taking another sip of her coffee. "He acted like he *was* just going to drive me home, but then..."

Her cheeks heated.

"Don't leave us hanging!" Amanda nearly shrieked.

"I basically begged him to give me an orgasm. Which he did. Thoroughly. With his fingers, right in the parking lot."

Layla's jaw dropped, and Amanda smirked.

"And then..."

"There's more?" Amanda asked excitedly.

"Well, after that, we started heading back, but I noticed he was still hard as a rock. You know? So, I..." Willa covered her face with her spare hand, peeking through her fingers with one eye. "I gave him road head."

"Holy fuck," Amanda said, applauding. "I wouldn't've guessed you had it in you, but damn. I'm impressed."

"Me too," Layla said quietly.

Willa bit her lip. "And then—"

"There's *more?*" Amanda asked again.

"This part's G-rated," Willa amended. "But I fell asleep on the car ride home. And he carried me inside. Took off my shoes, put me in bed, the whole nine."

"That boy's a goner," Amanda said.

"That's the problem!" Willa responded. "I can't do serious right now. I just... I can't. I'm not over what happened with my ex. And I feel like... maybe I pushed too far. And now we have to have the 'what is this' talk, and I don't want to deal with it."

Layla grimaced in sympathy.

"Look," Amanda interjected, "don't overthink this. He already knows what you want. You've made it clear. If he caught feelings, that's on him. Just tell him you had fun last night and want to keep doing it casually, but if he hasn't changed his mind, you can just stay friends and pretend like it never happened."

"I don't know if I can pretend it never happened," Willa said. "I mean, we're neighbors. I see him every day."

"Yeah, that would be hard," Layla said.

"So then are you willing to lose the friendship over this?" Amanda asked.

"No," Willa said too quickly. "Definitely not."

"Well, then I think your options are limited, babe."

Willa sighed and headed into the lobby, her friends trailing after her. She knew Amanda was right, and she had to talk to Shawn one way or another. She just dreaded rehashing the same conversation they already had, and she harbored a ferocious guilt for everything they did last night when she knew he was only looking for something serious.

At least she had a yoga session and her whole drive home to try and find some zen and figure out what to say to him.

SHAWN WOKE up early that morning and checked on the bait shop. Saturdays were his busiest days, and he always liked to make sure everything was fully stocked and organized for the weekend. Plus, he liked to be there before his employees arrived for the day to make sure they had everything they needed.

He had a chartered fishing trip he was taking a tourist group on later, so he brought a few insulated buckets of shrimp home with him after squaring everything away at the shop. When he got back, Grams was busying herself in the kitchen making breakfast.

"Got any extra for me?" Shawn asked.

"Course, Scooby," Grams responded. "Sausage, bacon, eggs, the works. Help yourself."

He didn't need to be told twice. Scooping generous helpings onto his plate, he sat at the kitchen table as she joined him.

"What happened with Willa last night?" Grams asked, attempting nonchalance.

He'd expected it. After all, he'd bolted out of here last night after getting a phone call from her, and Grams was here to witness the whole thing.

"Just gave her a ride home," Shawn said.

"Hmm," Grams responded.

"Don't go getting any ideas, Grams. You'll just be disappointed."

"If you say so."

Shawn took a bite of his food before Grams jumped in with another zinger: "How come I haven't seen Tucker or Hanna in months?"

He stiffened, then sighed. "It's a busy season for Tuck, you know that."

"That's never stopped them from seeing me before," Grams said, her brow furrowing. "Besides, Hanna's a teacher. She has summers off."

Shawn's heart clenched. His idiocy—his unwillingness

to have a hard conversation—was hurting Grams' relationship with his best friends.

He knew if he told her the real reason, she'd tell him to get over himself and tell them. It was the right advice, but he felt his stomach drop at the thought of it.

"I'll call them and invite them over soon, okay?" he finally said.

Clearly displeased with his response, she said, "If you say so, Scoob."

They finished eating before Grams headed out on her morning walk. Shawn knew Willa wouldn't be back for another hour or so, and his skin was itching with a desire to be near her, to talk about what happened, to run his thumb along her lips again. He needed to keep himself busy until she got back.

Before he knew what he was doing, he'd grabbed fishing gloves and pulled on swim trunks, then headed to her house. He waded into the water from the beach below her wharf, and quickly came upon what he was looking for: the rusted chair she'd tried to pull out of the water on her own the other day.

He gave it a tug and it didn't move at all. He shook his head absentmindedly, disbelieving that Willa was going to try to remove this by herself. Widening his stance, he grabbed the edges of the chair and wiggled it a bit until it started to loosen from the sand. He continued to work at it, slowly easing it from the sand, until after a few minutes, he tugged it completely free.

Shawn heaved the chair up out of the water and carried it to the shore and up the stairs, setting it on the wharf. Once he got there, he took a quick look at it and noticed some clams had stuck to it. He began pulling them off and tossing them in the water, trying to preserve the few he could. It was tedious work, pulling off clams of all sizes from where they'd found a home on this chair. But he'd grown up listening to his grandfather talk about how much more life there was on the Bay—until pollution and overfishing had depleted the wildlife significantly.

When he was a kid, Shawn could remember swimming and finding clams underneath his feet all day long. Now, he was lucky to find even one clam during the summertime. They weren't as plentiful as they used to be, making the small, fingernail-sized clams on the chair even more precious. As much as he would've liked to have just left the chair in the water so they could continue to thrive, it was a hazard. Anyone could accidentally trip over it just like Willa had, or a net or fishing line could easily get stuck in it.

He heard footsteps behind him and turned to see Willa walking down toward him, her red hair pulled in a bun on top of her head, a few stray strands framing her face. She was wearing a baby blue pair of leggings and a matching sports bra, and she was sipping from a water bottle in her hand, her face slightly flushed. Memories of the way her tongue swirled around his length last night came back to him, and it took everything in him not to toss her over his shoulder and carry her inside.

"Hi," Willa said shyly.

She was acting timid for the first time since he met her, and he thought it was possibly the cutest thing he'd ever seen.

"Hi," he responded with a grin. "How was yoga?"

"Good." Her eyes flickered to the chair. "Thanks for doing that. I could've done it, but I appreciate it."

"No problem. It was pretty heavy, though, so I was happy to do it."

"Are you trying to imply that I couldn't have gotten it out

without a man to help me?" she asked, crossing her arms, all shyness gone.

"Me?" Shawn asked jokingly. "I'd never say such a thing."

Willa rolled her eyes. "I know I look scrawny, but I've been doing yoga for years. I could've done it."

"Isn't yoga, like, relaxing? Like getting a massage?"

"Ha!" Willa said. "It definitely can be. But you should come to one of my yoga classes one time. I'd love to see if you'd still compare it to a massage."

He smirked. "Next Saturday, then. I'll be there."

"Can't wait to watch you beg for mercy."

He chuckled, then cleared his throat. "So. Last night."

She bit her lip.

Opened her mouth.

Closed it again.

Sighed.

"I'm sorry if I took advantage," Shawn said, feeling his shoulders slump. "I didn't mean to—"

"Shawn, stop." Willa took a deep breath. "I was buzzed. Not drunk. I remember every moment of last night, and I enthusiastically consented to everything we did."

"I did remember that part of it, Greene," Shawn said with a grin, delighted when Willa blushed.

"I'm the one who should be sorry," Willa said. "You made it very clear that you aren't looking for anything casual, and I haven't changed my mind on that front."

"I have," Shawn blurted out before he could stop himself.

He'd figured it would come to this. Had prepared for her inevitably saying they needed to go back to being just friends—or worse, just neighbors.

"I mean," he started, running his fingers through his hair nervously, "I'm open. To keeping it... relatively casual."

Willa studied him for a moment.

"Relatively?" she asked.

He nodded.

"So what are your terms?" she asked, crossing her arms, seeming to take a battle stance.

"So you want to do it again?" he asked, trying to hide the hopefulness in his voice.

She rewarded him with rosy cheeks and a hesitant grin.

"I had fun last night," she responded. "A lot of fun."

"How much fun?" he asked.

He was just fishing now, and they both knew it.

"Look, you know what you're doing, okay?" Willa said. "And honestly, I don't know what it was, but that orgasm was... powerful. Must've been the reason I jumped at the opportunity to—"

She cut herself off, and Shawn smirked.

"Yes, that was a pleasant surprise," he said.

"Let's just say I've never been so enthusiastic to suck a cock before."

God, if she kept talking like this, he was going to spill in his pants.

Their chemistry was off the charts, and he couldn't wait to get her alone again. Preferably somewhere larger than the front seat of his car, where he could properly strip her down and palm those glorious tits and—

"Um, eyes up here," Willa snapped her fingers, drawing Shawn's eyes from the aforementioned glorious tits up to her face, where she was giving him a bemused look.

"Sorry," he said. "You said cock and my mind wandered."

"Clearly," she said drily. "So. Relatively casual."

"Right," Shawn shook his head, trying to focus.

He was flying by the seat of his pants and needed to keep a clear head if he was going to have a chance of getting inside her again. Or possibly, maybe making her fall in love with him. But that was a long shot, and he knew it. He'd take whatever she would give him.

"So, you're down to just be friends with benefits?" she reiterated.

"Yes, but I have two requests," he said. "First, we keep this exclusive. Let's not sleep with anyone else."

"That doesn't feel like a casual request."

"Fair, but it's an important one. I promise I won't, like, fall in love with you." He dropped eye contact and tried to sound lighthearted. "I'd just rather not share you. Clearly I'm the jealous type, even if we're just fucking."

Shawn looked back up at Willa and her eyes were squinted as she studied him.

"Fine, but you can date other people," Willa said. "In fact, you should. So I don't feel bad about keeping you from finding an actual girlfriend, since I know that's what you want. That's one of my rules."

He tried to ignore how it stung to hear her say that, but he found himself nodding.

"Alright," he responded.

"And the second thing?"

"We still hang out," Shawn said. "I don't only want to see you for booty calls. I like fishing with you. I don't want to lose out on the friends part of this friends with benefits arrangement."

Willa nodded.

"I agree," she said, and he jolted with pleasant surprise. "I like hanging out with you, and you're one of my only friends my age here. As long as we keep it to friend stuff only, that's fine with me."

"Friend stuff only?"

"Like, don't show up with an accordion player and a bottle of champagne."

Shawn chuckled. "Fair enough."

"I have rules, too."

"More than just making me go on dates with other people?" Shawn was anxious to hear what else she had in mind.

"Ida can't know."

Shawn sputtered. "You think I tell my grandmother about my sex life?"

"I think that woman is far more observant and intuitive than either of us give her credit for, and I don't want her getting her hopes up if she finds out something is going on between us," Willa responded. "She keeps trying to push us together. She'll become unbearable if she finds out about our... arrangement."

"Good point," Shawn said. "So that means we should probably only hook up at your place."

"And don't tell her every time you're hanging out with me."

"You live next door. How am I supposed to keep it a secret every time I come over to fish off the wharf, Greene?"

"I don't know!" Willa said vehemently. "Drive your truck down the road and park it at the Bayou, then walk to my place."

"You've gotta be kidding me."

"Whatever. We can work out the details later. But she's going to get suspicious if we're not careful. That woman has the nose of a bloodhound and the brains of a CIA agent."

Shawn laughed.

"I'm serious," Willa said.

"I know," he responded with a grin. "Imagine growing up with her."

"Also, no sleeping over," she continued, and he tried to keep his face neutral. "No cuddling after sex. No dates or date-like hangouts. And no hard feelings if one of us isn't in the mood or available to hook up."

"Should I be writing this down?" Shawn asked jovially, trying to lighten the mood.

Willa chuckled, then bit her lip.

"One last thing," she said. "I'm on birth control, but I'd still like to use a condom."

Shawn nodded. Of course she would want that. He'd basically told her he'd slept with every tourist who came through the area in his twenties.

"Whatever you're comfortable with," he said. "I'm clean, but if you'd prefer using a condom, we can do that."

"I'm clean, too," she said. "I just would prefer to use a condom."

"Alright," he responded. "We can do that."

A beat of silence passed.

"So... now what?" she asked. "Do you want to come inside and...?"

Shawn felt his brow furrow and he tilted his head in an unspoken question. Willa covered her face in her hands and groaned, then peeked through her fingers.

"I've never actually done this before," she said. "The casual sex. Or even initiated things like this. I don't... At the risk of sounding extremely full of myself, guys usually come to me. Wine and dine me."

Amusement trickled through Shawn as Willa dropped her hands.

"I've had boyfriends since I was, like, 13 years old. I don't think I've been single for longer than a few weeks since then, and I don't really know how to ask you to please, for the love of God, fuck me before I explode without sounding like all I've been thinking about is how you made me come last night."

She paused.

"Which, for the record, I have."

Shawn walked toward her, then grabbed her cheek with one of his hands, running his thumb along her jawline.

"You're cute when you're flustered," he said with a smirk.

She bit her lip.

"But for the record," he continued, "all you have to do is ask. And hearing you say filthy things like that only makes me want to bend you over the closest table and make you come so hard that last night seems like child's play."

Her mouth formed that adorable O, then she grabbed his hand and trudged up the hill toward the back door of the house as he trailed closely behind.

17

Willa had planned to lead him to her room.

But the moment they closed the door to the house and stepped securely inside the kitchen, he grabbed her hips, turned her to face him, and pulled her into a kiss so ferocious she thought her knees would give out.

Since last night, a small part of her wondered if it was a one-off.

An isolated, unrepeatable, sexy-as-fuck one-off.

But this kiss was making it quite clear to her that it wasn't.

His hands felt hot and firm on her hips, and she felt the press of his fingers into her skin, just firm enough that she thought she might swoon from the sheer possessiveness he was displaying. His mouth devoured hers with such ruthlessness that she felt completely consumed by him—like the only thing that existed was Shawn, his delicious lips, his wicked tongue. She clawed her fingers up his six-pack, marveling at the way they moved along the firm ridges of him. Her palms flattened across his chest, feeling the smooth curve of his pecks against her hands.

Suddenly, he leaned down and grabbed the underside of her thighs, bringing her legs to wrap around his waist as he picked her up. She wrapped her arms around his neck, clinging to him like her life depended on it, trying to get as close to him as she could, soaking up the groan he released when she grinded up against his growing erection. Their bodies were pure heat against each other, and with his shirt off, she could feel his firm muscles rubbing against her front.

He dropped her and she yelped before realizing he'd set her on the bed. Willa had been so caught up in the kiss that she hadn't noticed he carried her to her room.

Shawn climbed over her, kneeing her legs apart as he came to the center of her.

"Take your bra off," he growled.

She pulled her bra over her head, then shivered as she looked at Shawn. His eyes were rapt, ravenous. He didn't move. His still form hovered over her body as he stared at her with such pure lust that she felt both exposed and confident as hell.

"God, you're perfect, baby," he whispered reverently, bringing a hand to palm one of her breasts. He gave it a gentle squeeze, then rubbed a thumb over her already perked nipple. "Been thinking about these tits for weeks. Wondering what they look like under those little bikinis you wear. Wondering if your skin is freckled under there or not."

He leaned down til his mouth hovered over the nipple he hadn't been fondling, pausing just above it until Willa started squirming in anticipation.

He grinned wickedly up at her. "Is there something you want?"

"Please," she said.

"Use your words, Greene."

"Suck my fucking tit already, you idiot."

"Mmm," he hummed against her nipple, then licked it gently with his tongue. "But you asked me so sweetly last night. Why aren't you begging now?"

He moved a knee up to her center and she gasped at the pressure he expertly put on her clit before enclosing her nipple in his mouth, sucking and grazing his teeth so delicately that she began to tremble.

"Shawn," she gasped as he kissed up to her neck, tugging an earlobe into his mouth before kissing her lips.

"I'm going to take your pants off now," he said. "That okay?"

She nodded, hungry and feral with anticipation as his fingers gently tugged at her leggings.

"You're not wearing panties," he said, stopping briefly before tugging her leggings off.

Willa had forgotten about that minor detail.

"Ran out," she panted as he tugged the leggings down her thighs, barely touching her, his eyes glued to hers.

"How often do you go commando because you need to do laundry?" his tone was steely, his eyes dark.

She squirmed as his hot breath fell over her thighs, his lips softly trailing kisses up her legs, up, up, up. Realizing where he was headed, she sat up and tried to stop him.

"Shawn, I haven't showered since yoga this morn—"

"If you think that'll stop me from tasting you properly, you've got another thing coming." He locked eye contact with her. "I asked you a question, Greene."

"I go commando a lot," she said breathlessly as he pinned her hips to the edge of the bed. "Never wore panties as a ballerina. Carried over to yoga, I guess."

"I'm always going to be wondering if you're wearing panties now," Shawn said as he stared reverently at her pussy. She watched his Adam's apple bob before he looked back up at her. "I want to make you come on my tongue."

"You don't have to."

"I want to. If you're okay with it."

Willa laughed breathlessly. "I'm extremely okay with that."

She'd barely gotten all the words out of her mouth before he'd parted her folds and pressed his lips against her clit. She gasped as his tongue ran all the way up the center of her before coming back to her clit, sucking it so hard she released a breathy moan.

He grabbed her thighs and tossed them over his shoulders before pulling her closer to him and burying his face between her thighs, his thumbs digging into her hips as he pulled her closer. Willa let out an embarrassingly loud whimper, and he growled his approval against her. She squirmed underneath his attention, but he held her still, lapping his tongue against her in steady rhythms as she felt an orgasm build.

"Shawn," she panted, shutting her eyes as she felt her climax build. "Fuck, I've never finished this quickly before but I'm gonna—"

Her body shuddered as he thrust two fingers into her and sucked her clit, her thighs tightening over his shoulders as she had a blinding orgasm. Moaning and rolling to her side, she felt his hands run up her legs and tug them back onto the bed.

He tugged his boxer briefs down, and her mouth watered at the sight of his cock, recalling every moment of what it felt like to have him in her mouth last night. She sat up in her sated state and moved toward him, but he stopped her.

"I want to finish inside you," Shawn said, his eyes flashing with heat and desire. "I need to. Tell me you have a condom."

Shit.

She'd come up with that rule on the spot. It felt silly in hindsight, but she'd always been extremely cautious when it came to having sex. She didn't want to have kids, so an accidental pregnancy would have been a nightmare. Even though she was on the pill, she had friends who'd still gotten pregnant on it. Nothing was perfectly effective, and she wasn't taking any chances.

But the real reason she came up with that rule?

If she was honest with herself, it was one more barrier between them. A layer of separation when they had sex so she could keep her emotions in check.

Like that would help her when he was looking at her like she held the sun and moon in her hands, when he ate her pussy so expertly she came in a few minutes flat, when he took that hazardous metal chair out of the water for her while she was gone.

"Do you have a condom?" Shawn repeated.

He licked his lips, still tasting her on them. She was heavenly. Sucking her off his fingers last night was like an appetizer compared to the meal he just had, and if he wasn't about to explode, he might do it again.

But now, he needed to sink his cock into her.

He'd only been fantasizing about it every day since she put him in his place in his bait shop weeks ago, and after last night, it was a miracle he'd made it through the morning. Then again, he'd taken care of himself in the shower right after he woke up. Fisted his dick until he came all over his hand at the memory of how her pussy clenched around his fingers.

But still.

He hoped to hell she had a condom. If she didn't, he'd have to figure out a nonchalant way to go grab one from his place. Which meant he'd have to walk home, hard as a rock, and somehow hide his massive erection from his extremely nosy and intuitive grandmother.

"I think I have one in one of my bags," Willa said, standing up and heading to the bathroom.

He heard some shuffling around for a moment before she returned with a small square parcel. She was still naked, and he let his eyes wander along the entirety of her body. When he'd gotten her leggings off earlier, he studied every inch of her, trying to memorize her perfect figure.

But he should've known he'd never get enough of it. Never get enough of her.

Willa delicately opened and pulled out the condom, then approached him hesitantly. He nodded, and she bit her lip as she rolled the condom over his cock. He couldn't hold back a groan as her slender fingers held his cock firmly and pulled it down to the base.

Shawn grabbed her face and kissed her lips messily, his tongue thrusting into her mouth, trying to taste every last inch of her. She gasped at the contact, and he swallowed up the sound she made, pushing her back against the bed and laying her down on her back before he nudged against her entrance with his cock.

"Shawn," she gasped. "Please."

He pushed it in slightly more, and she wriggled, trying

to push her hips up to meet him. He held her down, though. Steady, still. Fuck, she felt so good. He wanted to tease her, wanted to have her begging for every last inch of him. But he also knew if he took this too fast, this would be over before it even started.

Deeper, slowly. Inch by inch, kissing Willa gently on the lips, then sucking her tits as he sunk into her.

"Please," Willa begged. "Shawn, I need you."

He groaned as he pushed his last few inches inside her, until he was so deep into her that he could feel the head of his cock against her. She moaned breathily, and it was almost his undoing.

"I'm not gonna last long, baby," Shawn rasped, his palms flat on either side of her head as he slowly began thrusting into her.

"Fuck me hard, then."

Shawn didn't need to be told twice. He reared back and thrust into her as hard as he could, her screams egging him on more. He was taken over by primal need that lived deep inside him, and all he wanted was to come inside her, to keep making her scream his name, to fuck her so hard that she forgot they were nothing more than fuck buddies.

He felt his lower back tingle and let out a sound he didn't know he was capable of making, knowing he was about to finish.

"Shawn, I'm—"

She arched underneath him and her pussy clenched around his cock as she finished again, with just enough force to push him over the edge right behind her. It felt like his orgasm went on forever, like it would never end, like maybe time had just frozen in this perfect moment of plea-sure. He collapsed on the bed next to her, then tugged her on top of him. She rested her head on his chest as he tried to slow his breathing.

"Wow," Willa whispered against his chest.

He looked down at her and pushed the red hair out of her face, tracing a thumb over the constellation of freckles on her cheek, marveling at her beauty, at what she did to him.

"What?" he whispered.

She blushed, and he grinned at her as his thumb stilled over that reddened cheek.

"I've never..." she bit her lip, then buried her face in his chest. "I've never come from just penetration before like that."

Pride flared through his chest. He tugged at her chin with his forefinger until she looked at him. Then he pulled her closer to him and delicately kissed her lips. He wanted to tell her that if she let him, he'd make her come every day for the rest of her life, morning, noon, and night. That if she just stuck around long enough, he'd be begging her to sit on his face and let him taste her every minute of the day. That if she wanted to come on his cock, all she had to do was ask and he'd comply. That he'd never get tired of the little moans she made underneath him.

But she scared easy. Like a dolphin in the Bay, he knew she'd bolt at the first sign of trouble. And he didn't want to scare her off. He knew he had to play it cool.

"Seems like you're having a lot of firsts with me," he said.

He brushed his thumb along her lips—the lips he couldn't stop thinking about—and he felt her stiffen slightly under his scrutiny. Knowing he needed to bring this post-coital moment to an end so she wouldn't think he was trying to turn it into something it wasn't, he cradled her in his arms and carried her into the bathroom.

"You should pee," he told her as he set her down.

She smirked at him. "And you should take that condom off, wrap it up in toilet paper like a mummy, and toss it in the trash."

He laughed. "Okay, sorry for being heavy-handed. I'll get out of your hair."

Shawn grabbed a few pieces of toilet paper and stepped out of the bathroom, took care of himself, and got dressed. He vaguely heard the toilet flush and the shower turn on, and he figured that was his cue to leave.

As he left the back door of her house, he couldn't help but wonder what he'd gotten himself into.

18

Willa had been dodging Charlie's calls.

She knew that made her a shitty friend, but she didn't want to call her back until she'd nailed down a therapist like she promised. And she hadn't yet.

But there was no putting it off anymore. Willa desperately wanted to call Charlie and tell her about the friends-with-benefits situation she'd gotten herself into with Shawn. She wanted to tell Charlie about the not one, not two, but *three* orgasms he'd given her in the past twenty-four hours.

Which was why she'd furiously researched therapists in her area before deciding to use one of the apps that had hundreds of licensed therapists available. She'd scrolled through a few profiles before deciding to schedule an appointment with a woman who had experience working with women and couples. It was scheduled for the end of the week.

And now she had her phone on speaker on the kitchen counter as she thumbed through the mail, impatiently waiting for Charlie to pick up the phone.

"Well, well, well," she said by way of greeting. "Glad you aren't dead or something. I was beginning to worry."

"I suck, I know. I'm sorry," Willa said.

"What gives?"

"Honestly, I was dragging my feet on therapy," she said. "But I did it! Scheduled for Thursday."

"Getting started is hard," Charlie responded, voice full of concern. "I get it. And I'm really proud of you for making it happen."

"Thanks," Willa's eyes burned with gratitude for her friend who was unafraid to say the hard things and still more compassionate than anyone knew.

"So I'm assuming there's another reason you called?" Charlie asked.

Willa sighed.

"That bad, huh?"

"My hot neighbor gave me three orgasms."

Charlie cackled. She didn't giggle, didn't chuckle, didn't laugh. *Cackled.* If Willa were with her, she was certain she would've seen Charlie tip her head back and grab her belly in mirth.

"Well no wonder you haven't answered my calls!" Charlie shrieked. "You've been busy!"

Willa rolled her eyes.

"I took your advice, and—"

"Uh, my advice was to hook up with a rando," Charlie cut in. "Remember? Go to a bar? Dance with a guy? Bring him back to your place and kick him out before you go to bed?"

"Okay, well I tried that," Willa said. "But I found a friends-with-benefits situation instead."

"Wait, wait, wait," Charlie said. "Back up. You *tried?*"

Willa sighed. "I have these work friends and they took me to this place called Flora-Bama—"

"Dude, everyone knows what Flora-Bama is. I spent an entire spring break there when I was 20."

"Okay, well, my friend Amanda told me to stare at this guy until he noticed me—"

"Smart woman. I like her already."

"And we danced for a while. But then I called Shawn in the bathroom—"

"Sexy neighbor?"

"Yes, and then, like, forty-five minutes later he prowled onto the dance floor and pulled the rando off me—"

"Holy shit, you've really been holding out on me."

"And Shawn also happened to walk in right as the rando I was dancing with started to kiss me, so—"

"So you did kiss a rando! I'm proud of you."

"But then, Shawn started dancing with me. And he said all these things..." Willa bit her lip as she remembered the way he whispered into her ear. "Let's just say, the man has a filthy mouth."

"Love a man who knows how to talk dirty. So when do the orgasms come in?"

"We left the bar and I basically begged him to fuck me in the parking lot. So he fingered me in the front seat of his truck like we were a couple of teenagers—"

"Nothing wrong with some car sex."

"—and then I gave him road head on the way home."

Silence passed between them.

"You there?" Willa asked.

"Holy fuck, what is in the water down there?" Charlie asked, choking back a laugh.

"Salt, mostly. And fish poop."

"Since when do you even like giving head?"

Willa laughed. "I've always felt... neutral about it? But I don't know. He made me come so hard with his fingers—"

"Respect."

"—and I just looked at his rock hard dick bulging against his pants, and I didn't really think about it."

"Damn girl."

"So then, he came over this morning after I got back from yoga and basically said he'd do the friends-with-benefits thing. And then he carried me to my bedroom and fucked me so hard I thought I'd pass out."

"And that's where orgasms number two and three come in, I'm assuming?"

"Yes."

Willa heard Charlie suck in a breath and knew she was in for a lecture.

"Look, I'm happy for you," Charlie said. "And I'd love for you to please send me a shirtless photo of Sexy Neighbor the moment we hang up. But are you sure this is a good idea? I just don't want you to catch feelings and then end up even more hurt."

"We set up rules," Willa responded.

Willa absentmindedly thumbed through her mail, trying to avoid thinking too hard about Charlie's words. The truth was, she was a little worried about catching feelings. It was easier to think about doing a friends-with-benefits situation with Shawn a few weeks ago, when she thought he was a Grade A asshole. Now, she'd realized he was secretly a Golden Retriever behind all the grunting and frowning. He occasionally put his foot in his mouth, but he was kind and sweet, and so caring toward his grandmother.

Nothing like anyone she'd dated in the past, that's for sure. And maybe that was part of the reason Willa was concerned. Because she'd made it clear to Shawn that, under no circumstances, could this turn into more. And even though he was uncertain at first, he ended up hopping on board with the ease of a shark eating a minnow. She knew he had a history, so maybe he was just as horny as she was.

"I appreciate the concern, I really do," Willa said. "But I'm a big girl. I can take care of myself. And I know who to call if things go south."

Charlie sighed. "Alright, Willa. If you say so. Consider the subject dropped. Onto more important matters: when can I come visit you?"

"Whenever you want," Willa said as she opened an envelope. "You know I'd love to have you anytime."

"Hmm, let me check my calendar and see when flights are cheap," Charlie murmured.

Willa barely heard her as she stared, dumbfounded, at the invitation she'd just gotten in the mail.

"Holy shit." She held the invitation up and reread it, then laughed so hard she had to put the phone on speaker and wipe tears from her eyes while Charlie demanded to know what was going on.

"You'll never believe what I just got invited to," Willa said through her laughter, then took a picture of it and texted it to Charlie.

A few moments later, she heard her phone buzz with the text message through the call, and Charlie gasped.

"What the fuck is a Bingo Ball?" she asked.

"The event of the year, apparently," Willa responded, still chuckling. "Oh, my god."

Willa started laughing hard again, then harder when Charlie joined in, reading more information off the invitation with increasing incredulity.

"It's a Black tie event!" Charlie shrieked. "'Join us as we

crown the Bingo King and Queen.' Holy fuck, you're being pranked. There's absolutely no way this is real. My God, a ticket is $100!"

"Bingo is serious business for the elderly here," Willa said, wiping a tear. "This is definitely real. I'll ask Shawn."

Willa sent a picture of the invitation to Shawn along with a pressing question.

> Please tell me this ridiculousness is real.

"I went to Bingo with Ida a couple of weeks ago and I've never seen anything so intense in my life," Willa said. "And I was a fucking ballerina, for God's sake."

Her phone buzzed.

> So real that you should definitely not let Grams hear you call it ridiculous.

Willa chuckled. "Shawn says it's real. Holy shit. I can't wait to go to this."

"Well, this makes my decision of when to visit you a million times easier," Charlie said. "I'm coming to the Bingo Ball."

"Immediately, yes. I'm so into this plan. Sending our RSVP now."

Willa quickly sent an email to the contact listed letting them know she'd be coming with a guest, then texted Shawn.

> Just RSVP'd yes. Can't wait for this nonsense.

He responded almost immediately.

Don't let them hear you call it nonsense, either.

"Alright, I found perfect flights. Gonna book these and I'll send you the details later. This means I get to see you in a month!"

"Can't wait," Willa said, then in an exaggerated British accent, she added, "Bring your finest gown."

"But of course, darling," Charlie responded in kind.

19

How soon was too soon to text Willa for another hookup?

It took everything in Shawn not to text her immediately when he got home from the chartered fishing trip he took a group of tourists on yesterday. But he didn't want to seem overly eager, and he'd already told her he wouldn't be back in time to fish off the wharf like they usually did.

By Sunday morning, he was already counting down the seconds until the sunset so he could go to her place and see her. And those seconds ticked by agonizingly slowly.

Grams didn't typically go on her walk on Sundays, opting instead to go to church, so Shawn knew there was little chance of Willa coming over. He tried to keep himself busy.

He'd already been kicked out of the kitchen by Grams for hovering. He went to the bait shop to check in, but things were always slow on Sundays and the kid who was working today seemed a little confused about why Shawn was there. So he came back home, cleaned his room and bathroom, mowed the lawn, read a few chapters of the book sitting on his desk, and checked on all his crab traps.

All the while, he tried not to check his phone every few minutes to see if she texted him back. Each time he pulled up their thread, all he saw was the text he'd sent her yesterday after she texted him to see if the Bingo Ball was real. She'd left him on read, so he knew she saw it.

After Willa told him she'd be going to the Bingo Ball, Shawn asked Grams if he could go with her.

"You usually hate things like that," Grams said. "Last year, you told me you'd rather let crabs eat you alive than be my date to a Black tie event where all the old ladies would try to set you up with their granddaughters."

Most days, Shawn was grateful for Grams' memory. Unlike most people her age, she was still sharp as a tack. She still told stories about the early days of dating his grandfather with the same charm and wit as she did when he was a child, and he knew that wouldn't last forever. He knew eventually her age would catch up with her, and she'd start forgetting little details she typically remembered.

Most days, Shawn was grateful. Today, he wasn't.

"You're right," he responded, turning his back to her so she wouldn't see that he was messing with her. "Maybe I shouldn't go."

"Now, wait a second," Grams said. "I never said that. I was just wondering—"

"How about this, Grams?" Shawn grinned, turning back around. "I go with you as your date to the Bingo Ball, and you don't ask any follow up questions."

"Hmmm."

Figuring he'd won this round, Shawn started heading back to his room.

"You'll wear a tux?" Grams asked.

Shawn turned around and gave her a curt nod, then left before she could ask any other questions.

He was a goner. That much was sure. He hated dressing up. Anything more than his swim trunks and a t-shirt was outside of his regular dress. Shorts and a button-up were often pushing it for him, but a tux? He'd never worn one and didn't have a particular desire to start now.

Except Willa.

She'd be there, and he wanted to be where she was. Even if he had to wear something that was bound to make him look like an idiot. Even if his agreeing to go made Grams suspicious.

It wasn't just Willa's beauty or the way she tasted—and fuck, she tasted so good. It was her—how she was so at one with the water, how she knew this bay almost as well as he did, how fierce she was, a spitfire. She was fearless, but emotional. She was strong, but vulnerable. She was powerful, but soft. She was walking contradictions that he wanted to know better.

And she didn't want a boyfriend.

Shawn couldn't blame Willa. From what little he knew of her dating history, he could understand why she'd be skittish. And he'd take whatever she gave him. He'd follow her rules, do whatever it took so he could sink into her again.

And if she ended up falling for him in the process because he made her orgasm better than any other guy?

All the better for Shawn.

On the other hand, if their friends-with-benefits situationship ran its course after a few months and she dropped him like a fly...

Well, he'd figure it out if it came to that.

His phone buzzed, and Shawn reached for it so quickly

he almost fell over. A quick look at his phone told him it was a text from Tucker, and he felt a twinge of disappointment that it wasn't Willa. He cleared the text, deciding he'd respond later, and took a deep breath.

The sun was about to set, and he headed into the kitchen to have dinner before walking over to Willa's. He grabbed some leftovers out of the fridge and put them in the microwave, then went to grab utensils.

There, sitting on the counter, was a polaroid picture of Willa. She was wearing one of those workout sets she had, and her back was facing the camera. Her hair was splayed out in the wind, her head spun around as she beamed at the camera. Her eyes were squinting as if she was looking into the sun.

Shawn picked up the picture and ran his fingers along the edges of it.

"It's a good picture, isn't it?" Grams said as she entered the kitchen behind Shawn.

He set the photo back down and grabbed his food from out of the microwave.

"Getting out the old polaroid again?" Shawn asked instead of answering.

She kept a polaroid camera in the foyer at all times "in case the creative mood strikes," and occasionally, she took it with her on her outings. When that happened, she'd take about fifty photos and then wouldn't touch the camera again for a couple of months.

"Felt like taking it on a walk earlier this week," Grams said. "I saved all the polaroids in my fanny pack, but thought she'd want that one."

Shawn looked up from where he was eating and nodded. "It's a good one."

"I'll give it to her in the morning."

"I'll take it to her tonight," he responded before he could stop himself, pocketing the photo.

"You sure are spending a lot of time over there," Grams said.

Shawn scarfed down the last of his leftovers and stuck his plate in the sink.

"Just trying to be a friendly neighbor like you always taught me," he responded, throwing a wink over his shoulder.

"Sure that's all there is to it?"

"Course," Shawn said. "We're just fishing."

"Hmmm."

"Grams, stop. You promised, no more meddling."

"I believe the terms of our agreement were that I wouldn't set you up with anyone else," Grams said. "But I can still speculate about your romantic entanglements with people, as far as I'm concerned."

"There are no romantic entanglements to speculate about," Shawn said, getting frustrated as he stood with his hand hovering over the doorknob. "And I'd appreciate it if you'd stop assuming there were. She's not really my type. Plus, you know as well as I do that she just got out of a bad breakup. Even if I *were* interested, she isn't. Case closed."

"Not your type?" Grams drawled. "What, you're not interested in beautiful yoga instructors who know how to fish?"

Shawn felt heat creep up his cheeks.

Grams damn well knew that was exactly his type, and he was losing steam in this argument, getting dangerously close to breaking one of Willa's few rules.

"Grams, it's not 1950," he said. "Men and women can be friends without there being anything else between them."

"Hmmm."

"I don't want you to get your hopes up that something is going to happen between us when it isn't. Let it go, alright?"

Grams studied him for a moment.

"Okay, Scooby. I'll let it go."

Not entirely convinced that he'd gotten her to drop it—but unwilling to stay behind and try to further his point—he stepped out to the backyard and breathed in the salty air. the Bay glistened in the sunset, the sky cotton-candy pink, and he grabbed the bucket of shrimp he'd brought over from the shop this morning. He was technically a little earlier than usual, but as he started walking toward her house, he saw her sitting in a beach chair on the edge of the wharf, wearing loose-fitting shorts and a tank top, sipping a glass of wine.

And she looked fucking stunning.

God, he'd never get tired of looking at her. The way her hair framed her face, the curve of her cheeks, the delicate curve of her neck. Her head was tipped back, eyes closed in peace. As he got closer, he heard some light music playing—something instrumental, classical.

Shawn didn't want to disturb her. He wanted to freeze this moment in time, bottle up the way she looked and made him feel just by *being*, and stay there forever, watching her soak in a perfect sunset and salty air that reminded him there were depths of this earth yet to be explored. He wanted to watch her from afar, count the freckles on her face and the hairs on her head. He wanted her to always be this content, this peaceful, this happy.

But as if she felt his gaze, she sat up and made eye contact with him, heat blooming in her cheeks as her lips curved.

"It's creepy to stare," she said with a smirk.

"Can't help myself. You're too goddamn pretty," Shawn said before he could stop himself as he walked toward her.

Her lips parted and she looked away.

"I know I'm a little early, but we can get started before the sun is completely down if you want," Shawn said, trying to break the silence that came between them.

"Or we can go inside and do something else," Willa said, her eyes darting to his mouth.

He groaned, shifting as his cock hardened.

"As much as I would love that, we shouldn't," Shawn said, and Willa frowned. "Grams asked some leading questions about the nature of our relationship earlier, so I wouldn't be surprised if she's watching us with her binoculars."

Willa clapped her hand over her mouth, then tipped her head back and laughed.

Shawn reached in his pocket to grab the photo and hand it to her, but as she grinned at him, he decided against it. Nobody had to know if he kept this picture of her all to himself.

"I knew she would be a menace," she said. "Alright, then let's get this show on the road."

They walked out to the edge of the wharf in companionable silence. The sky was now gray, the pink and purple gone as the sun set lower, and the LED light Willa left permanently on was shining over the water where some minnows were swimming swiftly.

They wordlessly grabbed fishing rods, baited them, and tossed their lines in the water as the darkness covered the Bay like a blanket. Part of the reason Shawn wanted to make sure this part of their arrangement didn't go away—the friend part—was because of how easy it was to be around her. He wanted to learn everything there was about her, sure, but it was just as relaxing to sit in silence with her. He didn't feel like he needed to fill it with mindless babbling or thoughtful questions. He could just *be*.

Shawn had few friendships that were so quickly comfortable for him. And he didn't want to risk losing what he had with Willa.

"Do you miss California?" he asked, breaking the silence.

She glanced over at him, then back to where her line was resting in the water.

"Not as much as I thought I would." Her voice was quiet, but piercing in the stillness of the night. "I lived there for ten years. There are a lot of amazing things about California. The weather is always pretty temperate. There are so many things to do, especially in San Francisco. The restaurants are amazing. As a yogi, there were always trainings I could take part in or lead. And a lot of my college friends lived there."

Shawn waited for a moment before saying, "But?"

"But." Willa laughed. "But, we got older. A lot of my college friends left SF for other places. Cheaper places. I couldn't blame them. And I think I always craved a slower pace. That was the one thing I could never quite get the hang of—the hustle and bustle, how fast everything moved. My best friend, Charlie, loves it. She'll live in SF until she dies. But I think I always knew I'd end up back here."

Maybe they were kindred spirits in that way. Shawn couldn't imagine living anywhere else.

"Why's that?" he asked.

She smirked at him. "You'll have to tell me your deep, dark secrets next. It can't just be me."

"Fine. A question for a question. Answer mine and then I'll answer yours, Greene."

"You'll answer two of mine."

"You drive a hard bargain," Shawn said, then stuck his hand out to shake hers.

She laughed, then put her hand in his, sending a shock of electricity down his body that he desperately tried to ignore.

"I moved a lot growing up," she said. "This place was my only constant. I came here every summer. It's where I grew up. Where I learned to ride a bike. Where I took my first steps. Where I had my first kiss."

Her eyes darted to him nervously.

"This house is the only place that's been a real home for me through the years," Willa continued. "And I've always had this pipe dream that I'd move back here and start my own yoga studio. Teach some classes for seniors, do some classes on the beach for tourists."

Shawn felt a pang of guilt for how he'd acted when she tried to help Grams after her fall. Clearly Willa knew what she was doing. This dream of hers only made it more obvious.

"I like the slower pace of life here," she whispered. "I feel like I can hear myself think when I sit on this wharf. And there's something almost carnal about catching my own food that makes me feel... not just satisfied, but empowered. Like I don't need anyone else but me."

"I know what you mean," Shawn said.

She smiled at him. "So it's my turn now."

He groaned internally. "Give me your best shot."

"What do you like most about running the bait shop?"

He was sure she thought that was an easy question, but there was more to it than she knew.

"My grandfather started that shop," he said. "It was a project he started later in life. He'd been able to retire relatively early and still had some energy in him, I guess. So I grew up learning the ins and outs of the business and helping him out. People always came in asking him for advice. Where should they go if they wanted to catch flounder? What kind of bait should they use off their wharf? Which rod was best for a beginner? I thought he was the coolest man alive when I was a kid."

Shawn was quiet for a moment, and he could feel her eyes on him.

"When I was 13, he told me I could take over the shop for him when I grew up, but shortly after that was when the dementia came on. It was slow at first, but by the time I was 15, he didn't always know who I was. I was working there during the summers, but I was worried the business wouldn't make it. Luckily, some locals helped keep it alive until I was 18. That's when I took over."

He held her gaze for a moment, mesmerized by the compassion in her gaze.

"The business was a wreck when I took over, to say the least. And I didn't have a formal education. Didn't go to college. So I just researched how to run a business, watched YouTube videos about bookkeeping, and experimented with some things. I started doing the chartered boat tours a year later. I honestly didn't think the business was going to survive, so it was my last shot at keeping it alive. And I made more money in the first month of summer than I had the rest of the year combined. I knew that's when I had something good going."

Shawn closed his eyes.

"It reminds me of my grandfather. That's what I like most about the shop. People come to me and ask the same questions they asked him, and I get to help them do something I love. The chartered tours are really just to keep the business alive. I make good money from them, but what I love most is the day-to-day of the shop. I can still feel my grandfather in there sometimes."

Willa was silent for a moment, then said, "I think that's the most words you've ever said to me at once."

Shawn opened his eyes and belly-laughed, trying to avoid the creeping feeling of self-consciousness that crawled over him whenever he was vulnerable.

"So what's your other question, Greene?" he asked.

"Well, I'm assuming your least favorite thing is the tourists?"

He felt his jaw involuntary clench. He blew out a breath, then set his fishing rod down.

"It didn't used to be that way," Shawn said. "For the record, I don't hate all the tourists. There are some tourists who come here to experience the Bay, and I love showing them around. Families, groups of friends—those can be really fun. Especially with kids who are learning to fish. Those are my favorite groups."

He grinned. "And not all of the women are like the one you saw at the shop the other week. Most of them take no for an answer. But after a few drinks, they get bolder. And they're always drinking on the boat. But yeah, to answer your question, it is my least favorite part. Dealing with the women who shamelessly flirt with me, or the men who think they know better than me. It's worth it, though. I'd deal with a thousand terrible tourists to be able to take one great family on a tour."

"You said it didn't used to be that way," Willa said. "What changed?"

"Me, I guess," he let out a humorless chuckle. "I used to welcome the attention from women. Jump in bed with them the first chance I got. But then my best friend, Tucker, fell in love with this girl, and I was pissed. Don't get me wrong—

Hanna's awesome. I love her like a sister. But I saw how happy they were, and it took me months to figure out I was jealous. They had what I wanted. What I craved.

"I have no shame in my playboy ways. I learned a lot from all that sex, and I think you'll probably reap the benefits of that," he said, winking at her in an attempt to lighten the mood. "But I just realized I was ready for more than sex. I wanted companionship. Someone to come home to. To talk to about how my day went. To go fishing with."

Willa nodded.

"I get it," she said. "Well, I guess I don't. We're opposites. I've always had boyfriends. Never any good ones, obviously."

She huffed.

"But that desire to have a person like that? Who's there for you no matter what, who *gets* you, who listens to you when your day is shitty? That's always appealed to me. Probably why I'm terrible at being single."

"You're not terrible at it," Shawn said. "You're single now. And I'd say you're pretty damn good at it. You fish for your own meals, for Christ's sake."

She grinned, and his heart fluttered at the idea that he made that happen. "That's nice of you to say."

"So can I ask another question? Since, technically, I let you ask three?"

She groaned. "I was thinking I could reward you for your vulnerability with sexual favors, but if you'd prefer to ask me a question, go for it."

Shawn stifled a groan.

He was going to die from how much he wanted her. God, she was so hot, so perfect, with lips begging to be kissed. But he wanted to *know* her, wanted to be an expert in everything that had to do with Willa.

"You drive a hard bargain, Greene," he said. "But I'm going to ask my question now, and I'll make you come later."

Her eyes flitted to him, half-lidded with desire. Good thing she was feeling that way now, because he was about to bring down the mood significantly with his question.

"What happened with your ex?"

Just like that, her eyes shuttered and her body stiffened.

"You don't have to tell me if you don't want to," Shawn said quickly, already feeling overwhelmed with guilt for making her feel so bad that her body gave outward signs of discomfort.

She took a deep breath in and out, so slowly that Shawn felt like the Earth might've stopped spinning.

"I met Leo just over two years ago," Willa said. "He'd come to one of my yoga classes. We dated, and things were getting serious. Before I moved here, I'd just asked him to move in with me. We were about to start looking for apartments. But then I saw him at my favorite brunch place." She took a deep breath and closed her eyes. "With his wife and child."

"You're shitting me."

He wanted to throw up.

No, he wanted to find this Leo and chop his balls off and feed them to him.

Then throw up.

"I wish I was," she whispered, bringing her legs up to cradle them in her arms. "The worst part is how... embarrassing the whole thing feels. Does it hurt that he did this? Yes. Is it shitty that he led me to believe we'd move in together and maybe get married one day? Abso-fucking-lutely. Am I constantly replaying the last two years in my mind, reminding myself that every second was a lie? Yup.

Do I feel like a piece of trash knowing I was a married man's side piece for two fucking years? You bet."

She bit her lip. "But what sucks the most is how stupid and idiotic I feel. It's the twenty-first century, for fuck's sake. I should've looked him up on social media. I should've Googled him more thoroughly. When he told me he wasn't on Instagram or Facebook, I *believed* him. And his place—that apartment was so *bland* and *boring*. I mean, it was nice, but it had almost zero personal touches. I thought it was just a guy thing. Now, I know it was probably a pre-furnished place he kept secret from his wife. I'm hurt, yes, but more than that, I'm mortified. That I didn't know any better. That I didn't think to question anything. That he got me to believe his bullshit."

"You couldn't have known, Wi—"

"I should've. I should've known. This is not the first time a man has cheated on me, and I doubt it'll be the last." Willa quickly shut her mouth like she'd said too much, and Shawn's heart ached.

He wanted to cradle her in his arms and tell her how perfect she was. How beautiful. How brilliant and kind and funny. He wanted to wrap her up in him so thoroughly that she forgot Leo's name, forgot anything he ever did or said. He wanted to bottle her pain and take it from her.

"Why should you have known, Willa? How could you have known?"

She buried her face in her knees, then turned so her cheek was resting on them and her eyes were trained on Shawn.

"Every boyfriend I've ever really cared about has cheated on me," she whispered. "The ones where we said we were exclusive never actually were. I've found them in bed with someone else. I've gotten the frantic call from the other woman. I've accidentally seen the texts. And this was the worst fucking one. He was married. With a two-year old. And I missed every goddamn sign."

A few tears slid down her cheek, and before he could stop himself, Shawn swiped it away.

"There's nothing wrong with you," Shawn whispered, his hand still resting on her cheek. "But there is something wrong with any man who treats someone that way. And any man who has you and does something stupid enough to lose you."

20

S hawn couldn't remember why he agreed to this.

He was wearing what he normally wore for a workout: gym shorts and sneakers. The yoga class was taking place on the beach, after all. It would be hot.

He should've known it would be mostly tourist women at this class. Then maybe he would've worn a t-shirt. Or, at least, brought one. But most men were constantly shirtless around here, especially in the high heat of July.

And a small part of him knew he'd decided to go without a shirt to taunt Willa.

Maybe give her a reason to look at him.

He stood awkwardly in the middle of a group of women on the beach, hands in his pockets, awaiting further instruction. Meanwhile, she was busy chatting with a few of the people here for the class. He vaguely recognized a couple of women sitting on yoga mats a few yards away from him as the friends she'd gone to the bar with from the selfie she'd sent him. He felt the eyes of strangers on him, and his jaw clenched as he crossed his arms and kept his eyes on Willa.

She was wearing her signature yoga outfit—a matching

exercise set of leggings and a sports bra. Her auburn hair was pulled into a messy bun, and she was gesturing animatedly in conversation with people. He'd gone over to her place every night this week, and they'd fished for a while before she dragged him into her bed and he sunk so deep into her that he thought he'd never feel this kind of bliss with anyone else. Just last night, she'd crawled onto all fours on her bed before he plunged into her pussy from behind, and he barely lasted two minutes before exploding inside her.

As if sensing his eyes on her, she glanced at him and smirked. Then she checked her watch and clapped her hands.

"Alright, yogis!" she exclaimed, her voice carrying over the sound of waves. "I'm so excited by today's turnout."

Shawn looked around. There were about fifteen people gathered around her. Some stood waiting for guidance, while others sat on towels or yoga mats they brought.

"I love seeing familiar faces, so a special thank you to those of you who are back to practice with me today," she said. "If you need a mat or a towel, I have some extras over here. We'll begin in a seated position, so feel free to settle in and start taking some deep breaths."

Shawn walked toward Willa and picked up a towel, then settled on the ground on the outskirts of the group and sat down. He peered at other people around him, and noticing that many of them rested their hands on their knees and shut their eyes, he followed suit.

"As you breathe in and out, soaking up the salty air, begin to set an intention for your practice," Willa said, her peaceful voice floating over him like a blanket. "Maybe you want to challenge yourself and try something new. Maybe you want to simply honor your body. Maybe you're looking for peace or contentment. Or maybe you just need to work through your hangover from last night."

A few soft chuckles carried through the group, and Shawn felt his lips curve up in a slight smile.

"Remember that it's perfectly okay to skip anything that's too challenging for your body," she continued. "While I want you to push yourself, more than anything, I want you to listen to your body and respect what it's telling you. If you need to just lay on your mat for the entirety of this class, nobody will judge you."

Shawn felt comforted by her words. He'd never done yoga before—never had any interest in giving it a shot. So far, it was what he expected. Calm and easy. But her words healed something in him—something that told him he needed to do everything perfectly, even at the expense of his own happiness. He doubted there would be anything challenging enough in this class that he'd need to skip it, but knowing that the option was there made him feel better.

Willa began to lead them in a series of poses and actions that he was unfamiliar with, but was actually enjoying. Some of the stretches reached his muscles in new ways, though he had to often look around him or glance at Willa to accurately follow the instructions.

It was fun seeing Willa in her natural habitat, teaching people the thing that had saved her during one of the hardest times of her life. She was confident and kind, grinning through the entire class and going around, gently helping those who were struggling.

But about twenty minutes into the class, Shawn found himself profusely sweating as he settled into downward facing dog. This was the pose he saw her in a few weeks back, where her ass was pointing perfectly in the air. She made it look so easy—even now, she was talking to the class without even the slightest hitch to her voice.

As Willa led the class through a sequence, Shawn struggled to follow along. He could reel in a 100-pound swordfish on a chartered fishing trip without breaking a sweat. But balancing on one foot while extending his other leg in front of him? Holding a plank after doing a myriad of movements he didn't totally understand? Sitting in a half split, stretching muscles he'd sorely neglected for years?

Willa was right.

This was not easy.

And even though she'd proven it time and time again, it seemed she had more ammunition to showcase his idiocy for doubting her.

"Now, today, I thought we could be brave and experiment with handstands," Willa said as she came back into downward facing dog. "It takes regular practice to be able to hold a handstand, but it's worth it. We'll start with handstand hops."

Shawn placed his hands underneath his shoulders and looked between his wrists, like Willa demonstrated, before pushing up on his toes and kicking up into a handstand. But he overestimated the amount of strength he needed, and the next thing he knew, the breath was knocked out of him as he laid on the ground in simultaneous embarrassment and horror.

"Nice try," Willa said with an encouraging smile, standing over him.

He looked around and noticed everyone else doing handstand hops, and a few of them were able to hold a handstand for a few moments. He glanced back to where Willa was standing with an arm outreached, giving him a playful smirk.

"Let's try again, shall we?" she asked.

He grabbed her hand and gave it a squeeze before allowing her to pull him up. Then he went back into downward facing dog. She grabbed his hips and pulled them up, and he tried not to focus on the way it felt for her fingers to brush against his body.

"You should bring your feet closer to your hands," she said, still guiding his hips back. "Now, take a breath. Relax your neck. Relax your face, your jaw. Even your tongue."

He shook his head, wiggling his neck and loosening the muscles in his face.

"How did you know my tongue wasn't relaxed?"

She chuckled. "Just a guess. Now, don't forget to breathe as you push into your handstand. Alright?"

He took a deep breath and nodded. She released his hips and went to stand toward the side.

"Whenever you're ready," she said. "I can spot you."

He took a deep breath, then kicked his way up. He went up slower this time, but his legs still hit her arms as she held him in place.

"Good," she said. "Now breathe."

He didn't realize he'd been holding his breath. He sucked in a gust of air, then released it, repeating it over and over. His arms began to shake as she let go of him.

"Now can you hold it on your own?"

He focused on his breathing, willing his arms not to give out, then after a few moments, kicked down and sat on his knees. Sweat dripped down his forehead as he looked to her for approval.

"Amazing," she grinned. "Not a lot of newbies could pull that off, but you're a natural."

Willa winked, and he basked in her praise as she headed back to the front of the class and led them in stretches to close them out. As Shawn laid in savasana, which was apparently a pose even though it literally just meant laying on your back and soaking in everything your body just did, he felt his body go limp and relax.

"Shawn?"

His eyes sprung open and he looked around, noticing everyone else had started packing up their supplies and chattering amongst themselves.

"I think you fell asleep," Willa said, biting her lip to hold back a laugh.

"That was amazing," Shawn responded, sitting up and airing out his towel. "Fucking hard. But awesome. You were right."

"The three sweetest words in the English language," she said, faking a swoon. "Say them again."

He rolled his eyes, then stepped closer to her, cradling her cheek with his hand. "You. Were. Right."

A throat cleared a few feet away from them, and Willa turned out of his grip to face a man who somehow appeared clean cut even though he was sweaty and shirtless from running on the beach. Shawn felt his body stiffen as she stepped out of his embrace and crossed her arms.

"Blake," she said, a tight smile on her face. "Out for a run?"

He gave her a dazzling smile. "Thought about coming to yoga again, but I'm not sure it's for me."

"It can definitely be challenging to get started if you've never done it before."

Blake stepped closer to Willa. "Maybe you could give me those private lessons we talked about."

His voice was thick with meaning, and Shawn saw Willa's body stiffen. Instinctively, he stepped forward and put his arm around her.

"This your boss, babe?"

Willa bit her lip and looked up at him beneath her eyelashes. Amusement and gratitude shone there.

"Yes, this is Blake," Willa said. "Blake, this is Shawn."

"Her boyfriend," Shawn added as he stuck a hand out.

Blake glanced between Willa and Shawn, looking sullen. "Didn't realize you had a boyfriend, Will."

Blake grabbed Shawn's hand tight and shook it in a stiff up and down motion. It took everything he had not to roll his eyes at his blatant use of a nickname he was pretty certain Willa hated and his attempt to break Shawn's hand with the force of his handshake.

Shawn smirked. Blake would have to try harder if he wanted to overpower Shawn; he'd been stung by jellyfish, hooked by stray lines, and bitten by crabs. A pretty boy's attempt to intimidate him didn't hurt in the slightest.

In fact, Shawn would find it amusing if it weren't for the blatant discomfort radiating from Willa.

"Not sure if it's appropriate for your boyfriend to be attending your yoga classes," Blake added.

It took everything in Shawn not to punch this guy in the face.

"But let's talk about it at our one-on-one," Blake continued. "I want to hear how it's been going. Attendance has been pretty good, but clearly we need to review some things. How about we grab a drink Thursday night after your class?"

Willa gave a stiff nod. "Sure."

"Alright, then," Blake winked, putting his headphones back on. "Better finish up my run."

As he ran away, Shawn turned Willa toward him and cradled her head in his hands again. He searched her face for any lingering sign of discomfort, but he only saw relief.

"Thanks for being my fake boyfriend to scare away my creepy boss," she said with a smirk.

Almost immediately, Shawn felt his stomach drop. He hoped he hadn't overstepped, but more than anything, he wished he weren't her fake boyfriend. He was beyond the point of lying to himself. It was more than just a crush, now. He wanted to date her. For real. And it would likely never happen. He couldn't blame her after what her exes had put her through. And with his history, Shawn figured he probably came off like the exact kind of guy she'd want to avoid dating.

"Anytime," he said, pressing a gentle kiss to her forehead.

It was too far.

Too intimate.

But he couldn't help himself.

She gaped up at him as he stepped back.

"Do you have plans for the rest of the day, Greene?" he asked.

"No..." she raised her eyebrows at him.

"Good," he said. "Because I have an idea."

21

Shawn had told her to wear "normal Bay clothes." When Willa asked for clarification, he said a swimsuit and something to cover up with. So that's how she ended up wearing her favorite navy bikini underneath jean shorts and a tank top.

Willa sat on the steps of her front porch waiting for him. They'd started to be more careful around Ida, so they agreed that he'd pick her up rather than have her walk over to his place. That woman was too nosy for her own good, and Willa's walks with her were slowly turning into an inquisition. Usually, asking about Bingo or the latest birds she'd seen on the wharf would pivot the conversation well enough for Ida to drop it, but lately, she'd been asking more about Willa's dating life and talking up Shawn like it was her job.

Willa grinned to herself. It was sweet how much Ida loved Shawn, and how well Shawn took care of her in return. The wall she'd built around her heart was cracking, and she had to admit that the way he treated his grandmother warmed her to no end.

And his way of seeing her—of *really* seeing her—and

somehow saying the exact thing she needed to hear endeared her to him as much as it scared the shit out of her.

There is nothing wrong with you.

Willa squeezed her eyes shut. She hadn't planned to open up to him about Leo the other night, but he'd told her so much—he was so open, so vulnerable. She felt like she owed it to him to do the same, even if he'd given her a clear out. And before she knew it, she was spilling her guts, saying things she hadn't even said to Charlie—things she'd been working up the courage to say in therapy.

So she'd told him the whole story, but held back sharing that she felt like she'd never get it right, that she was inherently messed up somehow for always choosing the wrong guy.

And then, he said that, wiping away her tears.

Somehow, he read her mind. He knew she was thinking that something must be wrong with her. That had to be the case, otherwise, why would so many men cheat on her? She hadn't said it outloud, but he responded anyway.

There is nothing wrong with you.

Words she'd needed to hear for far longer than she realized. All the cascading emotions she had been feeling vanished in an instant, once he was touching her. He'd wiped away that tear, and his hand hadn't left her face since. He'd come closer, kneeling beside her, looking deep into her eyes as if extended eye contact could somehow convince her of what he said earlier.

There is nothing wrong with you.

The sinking feeling in her stomach was still there, but only slightly. Saying it outloud had taken away some of the fear in that sentiment, and now Shawn had looked at her like he wanted to take her pain away.

His truck pulled into the driveway, taking her out of her reverie.

"You gonna tell me what we're doing?" she asked as she climbed into the truck.

"I'm surprised you haven't figured it out."

She chuckled and put it out of her head as he pulled out of the driveway. She'd find out eventually. Though she'd usually have her suspicions, but she just wanted to turn her brain off after the morning she had. Letting Shawn take the lead so she could relax for a minute felt like a gift she didn't know she needed.

Blake's appearance at her yoga class today left her feeling unsettled. She wanted to give him another chance—*hoped* she'd been wrong about him at first, but he proved her initial judgment right today. Distantly, she thought back to when Layla first mentioned him, and she hoped her friend's work situation wasn't as toxic as Willa suspected.

Of course, when Shawn stepped in and saved the day as her fake boyfriend, she thought she might swoon on the spot.

But she still had that meeting with Blake to contend with, and she didn't quite know what to expect. Willa had been kicking herself all day for agreeing to meet with him over a drink despite her best judgment. A business meeting over a drink seemed harmless enough for most people, but with a man like that—one who clearly was used to getting his way with women—she wasn't so sure. She didn't feel like she could decline, though. She was rarely rattled, but something about Blake bothered her. And it wasn't just Layla's warning; it was a gut reaction, something that screamed for her to be careful.

And she hated to admit it, but Blake reminded her a bit of some of her exes. It made her feel stupid. Shouldn't she have seen through their bullshit the way she saw through Blake's?

Willa had her first therapy session a few days prior, and they talked about her sordid history with men—how they always seemed to disappoint her in the long run, with their cheating and their lying and their hurtful words.

Her therapist said that in their next session, she wanted to dig into self-love and self-trust, and how to rebuild it. Willa felt like that was a big task for her to undertake, but she had to admit, she felt better after her first therapy session. Even if she was emotionally exhausted.

"Are you thinking about that jerk?" Shawn asked, his knuckles white as he held the steering wheel. "Blake, or whatever the fuck?"

She leaned back in her seat and propped up her legs on the dash. "How did you know that's what I was thinking about?"

"I can read you like a book, Greene," he responded with a smirk, then grew serious. "I didn't like the way he talked to you."

"That makes two of us."

"He tried to break my hand with that handshake of his."

"Shit, I'm sorry," she said, looking over at him with sympathy. "You ok?"

Shawn chuckled. "I said 'tried,' Greene. It'll take a lot more than a pretty boy like that to hurt me."

Willa laughed with him and rolled her window down, closing her eyes as the salty breeze covered her. She breathed it in deeply, sucking it into her lungs in an attempt to calm her racing mind. Before she knew it, Shawn was pulling the car to a stop.

She opened her eyes and looked around.

"The marina?" she asked.

He nodded, giving her a grin as he sat back and waited for her to finish connecting the dots.

She looked out the window toward where the boats were docked. One of them was a nice little speedboat with the name "Ida" painted on the side. She turned back toward him suddenly and sucked in a breath.

"You're taking me on a boat ride."

"You won it, fair and square," he responded.

"But don't you have a paid tour today?" she asked, remembering that he usually did tours on Saturday afternoons, and she'd never forgive herself if he'd canceled it for her. "I thought you were booked solid for the month."

"They canceled at the last minute," he said. "Which means I have all the makings for the perfect boat picnic."

"But—"

"They had to eat all the fees, so it's completely free and it'll be fun."

Willa bit her lip and looked back out the window.

This felt an awful lot like a date.

But Shawn was her friend, and he'd insisted on them maintaining the friendship part of their arrangement, and he was just trying to cheer her up after a weird day. Plus, she had won a free, chartered boat ride with him. So no point in overthinking it.

Right?

Shawn was staring at her hesitantly. She beamed at him and threw her arms around his neck.

"Thank you," she whispered into his ear. "But I have one stipulation."

She pulled back and he grinned. "Name it."

"I want you to fuck me on that boat."

His eyes darkened and dropped to her mouth.

"I've never done it on a boat before," she continued.

"Me neither."

Her jaw dropped. "You're joking."

He shook his head, his lips curving up slowly.

"I don't believe you."

"There have certainly been... opportunities," he said. "But I was always captaining the boat. And it felt unprofessional, not to mention unsafe."

"So are you saying you won't do it, then?"

He winked. "I might be willing to make an exception."

IT HAD BEEN a long time since Willa had seen this much of the Bay. She grew up taking boat rides in the nooks and crannies of Perdido Bay, had gone back in the Bayous and rivers that only locals knew about, but it had been years.

Once her grandparents started getting older, it became more challenging for them to get the boat out and ready. She knew how to drive it, of course. She'd had a boating license since she was a teenager. But the upkeep and management of boat ownership became too much for her grandparents, and over the years, the boat rides became less and less.

Shawn took her all over the Bay, to all the places she remembered experiencing as a kid. All the while, he had a backwards cap on and a beer in his hand. She was feeling the inklings of a light buzz and leaned into Shawn's side, then looked up at him.

His strong chin jutted out, and she wanted to run her fingers along his jawline. But such casual familiarity felt beyond the scope of their arrangement.

They'd been boating around for hours, occasionally tossing a line in the water to see if any fish would bite.

They'd caught a few flounder and one trout, which Shawn said Willa could keep. She was itching to get home and filet them, maybe fry them for dinner or breakfast tomorrow.

The sun still shined brightly in the sky, and Willa suddenly felt the desire to swim.

"Can we anchor and jump in?" she asked him, her voice barely carrying over the sound of the engine.

He nodded. "We're close to a good spot for that."

A few minutes later, she was tossing the anchor in the water as he turned the boat off. They were in a relatively private area. Some boats went by occasionally, but it wasn't the most popular spot for swimming or fishing. It was hidden away behind some grasslands with water deep enough that Willa couldn't see the bottom.

She took off her shirt and shorts, and without preamble, she jumped into the water with a shriek. As she surfaced, she pushed her hair back and looked up at the boat. Shawn was nowhere to be seen.

"Shawn?" she asked, uncertain why she suddenly couldn't see him.

Suddenly, out of nowhere, he came running toward the edge of the boat.

"CANNONBALL!" he shouted as he jumped in the water right next to her.

Willa started laughing so hard she couldn't stop, even when he surfaced next to her and gave her an exasperated smile.

"You're ridiculous," she said.

He grabbed her and pulled her close to him, pressing a kiss to her lips.

"You don't seem to mind it too much," he said against her mouth.

She wrapped her arms around his neck and tugged him

closer, kissing him as they treaded water, feeling his muscular body against hers in the Bay.

"Is this the part where you fuck me on a boat?" she whispered.

He laughed and started swimming toward the back of the boat, where he'd released a ladder for them to climb back up. Once they got back on, she took a sip of her beer and laid out on the bow, allowing the sun to naturally dry her off.

"Thanks for this," she said. "Today. The boat ride. All of it. I feel like a kid again."

He laid down next to her on the front of the boat, resting his hands behind his head.

"You won the free chartered ride, fair and square," he said.

"It's more than that, and you know it," she said, curling her body into his. "Thank you."

He turned his face toward her and she pulled herself toward him before pressing her lips against his in a kiss that she hoped conveyed the depths of her gratitude. She kissed him lightly, at first, her lips barely skating over his. But it deepened as she kept going, her tongue swiping against his as she plunged into him, pressing her body against his. His hands came up to steady her hips as she straddled him, and she grinded against his length as she dragged the tips of her fingers up and down his muscled abdomen.

She sat up and admired him, and he gave her a quizzical look.

"You know, muscular guys are a dime a dozen in California," she said, earning a pointed glare from Shawn. "But the first time I saw you, I knew these muscles were the real deal. From reeling in 100-pound fish and rebuilding the wharf after hurricanes."

She pinched a bicep and then kissed him again, her hands splaying out on the soft ridges of his arms. Shawn rolled over their bodies so he laid on top of her and her back rested on the bow of the boat. He traced a thumb over the crook of her nose and the curve of her cheek, his eyes dark with lust and restraint and something else Willa couldn't figure out.

Something tender.

"I love your freckles," Shawn rasped. "I want to fucking memorize them."

The breath whooshed out of Willa, but as she digested his words, he claimed her mouth in a scorching kiss. She couldn't think about anything but the feel of his lips on hers, the way his body curved protectively around her as if hiding her from potential onlookers, the way his tongue moved with practiced precision against hers.

"If we're going to do this, you have to be quiet and do as you're told," he whispered against her lips before consuming her with another kiss.

She smirked, then saluted him. "Yes, sir."

His eyes narrowed. "Gonna have to fuck that sass right out of you."

"Please," she whimpered as he tugged her bikini bottoms down.

"That's more like it," he grinned devilishly at her, then tugged his swim trunks down and pulled a condom out of his back pocket. "This is going to be quick, but you're going to come."

"Have you had that with you the whole time?" Willa gasped, eyeing the condom in his hand.

"Been keeping 'em in my wallet since we started hooking up," Shawn said as he rolled the condom down his length. "Grabbed one after you laid out here in that tiny little bikini like you were begging me to make you come."

With no preamble, he thrust into her so hard she thought she'd elevated to another plane. She moaned, and his hand came up to cover her mouth.

"I need you to be quiet, Greene," he said. "Can you do that?"

Her eyes widened. He'd paused thrusting, his cock tauntingly deep inside her, and her body begged her to release another moan. But she nodded.

"You know where to let all your screams go," he said, removing his hand, and she turned her head into the crook of his neck. "That's right, baby. Save all those pretty noises for me."

He thrust into her again.

Hard.

She whimpered.

"Fuck, baby," Shawn grunted. "Love the way that pussy clenches around me."

Again, and again, and again.

He thrust into her with such slow force that Willa was close to begging him to pick up the pace, to make her *come* already. But she couldn't get out the words. Her breath came in slow spurts.

She longed to wrap her legs around him, but the way her bikini bottoms pooled at her knees made it impossible. She needed more—more friction, more force, more *Shawn*.

"I'm not gonna last, baby," he said. "Fuck, you're so goddamn perfect. Clenching my cock like you were made for me."

Willa whimpered.

"Touch yourself," he said. "I need you to come, baby."

She reached between them and began circling her clit

with her fingers. Shawn had brought her so close to the edge that it took only a few gentle strokes for her body to tremble with the force of her climax as she bit into Shawn's shoulder. As she quivered underneath his body, she vaguely felt him trembling with the force of his own orgasm.

Shawn leaned back so he was level with her face. He dropped a soft kiss on her nose, then gently pulled out and tugged her bikini bottoms back up her body.

Willa closed her eyes, soaking in the sun and the looseness that came with her orgasm. After disposing of his condom, Shawn came back to where she was and laid down next to her again.

"Boat sex, check," Willa said jokingly, her eyes still closed.

"Happy to be of service," Shawn responded light-heartedly.

Willa turned to look at him. "Today has been perfect."

"Yeah?"

"Yeah."

He lifted a hand to cradle her cheek, and she couldn't help but lean into it. His warmth. His comfort.

Feeling overwhelmed by the intimacy of the moment, Willa sat up and put space between them. She was starting to feel things.

Things she promised herself she wouldn't feel.

"Where are those sandwiches you brought?" she asked, rifling around in the supplies he'd put in one of the storage areas of the boat.

She pulled out a cooler that had finger sandwiches, chocolate strawberries, and a bottle of champagne. She lifted the champagne and looked at him quizzically.

"What kind of boat ride were you supposed to be taking the tour group on earlier?" she asked with a grin.

"It was a date," he said. "For honeymooners."

Her smile faltered and she put the champagne back in the cooler. This was beginning to feel like a date. But it wasn't. Right? It was just two friends who liked hanging out and also happened to occasionally have mind-blowing sex.

Fuck. This was only weird if she made it weird.

Shawn clearly had no problems keeping it casual. He was a goddamn pro, actually. So she took a deep breath and made a mental note to call Charlie later to discuss whatever weird situationship she'd gotten herself into, and started eating the finger sandwiches.

"Sun's setting soon," Shawn said, grabbing a sandwich and stuffing it into his mouth in one bite. "Should probably start heading back."

Willa nodded, eating silently as she pondered how much longer she could pretend she didn't have feelings for this man.

22

"Where'd you go, darlin'?"

Willa pulled herself out of her stupor and looked over at Ida, who was staring at her expectantly.

"Sorry, Grams," she said. "Just thinking."

About her grandson.

About the way he seemed to anticipate her every need.

About the perfect day they'd had on the boat together.

About the way it felt when he was inside her, trying to hold off an orgasm so she could finish first.

It'd been a few days since their boat trip, and like clockwork, Shawn had kept coming over every night to fish off the wharf. Of course, the amount of time they spent actually fishing had become less and less. Lately, they'd only lasted about 15 minutes before Willa dragged Shawn into the house and had her way with him.

Over.

And over.

And over.

That man had stamina, and Willa was all too pleased to take advantage.

"Well, I was saying that the Bingo Ball is next week, and I hope you have a nice dress picked out," Ida said.

Willa bit back a laugh. "How nice? I have a few sundresses I was thinking about."

Grams gasped and frowned. "Only wear a sundress if you want to embarrass yourself. This is the biggest event of the year. People go all out for it. And the invitation specifically states that it's Black tie. Don't make me regret putting you on the guest list."

"So you're the reason I got invited?"

"Of course, honey. Keep up. Now, what are we going to do about your outfit?"

Willa sighed. "I'll figure something out."

She made a mental note to talk to Charlie about ordering a few dresses from Rent the Runway for the event.

Ida huffed. "You'd better. Shawn will be wearing a tux, and I had a dress custom made for this event."

Willa's heart sped up. "Shawn's going?"

"Seems that way. He asked to come with me, though God only knows why. He hates dressing up. Every year, he comes up with an excuse not to come with me. Not this year, though."

The thought of Shawn in a tux made Willa sweat. She wondered if she could convince him to come over after the Bingo Ball and wear his tux while he fucked her with his tongue. She shook her head, trying to focus on the conversation with Ida.

"My friend, Charlie, is coming to town next weekend," she said. "She'll be coming to the Bingo Ball with me."

"Better make sure she knows the dress code," Ida muttered.

"I'll call her today and we'll figure it out," Willa said. "Promise."

"Is she single?" Ida asked. "Maybe we could set her up with Shawn."

Willa stopped in her tracks, her blood running cold. "Set her up with Shawn?"

"Yes, dear," Ida stopped and glanced back at her. "I promised Shawn I'd stop trying to play matchmaker after I tried to set the two of you up, but maybe he'll let you set him up. Since you're friends and all."

Willa's eyes narrowed at Ida.

She was baiting her. She knew it, but she couldn't stop the raging anxiety from flowing through her at the thought of Shawn dating someone else. Never mind that she'd insisted he date other people while they were friends-with-benefits. She took a deep breath.

"Unfortunately, Charlie's not much of a dater," Willa said. "She likes to play the field. Plus, she lives in California."

"Hmmm."

Willa rolled her eyes and they walked in silence for the last few minutes of their workout.

"Alright, Grams," Willa said as they approached Ida's house. "I'll get some dresses this weekend. Promise. And you can even give final approval if you want."

"That'd probably be for the best, sweetie. Send me pictures. And I'll see you tomorrow."

~

> FYI, the Black tie thing is not a joke. Come ready to impress for the Bingo Ball. Ida threatened me within an inch of my life that we better come dressed like it's the Met Gala.

WILLA SHOT the text off to Charlie as she headed inside the hotel lobby. Her sunset yoga class had gone great, and more and more hotel guests were coming every week. She'd been working with Layla to promote the class via text and email to guests at the Beachside Inn as well as other tourists staying nearby. Many of them ended up staying for a drink at the hotel bar after classes, and Layla was excited about the increased business coming into the hotel.

Willa's stomach churned as she thought about what came next: her one-on-one with Blake. She gave Layla a tight wave before heading to the bar, where Amanda was preparing drinks for a small group of women in one corner.

As she expected, Blake was already there, waiting. He'd found a secluded tall table and had two glasses of wine. His too-white teeth were bared at her as he gave her a smarmy smile, and she sat in a stool opposite him.

"I hope you don't mind that I ordered you a glass of our best red," he said, handing her the wine.

She did mind. She minded a lot.

Willa had planned on ordering a mocktail. Amanda made really good ones. Sometimes, her yoga students asked her to join them for a quick round before she headed home. She didn't really like to drink before getting behind the wheel, especially wine. It made her sleepy. So Amanda had been making her various mocktails, and she'd loved them.

She felt like she had no choice but to accept the glass Blake extended in his hand. But that didn't mean she had to drink it.

"So, what would you like to cover in this meeting?" Willa asked, setting the wine glass down in front of her.

"Where's the fire?" Blake responded with a teasing grin. "Let's visit for a few minutes before diving into business."

Willa ground her teeth together.

"So, how are you?" Blake asked. "How are you settling in?"

"Fine, thanks. What about you?"

"Aren't you going to drink your wine?"

It took all her self control not to roll her eyes. She took a small sip, then shared a look with Amanda and flagged her over.

"Could I get some water?" she asked

"You bet," Amanda said, her tone overly chirpy as if trying to sound normal.

"Feeling a little dehydrated after yoga tonight," Willa said.

"Of course," Blake responded. "It seems like your classes are picking up popularity around here."

Willa almost sighed in relief.

Finally, time to talk shop and get this over with. "Yes, they're going very well. Layla has been helping me market my classes and spread the word to guests. I don't know if you've noticed, but a lot of them stay after class and have drinks here."

Blake nodded. "There is one problem, though."

Willa quirked a brow. "What's that?"

"That boyfriend of yours probably shouldn't be coming to your yoga classes."

"Why's that?"

"It's just unprofessional."

Willa frowned. "That makes no sense. How is it any

different than if one of Amanda's friends or family members came to the bar for a drink?"

Right on cue, Amanda set a glass of water in front of Willa and locked eyes with her for a brief moment before retreating.

"It's different because they're paying customers, and your boyfriend, Shane, isn't."

"His name is Shawn."

"Well, the point stands."

Willa felt her body vibrate with rage. "So if he comes to the bar after, would that be fine? What if he pays a fee to participate?"

She was digging her heels in for no reason and she knew it. Willa doubted Shawn would come back to one of her classes, and even if he did, would Blake ever find out?

"Look, I didn't want to have to go here, but it's more than just that other people are paying customers," Blake said, setting his wine down and locking eye contact with Willa. "He seemed a little rough around the edges. Out of place. You know?"

"Rough around the edges?"

"Just not the kind of guy our guests would appreciate having around here."

Willa opened her mouth to respond and shut it. She couldn't believe what she was hearing.

"He doesn't really seem like your type, either," Blake said. "Not sure what you're doing with him, anyway. Is he really your boyfriend?"

This meeting had gotten way out of control, but Willa couldn't seem to regain her ability to speak. She was utterly confused and frustrated, but more than anything, she was fucking furious. How dare he talk about Shawn that way? How dare he make assumptions about Willa? And how dare he talk to her about something personal when they barely knew each other and this was supposed to be a business meeting?

Blake reached across the table and grabbed her hand, which had been resting on the table near her glass of water.

"If it's company you're after, I'd be happy to oblige," he shot her another cheeky grin, and she felt dirty. "I'm sure I could make it worth your while. I'd even be willing to look the other way if you brought him to another one of your yoga classes."

She tugged her hand out of his grasp.

"What are you suggesting?" she asked through clenched teeth.

"I'm suggesting that you ditch the long-haired caveman and let me take you out instead," he whispered seductively. "And if you're a good girl, maybe we can even—"

She grabbed the glass of water on the table and emptied it over his head. He sputtered and his eyes turned black with anger.

"You little bit—"

"Shut the fuck up and listen carefully, you disgusting creep," Willa said, getting closer to him and setting the glass back down on the table. "Even if I wasn't with Shawn, I would never go on a date with you. You know why? Because you're the kind of guy women have nightmares about. You overcompensate for what I'm assuming is a tiny dick with your fancy suits and perfectly manicured hair. I doubt you even know where the clitoris is, you walking pile of human garbage. You think women want you, but you know the truth? You have to fucking blackmail them into sleeping with you."

"Get out of here, you fucking cu—"

"Gladly. But first, you should know that I'm done teaching yoga here."

"You're fired."

Willa laughed. "Always have to have the last word, don't you? Well, you can get fucked."

She turned on her heel and left, head held high as onlookers stared. She walked up to the front desk, where Layla watched with wide eyes.

"I guess you probably saw, but I just quit," Willa said.

Layla nodded.

"Don't let that guy fuck with you," she continued. "It's not worth it. Quit if you need to."

"I can't," Layla said. "I can't quit."

"Why?"

Layla shook her head. Willa didn't press.

"Well, be sure to let the guests know that there won't be any yoga classes anymore."

"I will," Layla whispered.

"I'm sorry." *That there's no more yoga. That you're stuck working for this asshole. That you're trapped here.* All things she wanted to add, but didn't know how to.

Layla shook her head. "Don't be."

Willa held eye contact with her for a few moments, then left without a backward glance.

23

The week since Willa had quit her job at the Beachside Inn had flown by. She'd reached back out to the gyms she'd initially applied to, but nothing had changed—they weren't hiring. She also emailed a few hotels, thinking maybe she could set up a deal similar to the one she had with The Beachside Inn— but no luck.

At least she had a trust fund she could dip into, if and when she needed.

Which she had—several times since moving.

But she didn't want to rely on Daddy's money—not if she could help it.

Anxiety about being jobless again creeped in, but she pushed it aside, deciding that was a problem for Future Willa to deal with. She needed to get through the Bingo Ball first. And she deserved to enjoy this weekend with her best friend.

Willa pulled into the airport and chuckled as she remembered Shawn's reaction when she'd told him she quit.

"Good. I didn't like your boss," he said.

"You're gonna lose it when I tell you what he said to make me quit," she responded.

His eyes shot to her and narrowed.

"He told me you couldn't come to my classes anymore," she said, and he visibly relaxed. "Then he offered to look the other way if you came to my classes. But only in exchange for sex."

Shawn stood up from where he was sitting on the wharf and towered over her.

"And what did you say to him, Greene?"

"I told him he could get fucked. Among other things."

He kneeled in front of her and dropped his head to her pussy.

"That's my girl," he said against her sex before tugging her pants down and eating her out so thoroughly that she didn't notice she'd caught a fish.

She clenched her legs at the memory before pulling the Jeep to a stop at the arrivals section of the airport. Willa pulled out her phone and saw a text had come through from Charlie that she'd landed about 15 minutes ago. She shot back a text telling Charlie where she could find her. Tossing her phone into the passenger seat, she got out of the car and leaned against the side of it, crossing her arms as she waited.

A few minutes later, Charlie walked out the automatic sliding doors dressed in a baby blue sundress and a beach hat, her blonde hair blowing in the breeze and tanned skin glowing underneath the sun. She grinned when she saw Willa.

"Ugh, let's never go this long without seeing each other again," Charlie said, tugging her into a hug.

"Deal," Willa said as she wrapped her arms around her best friend.

They put Charlie's luggage in the back seat and hopped in the car.

"So what's the plan?"

"The plan?"

"For the weekend!" Charlie said, exasperated. "Aren't you going to show me around, introduce me to some locals, charm me into moving here?"

"You would never move here."

"Well, not with that attitude."

Willa laughed. "Tonight, we're fishing off the wharf. I'll teach you how to throw the cast net. Shawn will probably come over."

Charlie fanned herself. "Can't wait to meet the hot neighbor. His six-pack better be as amazing as you said it was."

"The Bingo Ball is tomorrow night," Willa continued. "So we can just take it easy tomorrow. Maybe go swimming or something."

"As long as my hair doesn't get wet. I just got it colored."

Willa rolled her eyes. "I sweet-talked Shawn into taking us on a boat ride on Saturday."

"By sweet-talked, do you mean you sucked his dick until he agreed?"

"I plead the fifth," Willa laughed. "And Saturday night, we're having a girls' night with my friends from the hotel. Takeout, rom-coms, the whole nine."

"And then Sunday, we'll nurse our hangovers?"

"Just like old times."

"Perfect."

SHAWN'S first impression of Charlie was that she probably devoured men with those scorching eyes and innate sexuality. Of course, he only had eyes for Willa.

His second impression was that she had a lot to say. And she had no problem saying it.

"Can I see your six pack?" Charlie asked.

Shawn's eyes widened and he glanced at Willa, who'd covered her mouth with a hand in an attempt to hold back laughter.

"Uh…" Shawn wasn't sure how to answer.

"It's just that Willa said your abs are amazing, and I'm not convinced they're any better than other abs we see at the yoga studio all the time. You know?"

Shawn looked at Willa again, whose shoulders were now shaking with silent laughter.

"I guess?" he said, then lifted his shirt up.

He shifted a bit under Charlie's scrutinizing gaze.

"Wow," Charlie said, nodding appreciatively. "Willa was right. Your abs are amazing. Never seen anything like 'em. You even have the V and everything. Can I touch them?"

Shawn dropped his shirt and looked at Willa in alarm, who had abandoned all pretense of hiding her laughter and now was doubled over in hysterics.

"Sorry, Charlie," she said, wiping her eyes. "I doubt Shawn wants to let you touch his abs. He barely knows you."

Charlie looked at Willa with narrowed eyes, then back to Shawn.

"Look, I don't bite, I promise," Charlie said. "And I won't put the moves on you, either. I know you two are fucking. I just want to feel them. For research."

"Research?" Shawn asked skeptically.

Charlie nodded solemnly. "I have a lot of sex. I see a lot of abs. I want to feel how yours compare to the others."

Shawn looked at Willa, who shrugged as if to say, *Up to you.*

"Are you always like this?" Shawn asked.

"If you mean charmingly bold, then yes. Now lift your shirt back up."

Shawn did as she asked, and she ran fingers along his abs. He didn't love the way it felt; he'd rather it have been Willa caressing his abdomen, like she did most nights. But he didn't mind it, either. He knew Charlie was harmless, and she obviously cared for Willa a great deal.

Charlie turned around suddenly and looked at Willa.

"You were right," she said. "I'm impressed. Nicest abs I've ever touched. Kudos to you, my friend."

She turned back to Shawn and gave him a wink.

"Thanks…?" Shawn's voice trailed off.

"You're welcome. Now, aren't we supposed to be fishing or something?"

Willa rolled her eyes. "We *are* fishing, Charlie."

She pointed to the fishing rods nestled in the holders at the edge of the wharf. The sun had set about 30 minutes ago, and Shawn came over as always with a bucket of shrimp. Willa had let him know that Charlie would be in town for the Bingo Ball, but she hadn't given many details on what they'd be doing or what Charlie was like.

Shawn had been entertained by their good-natured back-and-forth since he got here.

"Wow, fishing is easy," Charlie responded as she sat down.

Willa shared a look with Shawn over Charlie's head and shook her head, a bemused grin tugging at her lips.

"We haven't caught anything yet, Charlie," she said. "You're scaring all the fish away with your loud, invasive questions."

"Who, *moi?*" Charlie pressed a hand against her chest in over-exaggerated astonishment. "So, what? You guys just sit in silence for hours until you catch a fish?"

"We don't sit in *silence.* We just talk quietly."

Charlie pressed her lips in a thin line.

"The only time I'm even remotely quiet is during savasana and you know that, Willa."

Shawn chuckled, and Willa grinned at him.

"I should've known it would end up this way," Willa said. "You barely even gave the cast net a try."

"That thing was heavy!" Charlie whined. "And it made me all sticky with salt water."

"Charlie, you can hold a handstand for a minute. You expect me to believe you can't pick up a cast net?"

"Easy for you to say. You've been throwing that thing since you were, like, in diapers or something."

Willa sighed and sat down. Shawn leaned against the side of the wharf and eyed them. They had the rapport of two people who'd known each other through the trenches of life, and it made his heart ache. He really needed to call Tucker back. Go to dinner. See Hanna. He needed to get over himself and just tell them the reason he'd stopped coming around was because he felt lonely—lonelier when he was around their happiness.

"Are you two always like this?" Shawn asked.

Willa said, "Like what?" at the same time Charlie said, "Yes."

The two of them looked at each other and then burst out laughing. He'd never get tired of Willa's laugh, the way her face lit up with joy.

Suddenly, one of the rods jerked down, and Charlie shrieked. "Is that supposed to happen?"

Shawn bit his lip, trying not to laugh. He'd taught

hundreds of people how to fish over the years. He'd mastered the art of keeping a straight face when people asked weird questions or had strange reactions to fishing. But for some reason, his poker face was breaking as he watched Willa look at Charlie with the patience a mother gave a toddler while Charlie inched away from the fishing rod.

"That means you caught something!" Willa exclaimed. "Don't you want to reel it in?"

Charlie tentatively walked up to the fishing rod and started to pick it up.

"Use both hands and hold it tight, otherwise the fish will tug it out of your hands," Shawn said.

Willa winked at him then looked back at Charlie, who was holding her fishing rod like it was a dirty sock.

"Okay, now hold the rod with your left hand and reel with your right hand," Willa urged.

Charlie clenched the rod so tightly with her left hand that her knuckles went white. Shawn resisted the urge to chuckle as she slowly started reeling in, her stance wide, looking like a deer in headlights. She slowly reeled, the steady ticking of the rod breaking the silence of the humid night.

"I'm doing it!" Charlie shrieked.

"'Atta girl," Willa said. "Now if you could just pick up the pace of your reeling, we could probably get this fish up here before the morning breaks."

Charlie's jaw dropped in feigned offense. "How dare you! I'm working hard over here!"

"Do you want help?" Willa smirked.

"Of course I do! I'm never going to reel this thing in!"

Willa stepped next to Charlie and held the fishing rod, encouraging Charlie to continue reeling it in. With less effort exerted on holding the pole, she was actually able to reel it in faster. Shawn watched them with amusement and awe, leaning against the side of the wharf. They didn't need him, and he was happy to watch his girl show her friend the ropes.

His girl.

Fuck.

He was really screwed.

He was falling for Willa and he knew it. Every day that she expertly reeled in a fish and actively listened when he told her about his day and led him to bed so he could eat her pussy, he fell for her a little more.

And he didn't have a goddamn clue what to do about it.

Charlie pulled him out of his stupor as she started jumping up and down and clapping her hands.

"I did it!" she whisper-screamed.

"You caught us a nice little redfish," Willa said, grinning as she unhooked the fish and held it out to her. "Want a picture with it?"

Charlie grimaced. "What, like I'm a dude looking for material to put on my Tinder? Hard pass."

"C'mon, Charlie," Willa said. "It's probably three pounds. Barely big enough for us to eat, but I'll fry it for you for lunch tomorrow. Get over yourself and let me take a picture of you holding it."

Charlie groaned. "Fine. But you owe me."

"I just reeled in this fish for you and I'm cooking you dinner and I'm hosting you for the week."

"Fine. Call it even, then."

Willa laughed and handed the fish to Charlie, then grabbed her phone from her pocket and snapped a photo as Charlie beamed.

"This thing is slimy. Can I put it down now?"

"Toss it in the cooler," Willa said.

"How can you tell it's a red fish?" Charlie asked, holding it underneath the light of a lantern near the cooler.

"It's got a black dot on its tail. See?" Willa went over to where Charlie was and pointed to it.

"Cool," Charlie said. "At least I learned something. That's the first and last time I'll be fishing. I was made for inside activities only."

Willa laughed and glanced at Shawn. His heart fluttered at the way her eyes twinkled at him, and he felt the desperate need to kiss her. Of course, it'd be a few days until he could come over. She'd warned him that they probably wouldn't hook up while Charlie was in town so she could maximize time with her best friend. Shawn understood, of course, but he already felt the lack of her.

"Nice job, Charlie," Shawn said gruffly, his eyes never leaving Willa.

24

"You're sure this isn't too revealing?"

Willa stood in front of the full-size mirror in her bathroom, staring at her reflection. She and Charlie had ordered a few Rent the Runway dresses to choose from, and she'd landed on a floor-length, silver dress that hugged her curves. It had off-the-shoulder sleeves and a low-cut V that showed off just enough cleavage. The slit in the side of the dress left her leg on display, and she wore black stilettos with a bow on the back. Her hair was pulled up in a loose up-do, with curls framing her face.

"Does it matter?" Charlie asked. "It's a bunch of old people and your fuck buddy."

"It matters," Willa said. "I'll never hear the end of it from Ida if I dress inappropriately."

Charlie stepped into the bathroom wearing a sparkling, gold dress with a plunging neckline. She wore gold heels and curled her hair.

"You look hot and classy," Charlie said. "It can be both! Like one of the contestants on The Bachelorette."

"Okay, not helpful."

"Well, it doesn't matter, anyway," Charlie checked her watch. "You don't have time to change. They'll be here any minute."

Before Shawn left last night, he'd offered to give them a ride to the Ball. Charlie agreed before Willa could say anything, but she figured it was for the best. While Bingo nights were typically held at the church down the road, the Bingo Ball was held at a local hotel. It was slowly becoming clear to Willa that this event was much more extravagant than she expected.

And she couldn't help but hope Shawn liked her dress.

She tried to squash the hope—push it away.

He wasn't her boyfriend.

Just her friend.

With occasional, very amazing benefits.

She shouldn't care what he thought.

Except she did, and she hoped he would nearly pass out from how good she looked. Because even though she wasn't sure if she was dressed appropriately enough, she knew one thing for certain: she looked hot as fuck.

Her phone buzzed and a quick look at it told her it was Shawn.

"He'll be here in a minute," Willa said. "Let's head out front."

Looked like she was stuck wearing this dress. They both grabbed their clutches and headed to the driveway, where they waited for only a moment before Shawn's truck pulled in.

He got out of the car and stopped in his tracks as he stared at Willa. The breath whooshed out of her as his steely gaze caught hers. His eyes dropped slowly—ever so slowly—down the length of her body. Willa felt hot under his scrutiny, like every inch his eyes touched were on fire. His eyes drifted back up the length of her body just as slowly, and he stilled once he reached her face again.

She'd barely registered that he was wearing a tux. The white shirt and jacket pulled tightly against his chest and arms, and the fit of the pants was perfectly tailored to his muscled legs. And he was clean shaven. He must've just shaved. He did so every few days, Willa had noticed. It was enough that a bit of stubble was always on his face, and she liked it. But tonight, the way Shawn had shaven perfectly showed off the chiseled jawline she loved so much. His hair was pulled tight into a bun toward the top of his head, and her mouth watered as she drank in the sight of him.

"Hi, Shawn," Charlie said perkily.

"Hi," Shawn said, not taking his eyes off Willa.

She felt frozen under his scrutiny, and she was torn between the desire to just look at him all night and the need to drag him to her bedroom and shove his head between her legs.

"Hurry up, Scooby!" Grams rolled down the window from the back seat and her voice broke the spell. "We don't have all night, and I won't have that she-devil arriving before me."

Willa glanced at Ida and bit her lip.

"Sorry, Grams," Willa said. "My fault. I'm not used to seeing Shawn in a tux."

"You and me both, hon. Now hop in the front seat and introduce me to your adorable little friend so I can get to know her in the back seat."

"This again?" Willa asked, glancing back at Shawn, who tossed her a bemused grin and shrugged. "Grams, why don't you sit in the front seat?"

"You know I get carsick, missy," Grams said. "Now do as I say."

Willa rolled her eyes and walked to the passenger side of the car. Before she could open it, Shawn reached over her and grabbed it, opening it for her and extending a hand while he helped her in. The moment her hand landed in his, she felt a buzzing course throughout her body. God, this should *not* be happening. They'd been fucking for well over a month now. Shouldn't her body stop reacting this way?

Charlie cleared her throat from behind them.

"Do I get the same white glove service getting into the car?" She smirked.

Willa bit her lip to hold back a laugh, and Shawn smiled at her before shutting the door and helping Charlie get into the car.

SHAWN GRIPPED the wheel so hard his hands went numb.

But at least it took his mind off his hardening cock. He glanced over at Willa again, who was peering out the window silently as Charlie and Ida chattered in the back seat. Shawn tuned them out, instead focusing on the stunning creature sitting next to him.

He thought he'd forgotten to breathe for a moment there when he first saw Willa. Her legs looked a million miles long in the silver dress she wore, with one peeking out of the slit. She'd done her makeup differently, too. She didn't often wear it, but when she did, she'd never worn it like this.

And her tits.

God, her fucking tits. Maybe it would be easier if he didn't know exactly what they looked like underneath that dress of hers, if he hadn't palmed them every day for the past month, if he hadn't grown addicted to sucking them between his lips.

He'd almost blown their cover in front of Grams. He wanted to kick himself, but he couldn't help it. She was too perfect. Too gorgeous. Too stunning. He lost his mind around her, and he didn't know how he was going to make it through the night knowing he wouldn't be sneaking over to her place later.

"You look good in a tux," Willa said quietly, and Shawn's head whipped toward her. "I like it."

If she liked it, he would wear it every fucking day. Screw the fact that it made absolutely no sense and was not at all suitable for his line of work.

"You look delicious, actually," Willa whispered.

His eyes flitted to the rearview mirror to see if Grams had heard, but she was happily chatting with Charlie.

"Delicious is too mild a word for how you look," Shawn said out of the side of his mouth. "You're testing my self control tonight with that dress, Greene."

Willa grinned at him, then raised her eyebrows as her gaze drifted down to his crotch. "I can see that."

He winked at her, then shifted in his seat and let his mind wander to other things. Fish guts. Cast nets. Shrimp. He started naming different types of fish in his head trying to get his boner to go down.

Trout.

Mullet.

Red fish.

Flounder.

Carp.

Catfish.

A few minutes later, they were pulling into a hotel parking lot and leaving their car at the valet. He helped Grams get out of the car and offered her his arm.

"Charlie's my date tonight," Grams said, as if it were obvious. "Go help Willa out of the car."

"Grams, you asked me to come as your date to this every year. I don't understa—"

"Well, my new friend, Charlie, is my date this year."

As if on cue, Charlie came up next to Grams and offered her arm. The two of them marched inside with purpose, leaving Shawn to watch them dumbfounded.

"Up to her matchmaking again, I see," Willa said. "I thought she promised you she'd stop doing that?"

Shawn turned around and took her in again. Now that nobody was watching, he did nothing to hold back the pure lust and desire from his gaze, and he walked slowly up to Willa, cradling a cheek in his hand. His thumb brushed her cheek, and she closed her eyes and leaned into it.

"You wearing panties tonight?" he asked, knowing he was torturing himself by asking. He'd already looked at her ass in that dress long enough to know the odds were slim that she had anything on underneath.

Her eyes opened slowly and she shook her head, a cat-like grin tugging at her lips. He groaned.

"What are you trying to do to me?"

"Nothing," Willa said, grabbing the hand that was on her cheek and tugging it to her side so she could clasp it as they walked inside together. "This dress is just too tight for panties."

Shawn shook his head. "I'm convinced you do this to fuck with me."

"You think I really think about you that much?" Willa asked lightly.

"I hope you do," Shawn responded before he could stop

himself.

She stopped in her tracks and looked up at him, eyes wide.

"Welcome to the Bingo Ball!" a piercing voice rung out, interrupting their conversation.

Shawn quickly looked at the source of the voice and found Amos. He nodded and they signed in before descending stairs into a long hallway that led to a ballroom. Willa's hand rested delicately on his arm, and that one touch was enough to make him feel like he might combust.

As they passed a deserted hallway, Shawn tugged Willa with him down it and toward a door that went outside.

"What are you doing, Shawn?" Willa asked. "The ballroom's back that way."

"We're making a quick detour," he said, walking her to where the doors led outside to a back alley.

"A quick detour for what?" she asked as he opened the door and led her outside, pushing her back against the brick wall.

"For this," he said against her lips before crushing his mouth against hers.

A small part of his idiotic brain knew he was being reckless and stupid. The chances that Grams would see them out here were slim, but somebody else could possibly come along. Still, he knew that this part of the hotel was rarely visited, and given that there was no parking back here and only a couple of trash cans, he figured they were safe.

Probably.

Really, though, most of his brain was focused on her lips. Her tongue. Her tight little body underneath his. The way her fingers trailed over his chest and then up to his jawline. He reached underneath her dress—the slit provided him easy access, and palmed her pussy.

"Just like I thought," he said, burying his face in her neck and breathing in her scent before nipping her neck. "Fucking drenched."

She whimpered as he teased her with his fingers, lightly touching her folds and her clit, pushing his forefinger inside her just barely before tugging it out again.

"Shawn, please."

He knelt in front of her.

"What are you doing?" she asked breathlessly.

"Tell me your pussy's not begging to be licked. Tell me you don't want my mouth on you. Tell me you don't want to come all over my tongue."

She spluttered. "But... here?"

"Nobody will come out here," he said confidently.

He grabbed her left leg—the one easily accessible to him through the slit in her dress—and tugged it over his shoulder before burying his head underneath her dress. He licked all the way up her pussy as slowly as he could, savoring every bit of her.

"Fuck, baby," Shawn said against her entrance. "You taste so fucking good. Like a fucking dream."

"Shawn," she moaned, digging her fingers into his hair.

He groaned against her pussy and he felt her legs quiver around his face. He reached his hands up and cupped her ass, digging his fingers into her. He ate like a starving man, lapping up every last bit of her arousal with his tongue. Her knee began to buckle, and the one leg that kept her upright began to give out as she got closer to a climax. He held her steady as he ruthlessly tongued her clit, sucking on it as she came on his face with a breathless sob.

"Another," Shawn said against her pussy.

"Shawn, I can't."

"Yes, you can, Greene."

He wanted her to come on his tongue so many times that he was tasting her for days. Wanted to make her so fucking loose and relaxed all night because of the force of the orgasms he gave her. Wanted to remind her that he was the one who made her come every fucking day. Wanted to swallow the sweetness of her arousal until he couldn't—

"Oh. My. God." A voice that wasn't Willa's pierced through the sound of her panting.

Willa tensed above him, and Shawn moved his head just enough so he could peak out from underneath where Willa's leg still rested over his shoulder.

"Respect," Charlie said, a Cheshire cat grin growing on her face. "Honestly, mad respect. I didn't know you had it in you, Willa."

"Oh, my god," Willa said softly, throwing her hands over her face in mortification.

Shawn felt like he was being taken over by a caveman. Where he should feel mortified, he only felt gratified that Charlie knew Willa was decidedly his. That she got to see first-hand the way Willa succumbed to every sort of pleasure when Shawn was involved.

"Listen, I love public sex as much as the next girl, but Ida's asking a lot of questions about where you two went," Charlie said with a smirk, crossing her arms.

"Shit." It was like a bucket of ice cold water was dumped over his head. He gently removed Willa's leg from where it rested on his shoulder and put it down on the ground. He tugged her dress back down, straightening it out with his palms, then stood and tugged her hands away from her face. "You okay?"

She nodded. A few of her hairs had fallen out of place in the shuffle of things, and he gently pushed a few pieces back into place and tugged a stray curl behind her ear. Some of her eyeliner had run a bit, and he tried to hold back a smirk. He must've given her one hell of an orgasm. He brushed his thumb gently along her eye, ridding any excess makeup and clearing away any smudges.

Her lipstick still looked fine, but a little faded. He traced a finger along her lips and got rid of any stray red that had smeared when he devoured her mouth earlier. He grinned at her.

"You still look perfect," he whispered.

She bit her lip and her eyes darted to his mouth. He tried to hide the smug look from his face, but he couldn't. She laughed.

"Probably need to reapply some lipstick, though," Charlie said, reminding Shawn they weren't alone. He looked over and found her studying him with an unreadable expression. "C'mon, Willa. There's a bathroom down the hall."

Shawn stepped back and Willa held his gaze for a moment before heading toward Charlie, who was still scrutinizing him from where she stood. As they headed inside, Willa turned around and shot Shawn a quick smile.

"See you inside," she said softly before going in.

As the door closed behind her, Shawn leaned his back against the wall and tipped his head up. His raging erection pressed uncomfortably against his pants, and he willed it to go down.

He was an idiot.

He knew that now.

Because he'd gone and fallen in love with the beautiful redhead next door who wanted nothing but sex from him. And Lord knew, he'd give her whatever she wanted—even if it meant he swallowed feelings that led him to do crazy things like eat her pussy in public.

25

Holy fuck.

Every time she was with Shawn, it only got better. Every time she thought he'd given her an earth-shattering orgasm that could never be matched, he proved her wrong. And every time she was around him, she did things she couldn't control.

Like let him eat her out in a weird alleyway behind a hotel, less than 100 yards away from his snooping grandmother.

She leaned against the countertop in the bathroom and looked at her reflection in the mirror. She looked...fine. Not at all like she'd just been ravished by a fisherman who had no business looking that goddamn perfect in a tux. Shawn had fixed her makeup and hair perfectly, and she didn't quite know what to make of how tenderly he helped her get cleaned up after being caught with his face buried between her legs.

"That man is in love with you."

Willa tensed as Charlie's statement brought her out of her head. She looked over her shoulder through the mirror at her. She was gazing at Willa with a mixture of bemusement and concern.

"What? No. We're just friends. Fuck buddies."

Charlie scoffed and shook her head. "I love you like a sister, but don't be stupid."

Willa huffed and turned around, crossing her arms. "What is that supposed to mean?"

Charlie winced. "Look, I'm sorry. That came out harsher than I intended. It's just that... fuck buddies don't look at you the way Shawn looked at you out there. And they sure as hell don't clean the makeup off your face after they make you come so hard that you ruin a perfectly good face of makeup that shouldn't get ruined at all because you used super expensive setting spray."

Willa shifted. "Well, we do."

"And that's my point. You guys aren't fuck buddies in anything but name. You're in a relationship."

Willa's eyes widened. "No, we're not!"

"I'm not trying to freak you out, but yes, you are. He comes over every day to hang out. Brings you gifts—"

"The shrimp is not a gift! It's bait."

"Free bait. That's a gift. For a weirdo like you, anyway."

Willa sighed, and Charlie continued.

"He took you on a romantic boat ride—"

"I told you, that was because honeymooners canceled on him and I won that prize at Bingo!"

"It was still a romantic boat ride where he made love to you—"

"We fucked. That's all."

"You can try to convince me that man is only fucking you, but you're wrong. If all the other stuff wasn't true, this is: he looks at you like you're the sun and he's lucky as fuck to be a planet in your orbit. He did it yesterday when I met him, and he definitely did it when he picked us up. Barely even noticed I was there."

"You're over-exaggerating, Ch—"

"Believe what you want. But he looked at you like that a few minutes ago, too. When he cleaned you up after going down on you."

Willa bit her lip and took a deep breath, trying to calm her racing heart. They had rules. They had been clear. Everything was going perfectly. Why was Charlie ruining it?

Except... maybe, she wasn't ruining it. Maybe, a small part of Willa had feelings for him, too. Even though she knew she shouldn't. Even though she didn't completely trust herself after Leo. Even though she was so terrified of getting her heart broken again that she wanted to throw up.

"You're freaking out," Charlie said, and Willa nodded. "Of course you are. Leo fucked you up a little bit. But listen. I've never seen anyone look at you the way Shawn does. Like he's the luckiest motherfucker in the world for existing in the same lifetime as you."

Willa's eyes burned.

"I can't."

A tear fell down her cheek, and she looked away from Charlie.

"Oh, Willa," Charlie said, her voice full of compassion as she tugged a tissue from a box sitting on the countertop. She wiped Willa's cheek and pulled her into a hug. "Loving people is scary. Letting them in... it's terrifying. Why do you think I avoid it?"

Willa choked out a chuckle, and Charlie gave her a squeeze.

"But I think you might have feelings for him, too. And I'll be so pissed at you if you pass up on a guy as good as Shawn. He's a good one, babe. I can feel it."

Willa pulled back from their hug and wiped her eyes one more time, then heaved a sigh. "I know you're right. But I'm just so scared."

"So tell him that. He seems like a reasonable guy."

Willa closed her eyes and nodded. She knew Charlie was right. Her best friend sometimes knew her better than she knew herself. But she didn't know if she was ready. Didn't know how she could be ready.

"It doesn't have to be all or nothing," Charlie said. "You can just have a conversation with him. That's it."

Willa opened her eyes and nodded.

"But for now, let's put more lipstick on you and head back before Ida comes searching for you, okay?" Charlie grabbed Willa's purse and pulled out the lipstick.

"Does she think something is going on between me and Shawn?" Willa asked as she grabbed the lipstick from Charlie and opened it.

"Yes."

"Fuck."

"Relax. She can just see what I can see," Charlie said, setting Willa's purse on the countertop and smoothing back her hair. "That Shawn is an absolute goner for you."

Willa's stomach fluttered at the thought. Could Shawn really have feelings for her? He was different from other guys she dated. For one, he didn't have a college education. Not that she cared. He made a good living for himself, and the community loved him. He took care of people, too. That was different from other guys she dated—most of them only looked after themselves. And then there was the fact that Shawn only ever wore swimsuits and t-shirts. All her exes had fancy suits and would never be caught dead wearing flip flops. Or having a man bun, for that matter.

And it really wasn't about how Shawn was different from

her exes, anyway. It was about whether she could take the leap and trust again—trust Shawn, yes, but mostly, trust *herself*. She didn't know if she could.

Willa needed to put it out of her mind until Charlie left town. Or at least until after the Bingo Ball. She couldn't overthink everything about Shawn while he was sitting right next to her. She squared her shoulders.

"Alright, let's head in there."

Charlie led the way into the ballroom, and Willa gasped as she stepped inside. She'd been to her fair share of fancy events over the years, so she knew she was looking at something of a professional caliber. At least now she knew why their tickets were $100. White table cloths covered the tables, and the lights were dimmed. Rather than table numbers, each table was labeled like a Bingo card—like B2 or I14 or O7. Cake pops decorated like Bingo balls were at the center of each table. At the front, a slideshow of Bingo regulars played. In the far right corner, Willa saw a booth that was clearly meant to be the voting station for Bingo King and Queen.

"Holy fuck," Willa said under her breath.

"Watch your language, young lady," Ida said from behind her.

Willa whirled around to find Ida holding a glass of red wine and extending one to her. "Thanks for the drink."

"It's for Charlie," Ida said. Charlie giggled and grabbed the drink from Ida's hand. "Where have you been, missy?"

Willa's heart jolted. She'd never been a good liar.

"Found her in the bathroom," Charlie said before Willa had the chance to respond. She took a casual sip, then continued, as if spilling hot gossip, "Willa's having lady problems."

Willa felt her face flush as she glared at Charlie, who was smirking behind her wine glass.

"Oh, dear," Ida said. "Are you alright?"

"I'm fine, Grams," Willa said through clenched teeth. "All good. Just have some cramps."

Willa was on the pill and hadn't experienced period cramps in years. But she could fake them to get Ida off her back. She gently rested her hand on her stomach, then felt the hairs prick on the back of her neck.

Shawn was behind her. She knew it. She could *feel* it.

"Shall we go to our table, ladies?" he drawled from behind her.

"Not until you vote, Scoob," Grams said. "I wore my best dress for this. I'll be crowned Bingo Queen if it's the last thing I do. And at my age, it very well might be."

"I already voted for you, Grams," Shawn said.

"Me, too," Charlie chimed in.

"I guess I'm the only one who hasn't," Willa said with a sheepish smile. "I'll go do that next."

"Shawn will escort you," Grams said before grabbing Charlie's hand and heading off.

"That's not necessary," Willa responded.

"Of course it is," Grams said. "Wouldn't want the cramps to slow you down."

Shawn came up beside her, and Willa kept her gaze on the floor. After the revelation she had in the bathroom, she was afraid to lock eye contact with him.

"Cramps?" he asked, his voice drenched with concern.

"Charlie told her I'm on my period," Willa said. "You know. As an excuse."

"Ahh."

"Yeah."

They stood there in silence for a moment before Shawn

extended his arm to her. She gently rested her hand on his forearm as he led her toward the voting station. She walked up to a station with an iPad and selected Ida's name. Apparently, to be eligible for Bingo Queen, you had to have attended at least 75 percent of the Bingo nights.

After she finished voting, they headed toward their table, where Charlie was animatedly chatting with Ida and her Bingo friends.

"Are you alright?" Shawn asked, his lips brushing Willa's ear.

Goosebumps covered her body as desire coursed through her. "Fine. Why?"

"You've barely looked at me the past five minutes. Is it... Did I do something?"

Willa's heart cracked, realizing her own discomfort was feeding Shawn's insecurities. She stopped in her tracks and turned toward him, tracing his jawline with her forefinger. "Sorry. Just Charlie getting into my head about our... arrangement."

"She disapproves?"

Willa sighed. Maybe she said too much, but she didn't want to keep things from Shawn. She didn't want to dive into this conversation right now, though. Preferably, she wanted to wait until after Charlie left—until she had some time to think about it.

"Not exactly," she finally said. "But don't worry about it. We're all good."

He stared at her for a beat longer, then nodded and led her to the table.

SOMETHING WAS OFF WITH WILLA. That much he knew.

He wished he could've been a fly on the wall in the bathroom when she talked to Charlie earlier. He wished he could reassure her that everything was fine. He wished he could fix whatever it was that made her avert her gaze from him all night. He missed those ocean eyes, that piercing stare, that perfect smile.

He had barely kept his eyes off her all night, hard as he tried. He hoped Grams was too caught up in the race for Bingo Queen to notice. He couldn't help it. She looked fucking perfect, and he swelled with male pride when he thought about how he made her come on his tongue earlier. The memories of that particular interaction had been replaying in his brain ever since.

Grams' friend from Bingo, Mary, was accompanied tonight by her grandson, Wyatt. Shawn remembered that he was a doctor. Mary had mentioned it a time or two or twenty. Shawn tried to make small talk with him, but his attempts to take his mind off Willa failed miserably. And he couldn't help but notice that Wyatt was eyeballing Charlie with a keen interest.

They'd eaten dinner and had done a ceremonial round of Bingo, which Nancy Siders won, much to the displeasure of everyone at their table. It was almost time to crown the Bingo queen. He glanced at Grams and saw that she was clutching her rosary and praying feverishly. He looked over at Willa and gave her a look that said, *Are you seeing this?* She giggled and nodded.

"Alright, folks," Amos came over the intercom. "It's time to crown our Bingo King and Queen."

Grams grabbed the hands of the people next to her, which happened to be Charlie and Shawn. He gave her hand a squeeze and held back a laugh. He loved his grandmother and all her eccentricities. She'd never been crowned

Bingo Queen before, so he hoped she would get it—only because he knew it'd make her so happy.

"Our Bingo King is Robert Ganden, by a landslide. Come on up here, Rob!"

Shawn clapped along with everyone else. He didn't know Robert well, but he was roughly about 80 and he regularly came by the shop.

"And our Bingo Queen—by a hair—is Ida Gray!"

Shawn didn't hear what came next because their entire table broke out in abrupt and overwhelming applause and shrieking. Grams looked thrilled and wiped away tears from her eyes. He didn't realize how much this meant to her—that she would be moved to tears by winning. He sprung out of his seat and offered her his arm, which she accepted, and he escorted her onto stage.

As he made his way back to their table, he noticed Charlie and Willa both snapping pictures and videos with their phone. Willa shot him a wink, and he thought his heart would melt on the spot. He passed by Nancy Siders' table and overheard her muttering to herself, looking full of disdain and anger.

Once settled back in his seat, he watched as his grandmother was crowned.

"Let's have a round of applause for this year's Bingo King and Queen!" Amos said through the microphone, to which everyone responded in kind with clapping. "And now, the inaugural dance. Feel free to join them on the dance floor, folks!"

A slow, jazzy song came over the speakers, and Shawn looked over at Willa with a lifted brow. Her eyes grew wide as he stood up and extended a hand to her.

"Dance with me?" he asked.

She bit her lip and looked over at Charlie briefly before accepting his hand and standing up.

He led her to the dance floor and pulled her close, placing one hand on her hip and grabbing her hand with his other. Out of the corner of his eye, he saw Wyatt leading Charlie to the dance floor, and he grinned over Willa's shoulder at him. In return, Wyatt gave him a thumbs up. Charlie rolled her eyes at the both of them.

Willa's eyes stared pointedly at his chest as he led her in a slow dance, until he couldn't take it anymore. Removing his hand from her hip, he used his forefinger to tilt her chin up.

"What's going on, Greene?" he asked roughly.

She shook her head and closed her eyes. "I'm not ready to talk about it yet."

His heart shattered.

Was she going to end things with him? He knew it would happen at some point, but he thought it would be later. Down the road. He wasn't sure if he could handle her walking away. Not when all he had to do to see her was peek out his front window and watch her cast a net like a pro in one of her little bikinis. Not when he knew now what she tasted like. Not when he'd buried his face between her thighs barely two hours ago.

"But this is nice," she said, a hesitant grin tugging at her lips. "You're a good dancer."

He gave her the best smile he could muster. "Well, I'm sure you can figure out who to thank for that."

"Ida?"

He nodded.

She leaned her head against his chest and he breathed her in.

"Remind me to thank her later, then," Willa said.

26

Charlie came around the corner carrying a buoy, her brows crinkled in confusion.

"What is this thing?" she asked.

Willa chuckled. Shawn had recommended they all meet at the bait shop before the boat ride so he could drive them all to the marina. Parking sometimes got dicey on Saturdays, and he had a reserved spot since he'd been a longtime customer there and did so many tours. It was a miracle he even had availability today.

"It's a buoy," Willa responded. "They're used for docking, providing direction, crab traps, and a bunch of other things. Haven't you seen them in SF?"

"Like I said," Charlie responded with a sniff, "I was made for indoor activities."

Charlie had been keeping herself busy snooping around the store and picking up random items, shaking them or inspecting them with a keen eye. Willa was having a hard time holding back her laughter. Charlie looked so out of place here in her long, sleek cover up, sun hat, and extra large sunglasses.

Willa had tried to put Shawn out of her mind after last night.

Tried being the operative word.

She could barely sleep; her mind was racing and she'd gotten used to having an orgasm or two before bed. She wasn't sure how she was going to be around him all afternoon without thinking about the fact that she might have feelings for him.

Okay, she *definitely* had feelings for him.

He'd texted her earlier that he'd be in the back when they arrived, gathering all the supplies they'd need for the day. She stood in his shop, surrounded by all the things that made her think of him, and she was already overwhelmed. She couldn't imagine what she'd do when she finally saw him today after spending a restless night thinking about him before pulling her vibrator out of her bedside table and succumbing to her need for him.

Even just a fantasy of him.

"Well, well, well," Charlie's voice carried to where Willa was. "Look at what I found."

Willa walked from where she'd been looking at hooks—she needed some new ones—and found Charlie peering over the checkout counter. Willa stopped in her tracks when she saw what Charlie was looking at.

She felt her jaw drop. It was a picture pinned prominently on the wall—a picture that Ida had taken of Willa on one of their walks. Ida had said something that made her laugh, and Willa turned around for a split second and grinned at her. Ida had texted her saying she'd bring it over to her, and Willa had just forgotten about it.

Willa glanced at Charlie, who had crossed her arms and was smirking at Willa with an *I told you so* smugness on her face.

"Like I said, that man is in lo—"

The bell at the front door jingled as Amanda and Layla walked in. Layla was wearing a modest swimsuit coverup and toted a colorful beach bag. Her hair was pulled up into a no-nonsense bun, and she had a visor on. Amanda was wearing jean shorts and a bikini with heart-shaped sunglasses. Her black hair was in space buns on top of her head, and she walked in like she owned the place.

"Where's your sexy fisherman?" Amanda asked.

Willa rolled her eyes. "*Shawn* is in the back getting some supplies."

"Hi, I'm Amanda," she stuck her hand out to Charlie. "You're Charlie?"

"Yes, it's so nice to meet Willa's work friends!" Charlie said. "And you're Layla?"

Layla nodded and shook Charlie's hand.

"We were just looking at the picture Shawn hung up of Willa," Charlie said. "Based on the look on her face, she had no clue it was here."

Layla bit her lip, trying to hold back a grin as Amanda released a melodramatic gasp.

"No, it's probably just to keep the tourists from flirting with him," Willa said, trying to convince herself as much as her friends. "He hates that. I told him he could use me as an excuse—say I was his girlfriend to keep them at bay."

Amanda laughed. "Girl, that man is head over heels in love with you."

"That's what I said!" Charlie said, high-fiving Amanda.

"Introducing you two was a terrible idea," Willa said, rubbing her temples. "Can we not—"

The back door swung open and Shawn moseyed out, his hands full with fishing rods, coolers, and life jackets. Willa gaped at him in all his glory. She loved seeing him in a tux last night, but nothing compared to the way he looked on a daily basis. Rugged and natural, like he was built for life on the water.

The shirt he wore clung to his pecs and biceps, his muscles perfectly on display. The muscles she touched, the ones she loved trailing her fingers down as he railed her so hard she saw stars.

And then he beamed at her. His face stretched in a smile so blinding, she couldn't look away. She felt her lips tug up in response, and she walked slowly toward him, as if drawn in by a magnetic pull.

"Ready to teach your girl gang how to fish, Greene?" he asked with a wink.

"I don't know if they have what it takes," she whispered as she grabbed a couple of fishing rods from his hand.

"Rude," Charlie said.

"Seriously, do you think we can't hear you?" Amanda said. "We're right here."

"I feel like it's worth mentioning that I grew up on the water and do not need a fishing lesson," Layla piped in.

Shawn chuckled and Willa noticed a teenage boy trailed behind him. She gave Shawn a quizzical look.

"This is Brodie," Shawn said. "He's a senior in high school and he works here on Saturdays."

They all said hello and introduced themself to the lanky, dark-haired teenager. As Willa introduced herself, she saw a look of recognition pass over Brodie's face. Then she realized he probably recognized her from that damn photo. It was sweet that Shawn had a photo of her in the bait shop, but confusing as hell given their current situationship. It's not as if she needed another thing to stress about today, and of course, she knew she could count on her friends to poke the bear.

Brodie gave them a shy smile before settling in behind the checkout counter, right near where the photo of Willa hung proudly.

"That's a great picture of you, Willa," Charlie said, grinning like a cat.

"It really is!" Amanda chimed in. "You look so pretty."

"That she does," Shawn chimed in, his cheeks reddening as he looked his fill at Willa.

Amanda and Charlie exchanged knowing glances.

"So what's the story behind it?" Charlie asked.

Shawn cleared his throat. "Well, my Grams took the picture. She and Willa go on walks together most days. And she asked me to give it to Willa but I decided to keep it and hang it in the shop. It's a good photo. Plus, it keeps the tourists off my back."

"The tourists?" Amanda asked.

"Ahh, well..." Shawn trailed off, then looked to Willa with wide eyes as if searching for help.

"The aggressively flirtatious tourists who show up to the shop drunk and try to get in Shawn's pants even after he's expressed that he's not interested," Willa said.

The girls nodded knowingly.

"Yikes," Layla frowned.

"People suck," Amanda said.

Out in front of the shop, they piled the supplies into the bed of Shawn's truck before climbing into it. Of course, the girls insisted that Willa sit in the front. As she walked around to the passenger seat, Shawn was preparing to open the door for her but stopped her.

"Sorry I didn't tell you about the picture," he said quietly.

"It's alright," she said. "Just wasn't expecting..."

"I know we're just keeping it casual, but having that

picture does help keep the tourists away," he said. Willa nodded, grateful, at least, that she could help in that department. "Plus, if I'm going to be honest, I like looking at it."

Her lips parted as he smirked at her, then opened the passenger door. She felt hot all over her body as he shut the door and then hopped in the driver's seat. He sent a quick glance her way and winked at her, then turned the car on and pulled out.

Willa rested her head against the window and willed her body to calm down. If she couldn't get herself in check, it was going to be a long afternoon.

SHAWN LAUGHED to himself as he hosed down the boat. It'd been a great afternoon on the Bay, and aside from a few suggestive remarks from Charlie and Amanda, he'd pretty much just acted as their chauffeur and taken them to all the best spots. He'd had a good time watching Willa have fun with her friends, and he was certain they'd be exhausted after swimming and fishing all over the Bay.

Of course, he'd had a raging hard-on half the afternoon. He was a man, after all, and being around Willa in a swimsuit still made him feel like he might explode.

"What are you grinning about?" A deep voice pierced through his thoughts.

Shawn turned around and saw a familiar tattoo sleeve on fair skin.

"Tucker," Shawn said, dropping the hose and hopping onto the dock to pull his best friend in for a hug. "Good to see you, man."

Tucker hugged him back, but when they parted, he said, "Gotta say, I'm surprised to be receiving such a warm welcome considering you haven't texted me back in months."

Shawn grimaced. "Sorry, man."

"How sorry are you? Because Hanna is in the car and we'd love to take you to dinner."

Shawn chuckled. "Pretty sure if I say no, she'll come yell at me."

"Probably," Tucker grinned.

"Give me ten minutes to wrap this up?"

Tucker nodded and turned around. Shawn hopped back on the boat and finished hosing it off, then headed to the parking lot where he found Tucker and Hanna leaning against their truck waiting for him. As soon as he came into sight, Hanna beamed and ran toward him, then jumped into his arms and gave him a huge hug.

"You're in trouble, mister," Hanna said as he lifted her off the ground.

"Will it help if I pay for dinner?" he set her back down and she chuckled.

"It's a start," she responded.

He told them he'd follow them to the restaurant, so he hopped in his truck and drove five minutes down the road to the main cafe in town. A few minutes later, they were seated in the restaurant with drinks on the table, and an awkward silence ensued.

Shawn didn't know where to begin.

"I'm sorry I went AWOL on you guys," he finally said. "I know that barely begins to make things right."

"You're right. It doesn't," Hanna said, crossing her arms.

"Babe, go easy on him," Tucker nudged her with her shoulder.

"Why should I? He disappeared on us." Her scowl melted into hurt. "Did we do something wrong?"

Shawn ran his fingers through his hair and sighed. He'd only known Hanna for a few years, but they'd become close after she started dating Tucker—and even closer when they got married. He'd hurt her. He'd hurt both of them.

"I was jealous," he said, staring at his twiddling thumbs to avoid eye contact. "Of what you guys have. It was hard being around you. I know that's not fair. I'm happy you two are happy. You know that. It's just... hard watching two of your closest friends be in love and have something I'm not even close to having."

Willa flashed through his mind, but he wasn't ready to bring her up yet.

"Then my grandpa died, and I moved in with Grams. And I guess it just got easier to flake on things. I was sad, and Grams needed me, and... God, I don't know. I was a shitty friend, and I'm sorry."

When he looked up at them, Hanna's hand was over her heart and her eyes were misty. Tucker was looking at him with a mix of regret and concern.

"I'm sorry, man," Tucker said. "We had no idea. I thought you just, you know..."

"We thought you were going to continue being a playboy for the rest of your life," Hanna finished his sentence with a smirk.

Shawn chuckled. Trust Hanna to get right down to the heart of things.

"That was the plan," Shawn responded. "But then..."

They looked at him expectantly as he trailed off.

"Then I was the best man in your wedding. And I saw how happy you two were. And it made me realize I wanted that too."

"Oh, Shawn," Hanna squeezed his hand. "I want that for you, too."

"I'm sorry I've been such a shitty friend."

"All is forgiven," Hanna said with a smile.

"It's all good, man," Tucker added.

"That easy?" Shawn said, breaking eye contact with his friends. "I've been putting off this conversation for a while. I should've come to you sooner. Way sooner. I know that. And I'm better than this, too. But a few weeks became a few months and it just became easier to avoid talking about it."

"Look, I won't say we aren't hurt," Tucker said as Shawn's eyes lifted from the spot he was looking at on the table. "We are. And you should've communicated with us. It's not like you to not tackle things head on. But..."

"I've been telling him we needed to just show up at your place for months," Hanna said. "Grams would never stand for it if she knew you basically ghosted us. We could've tried harder. We knew something was going on."

"Yeah, Grams misses you," Shawn replied. "So do I."

"We love you, Shawny," Tucker said. "You've been with me for my whole life. It'll take more than that to get rid of me."

What did Shawn do to deserve friends like these—so quick to forgive?

"I fucked up, guys. Big time. And I know I need to earn back your trust. It won't happen again."

"It's alright, man," Tucker responded.

"We get it, bud," Hanna added. "Like Tuck said, we love you."

Shawn breathed a sigh of relief.

"Well, now that I know you're ready to date, maybe I could set you up with one of my friends," Hanna said. "They've all been crushing on you for years."

Shawn grimaced and shook his head, and Hanna gave him a knowing look.

"I see," Hanna said. "So there's a girl."

Shawn felt his cheeks grow hot, then he covered his mouth with his hand to hide the smile that stretched over his face whenever he thought about Willa.

"Wow, you *really* like her!" Hanna said, elbowing her husband. "Are you seeing this? He's *blushing!*"

Tucker smirked. "Oh, I see it."

"Tell us everything!" Hanna said, clapping her hands in excitement.

Shawn shook his head, unsure where to even begin.

"She's not going to give this up," Tucker said, leaning back in his chair. "Trust me. Just give in now."

"You owe us, Shawn," Hanna chimed in.

"What happened to 'All is forgiven?'"

"Yeah, yeah, yeah," she responded, waving her hand in irritation. "All is forgiven with this one stipulation. Tell us about your girl."

His girl.

If only.

Shawn eyed them both warily before deciding to give in. Maybe they could give him some advice.

"Her name is Willa," he said softly. "She moved into her grandparents' house a couple of months ago. It's right down the beach from Grams' place. She's... God, she's fucking perfect. Gorgeous and kind and funny. And she knows how to fish. Like, really knows. Puts me in my place all the goddamn time. Tells me what's what. She walks with Grams every morning and helps her stretch. We fish together off her wharf most nights. She's a yoga instructor, and I went to one of her classes and it was actually pretty awesome."

Hanna was beaming, and Tucker was studying him.

"I'm sensing a 'but' coming," his best friend said.

"But... she's skittish," Shawn said, running his fingers

through his hair. "Men have let her down before. Her last boyfriend... well, he really fucked with her. And so I agreed to a friends-with-benefits arrangement with her because it was the only way I could have her. And now..."

"You fell in love with her," Hanna said matter-of-factly.

Shawn nodded, jittery that he was finally saying it out loud. "I'm so fucking in love with her. But she's made it clear she wants to keep things casual. Sometimes I think maybe... maybe she caught feelings, too, but she's just too damn scared. And I get it. Who am I to push her into a relationship when every relationship she's been in has ended so badly that she's basically sworn off all men?"

"Except she hasn't sworn off you," Hanna said, raising her eyebrows.

"You gotta talk to her, bro," Tucker said.

"But what if—" Shawn cut himself off, running a hand down his face.

He couldn't voice his fear—was too afraid to even say it.

"What if she doesn't want you?" Hanna asked, her eyes full of compassion. "Then it's her loss. But you need to know. One way or another."

Shawn knew Hanna was right. He'd known he'd have to talk to her for weeks now. He'd just put it off because he didn't want it to end. Even getting pieces of her was better than nothing. But it was getting to a point where it hurt too much. He wanted more. He wanted everything. And if she didn't want that, better to find out now than later.

27

"I can't believe you're already leaving me," Willa said, her eyes burning.

She hadn't expected to get so emotional over her best friend leaving, but they'd had an extraordinary weekend together. From the Bingo Ball to a full day on the boat yesterday, Charlie had gotten the full Bay experience—and Willa didn't want her to leave. Yesterday's boat outing was perfect.

Amanda and Layla had joined them, and as expected, they absolutely loved Charlie. Shawn took them all over the Bay to the ideal swimming and fishing spots. They'd had a picnic on a small island, where they anchored the boat for a couple of hours while searching for sand dollars and seashells. Then, all the girls came home and watched rom-coms until everyone fell asleep on the couch or floor, the coffee table littered with empty bags of chips and wine bottles.

"You left me first," Charlie retorted, then pulled Willa in for a hug. "You've got a great life here, babe."

Willa grinned, the past couple of months flitting through her mind. "I know. I just miss you."

"I miss you, too," Charlie said, pulling back. "But this is why you should answer me when I call."

Willa laughed. "Fair enough."

"I'll come visit again soon."

"Promise?"

"Promise."

As Charlie pulled her suitcase out of the trunk and settled her backpack on her back, Willa leaned against the side of the Jeep.

"Wait, what happened with that guy?" she asked.

"What guy?" Charlie responded, avoiding Willa's eyes.

"Don't play dumb. Wyatt or whatever? Who you danced with at the Ball?"

"Ugh, that guy." Charlie rolled her eyes. "He kept trying to, like, get to know me."

"The horror," Willa deadpanned.

"I offered him sex and he said no," Charlie continued in a whisper, her voice dripping with disbelief.

"God forbid somebody says no to you."

"That's what I'm saying! And then he has the audacity to ask for my number?"

"Did you give it to him?"

"Of course not."

Willa sighed and gave her best friend a grin. "Sorry I asked about it."

"I forgive you," Charlie winked. "So are you going to talk to Shawn?"

Willa's stomach dropped. "Yes."

She'd been doing her best not to think about it. But she knew she needed to be honest with Shawn and tell him she had feelings for him. The boat ride around the Bay was fun, but she knew he was confused. She'd barely talked to him all day unless absolutely necessary because she didn't know how to look at him without giving away the fact that she was falling for him. And she didn't know how he'd react to it. She barely even knew how she felt about it.

"Listen, babe. It's going to be fine. Just tell him how you feel. Be honest."

"Oh, is that all?" Willa asked.

"Easier said than done, I know," Charlie smiled. "And I'm not exactly a perfect example for communicating feelings. But you can do it."

Willa's eyes burned. "Remind me why you have to leave?"

"I pay $3,000 to rent an apartment in SF."

"Right, that."

Charlie laughed and tugged her into another hug.

"Love you," Charlie said.

"Love you, too."

SHAWN CAME PREPARED TONIGHT. He'd asked Grams if she'd make some brownies today, to which she happily obliged, and he'd brought a small plate of them to Willa's. He wanted to give her as many reasons as possible not to end their arrangement.

Taking Willa and her friends on the boat yesterday was fun, and when she'd asked him to do it, he was more than happy to help out. But she'd still been acting distant, and he was convinced she was ready to end it. He couldn't allow that to happen.

"What'd Ida make me this time?" Willa asked as Shawn

came into view on the wharf with the shrimp bucket in one hand and a plate of desserts in the other.

"Brownies," Shawn responded, extending the plate to her.

She squealed, and he felt like things were finally normal between them. She pulled out a brownie and thrust it into her mouth, groaning in pleasure before licking her fingers slowly. He felt his mouth go dry at the sight of her, his cock hardening as she winked at him.

"You're playing a dangerous game, Greene."

She laughed. "Sorry. I wanted to talk, anyway. Then, maybe after..."

His heart soared. If she wanted to hook up after this, that meant she wasn't ending it. Right?

He cleared his throat. "Oh. Okay. Cool."

He inwardly flinched. He was trying way too hard to sound relaxed when he was anything but that.

"Want to sit down?"

They left the fishing rods on the table and sat in their usual chairs at the edge of the wharf. She turned to face him, pulling her knees up to her chest and hugging them into herself. She twiddled her thumbs where they were wrapped around her legs.

"So," she said, then put her feet back on the ground and stood up, leaning against the railing. She crossed her arms, uncrossed them, then tugged her hair behind her ears. Giving him a quick glance, she said again, "So."

Shawn smirked. "You said that already."

She groaned and put her face in her hands. "Sorry. I'm nervous."

Her voice broke on the last word, and Shawn stood up, put one hand under her knees and the other under her back, and picked her up. Willa yelped, and he sat back down, tugging her into his body. God, he could get used to this—holding her out here, burying his face in her hair, pressing her warm body into his.

He whispered against her ear. "You don't have to be nervous around me."

She shivered and buried her face in his chest. "I can't help it."

He tugged her closer, tucking her head under his chin. "What if you don't look at me while you tell me whatever it is you want to tell me?"

She stilled, then took a deep breath. "I don't want to be friends with benefits anymore."

Shawn's smile dropped and his heart stuttered.

So he was right.

She was done with him.

He closed his eyes and tipped his head back, trying to calm himself down. He knew it would come to this eventually. Knew she'd grow tired of him, just like everyone else had. And he had nobody to blame but himself for agreeing to this in the first place. He had to let her go. Would she want to remain friends? He wasn't sure he could handle that —at least, not right away. But maybe down the road—

"Shawn?"

The way Willa said his voice made him realize she'd been trying to get his attention for a few moments. She placed her hands on his cheeks, tugging his gaze down to meet hers.

"Shawn?" she said again.

"If that's what you want," he said.

"Wait, Shawn. It's not because—fuck, I'm really screwing this up." She dropped her hands from his cheeks and buried her face in her palms.

"It's okay, Willa."

"No, Shawn. It's not," she lifted her face to his again. "I'm... Fuck, what I'm trying to say is that I don't want to be friends with benefits anymore because I have feelings for you."

Her voice trailed off as she spoke until it was barely a whisper. Shawn jolted, hope and shock coursing through him.

"And I can't... I can't just be friends with benefits anymore. I don't... Fuck." She buried her face in his chest, and Shawn's arms tightened around her.

"I have feelings for you, too," he whispered. "Been trying to pretend like I don't for weeks now."

Willa gasped, gazing up at him. "Really? Charlie said..."

"What?" Shawn asked when she trailed off.

"Charlie said she thought you might. The way you looked at me or something."

Shawn chuckled. "And how do I look at you?"

Willa bit her lip. "Charlie was a bit melodramatic about it, actually. Something about how I'm the sun."

The sun, the stars, the moon, every fucking planet in the galaxy.

But the sun was good enough for now.

Shawn kissed her. "Sounds about right. So why were you nervous to talk to me about this, baby?"

The endearment he usually saved for sex slipped out before he could stop himself, and she gave him a tentative grin before burying her face in his chest again.

"I'm scared," she whispered, eyes watering. "After Leo. I'm fucking terrified. I don't... I can't go through that again. And I don't trust myself when it comes to picking guys. I've always ended up getting hurt."

His heart splintered as he watched a couple of stray tears roll down her face. He cradled her cheeks in his hands, brushing them away with his thumbs. If he ever met this Leo guy, Shawn was going to punch first and ask questions later. He hoped for all their sakes that they never crossed paths.

"I'm gonna fucking kill that guy," Shawn said, earning him a humorless chuckle from Willa. "I know there's not much I can say to make you feel better about this. We'll have to figure it out as we go. But here's what I can promise: I'll always be honest with you. Always. And I'm willing to do whatever it takes to make sure you trust me."

"It's not you I don't trust. It's me," Willa whispered, tears streaming down her face as she let out a humorless chuckle. "My therapist and I are working on it."

Shawn rubbed his thumb along her lips. "I'm proud of you for getting the help you need. Listen, baby. I've never felt this way before. Ever. And I don't want to freak you out, but I'm all in on this. On you. On us. So whatever you need to feel good about it, I'll give you."

He was pretty sure he'd give her anything she wanted. She had him wrapped around her slender finger. But she'd figure that out eventually.

"So what do you need?" Shawn asked. "What can I say or do to make you feel better?"

Willa pressed her lips together in a firm line. "I still don't think I'm ready to tell Ida. I'm just worried about the pressure she might put on us. I want to keep it just to us for now. While we figure things out."

Shawn was a little disappointed—only because he wanted to scream from the rooftops that she was his. But he understood, so he nodded.

"I want..." she continued, but trailed off. "Can I call you my boyfriend?"

He beamed at her. "I would love nothing more."

She fidgeted nervously. "Has there been anyone else? Since we've been... you know. I won't be mad. I told you to date. I just want to know, you know? Just so I can—"

He cut her off with a kiss.

"There hasn't been anyone else since you walked into my bait shop looking like a goddamn queen." She blushed, and he kissed her cheek. "What else, baby?"

She wrapped her arms around his neck and laid her head on his chest. "I guess nothing else, for now. I just might be a little paranoid for a while. I'm sorry."

"You have nothing to apologize for," he said, planting a peck on her head. "Now if I ever meet that fucker, Landon, on the other hand..."

"Leo?" Willa laughed. "I'd love to see that interaction."

"Let's hope for everyone's sake that it never happens."

She sighed happily.

"One more thing," he said, fishing his phone out of his pocket and handing it to her. "My code is 7-9-4-5. Grams' birthday."

She looked at the phone in her hands, then back up at him with wide, disbelieving eyes. "What...?"

"You can look at my phone whenever you want," he said. He'd been thinking about this for a while—giving her this kind of access to him would undoubtedly show her that she was the only girl he would be talking to aside from Grams. And maybe Hanna. "I won't change the code. That's been my code for years."

"Shawn," Willa's voice broke, and a tear slid down her cheek.

"I want you to trust me. But I want you to trust yourself. And having access to my phone whenever you want... I think it'll help."

She bit her lip as he wiped away her tears.

"Thank you," she whispered, burying her face in his chest.

"Does this mean I can finally take you on a date?" Shawn asked.

She grinned at him and nodded, then weaved her fingers into his hair and tugged him closer until she devoured him with a kiss. Her lips pressed firmly against his as she tugged his bottom lip into her mouth, then worked to open his mouth more. He succumbed to her, his tongue lapping against hers. It was slow and loving, unlike their other rough kisses. There was an intimacy to it.

Willa tugged her legs over him until she was straddling him, her core grinding up against his growing length.

"Let's go inside," he whispered against her lips. "The first time you come around my dick as my girlfriend is going to be in your bed where I can see every inch of your perfect body."

She shuddered, then nodded, standing up slowly as she grabbed his hand and led him to the house. The moment they got into the kitchen, he tossed her over his shoulder as she let out a little shriek. He rested his hand on her rear and carried her to her bedroom as quickly as his feet could carry him. He tossed her on the bed, and she peered up at him through half-lidded eyes.

"Strip," he commanded.

Shawn watched Willa as she methodically tugged off a crop top and those little shorts she liked to sleep in. She wore nothing underneath, and it took everything in him not to immediately pepper her body with kisses.

He walked over to her bedside table and opened up the drawer, finding exactly what he suspected. Grinning to himself, he picked up a bright pink vibrator. As he walked over to her, she squirmed, a pretty flush covering her cheeks. Grabbing her ankles, he tugged her to the edge of the bed and palmed her pussy.

"Drenched, as usual," he said.

Turning on the vibrator, he pressed it against her core. She trembled as he dragged it up her belly and over her tits. He watched her nipples bud as he circled them with the tip of the vibrator.

"Shawn," she whimpered. "Please."

Bringing it back to her core, he rested it against her entrance tauntingly as she tried to grind against it. He pressed her hips down, forcing her to still as he continued to tease her.

"Remind me again what you think about when you use this, Willa," Shawn said.

Willa whimpered.

"You," she said between pants. "Always you."

He plunged it inside her and she screamed, her body convulsing. He thrust it in and out of her at a tauntingly slow place, watching her body trembling, her breathless whimpers piercing the gentle buzz of the vibrator. God, she was fucking gorgeous like this. Naked and screaming, completely at his mercy. His body begged him to touch her —to take off his clothes and tangle his limbs in hers.

But not yet.

Keeping his pace steady, he slowly knelt before her. Her eyes widened as she realized what he was doing. He hovered his mouth over her clit and she moaned. She tasted so fucking good, like absolute perfection. He'd die a happy man for tasting her more times than he could count. He licked her softly, slowly picking up the pace of the vibrator's thrusts with his hand. Then he buried his face in her, sucking and licking her clit, putting an increasing amount of pressure on it in tune with the thrusts of the vibrator.

Her body grew taut, then loose as she orgasmed, screaming his name and burying her face into the bed.

"I love watching you come," Shawn growled as he tugged his shirt over his head. He smirked as Willa's eyes dipped from his face to his chest and torso. She licked her lips. "See something you like?"

She blushed and nodded as he took his pants off.

His erection sprang free as he tugged his boxer briefs down, a bead of pre-cum dripping from the head of his cock. He grabbed a pillow and tucked it under Willa's lower back, then hovered over her, grinding against her entrance. Her arousal coated his cock, and she groaned as she sought friction against him.

"Shawn, please," she panted.

He thrust his cock inside her, and she instantly clenched around him. Their naked limbs tangled together, a welcome relief after he'd made her come with every item of his clothing still on. Her soft, warm body pressed against his as he thrust into her painfully slowly, savoring the tightness of her pussy.

He pressed his lips gently to hers as he increased the speed of his thrusts, the pillow underneath her giving him the perfect angle to slide so deep into her that he perfectly hit her G spot. Her eyes glazed over as he rested his forehead against hers.

Willa was perfect like this. Relaxed from her earlier orgasm while desperately seeking the bliss of another. Taking his cock like she was fucking built for him. Completely bare and vulnerable before him, her auburn hair messily splayed out around her head. Her freckles had increased over the summer—all that time in the sun had given her more, and he fucking loved it.

But mostly, he loved the way she looked at him. Like she

was hungry and satiated all at once. With tenderness and ferocity.

"I'll do everything I can to earn your trust, Greene," he said as her legs started trembling underneath the weight of a building orgasm. "Just know that you're it for me. You're all I want. This perfect pussy is mine. *You're* mine. And I'm yours."

She screamed with the power of another orgasm, and he followed after her as her pussy milked his cock perfectly. He collapsed on top of her, unwilling to pull out of her just yet.

He stiffened.

"Fuck," he said. "I forgot to use a condom."

He pulled out of her immediately and buried his face in his hands.

"It's okay," Willa said softly, sitting up and wrapping her arms around his center.

"No, it's not," Shawn said. "You asked me to wear a condom every time, and I—"

"I don't care anymore." He looked at her, eyes wide. Willa sighed. "I only made up that rule because... I guess, on some level, I thought it would help me not catch feelings. Obviously, that didn't work out."

She smirked at him, and his shoulders dropped with relief. "I thought you were worried that after my sexual history, I'd be... unclean."

"You told me you aren't," she responded.

"Still," he said. "I just thought..."

"I don't care about your past, Shawn," Willa said. "I just care about this. Right here. Right now."

He beamed at her and tugged her into his lap, pressing a kiss on her forehead. She rested her head on his shoulder for a moment before standing up, grabbing his hand, and leading him into the bed.

"I, uh…" Shawn cleared his throat as he got into bed next to her. "Not sure I can handle round two yet."

She laughed. "I know. I was just thinking…" she curled her body into his, running her fingers along his chest and resting her head on his shoulder. "You should spend the night."

Shawn tightened his grip on her body and tugged her closer. "I'd love to."

He shot a quick text to Grams that he'd be home late and not to wait up, hoping she wouldn't read too much into it.

"Maybe tomorrow you can bring a toothbrush here," Willa sleepily whispered. "And some clothes."

Shawn thought his heart would burst from happiness, as he gently moved wisps of hair out of her face.

Exhausted from the orgasms he gave her earlier, Willa quickly drifted, her eyes shuttering as her breathing turned heavy. He watched her fall asleep, still disbelieving that she was really his. And as she started lightly snoring, he whispered into her hair, "I love you," before shutting his eyes and falling asleep.

28

The sound of a zipper woke Willa up. She blinked her eyes open and reached her arm to the warm space next to her where Shawn had been.

"Shawn?" she mumbled sleepily.

"Right here, Greene," he said, kneeling next to the bed and kissing her forehead.

"What'reyoudoin?" Willa asked, her words slurring together as she fought the urge to fall back asleep. She felt a warm hand cup her cheek and she smiled. "What time issit?"

He chuckled. "It's 5 a.m. I'm heading back home so Grams doesn't get suspicious."

A pang of sadness hit her chest, and she felt stupid for being so bummed. She wasn't ready for Ida to know. He was just respecting her request. But she didn't want him to leave —his warmth, his presence made her feel safe. She grabbed his shirt with her fingers and tugged him in for a kiss.

"You're making it hard to leave," he whispered against her lips and she giggled.

"I don't want you to."

He groaned. "Willa..."

Shawn pulled away from the kiss and she pouted. He laughed as he tugged the blankets over her and tucked her in.

"Go back to sleep, baby," he whispered. "I'll see you later, okay?"

"'Kay."

She rolled over and closed her eyes. She heard the door click shut as he left, then drifted back to sleep shortly after that.

When Willa woke up several hours later, her clock read 10 a.m. and she smiled to herself as she remembered everything that happened the night before. She was nervous—scared to end up in a bad situation again. But she trusted Shawn, and she was starting to trust herself again, too. Having him spend the night was the best way to seal their new deal.

She rolled out of bed, and after lighting incense, stretching, and mediating, she checked her phone. She had a few texts, but the one from Shawn made her heart leap.

> Date night tonight? Pick you up at 7?

She grinned and texted back.

> Sounds perfect.

～

"Where ya goin', Scooby?"

Shawn had briefly considered climbing out his window to avoid this encounter. After all, he wasn't wearing swim trunks or a t-shirt.

He was wearing real clothes. Jeans. A button-down shirt. A belt.

His hair had been brushed, for Christ's sake.

As much as he wanted to tell everyone he knew that he was taking Willa on a date, he understood why she wanted to keep things private for now. And he respected it, even though it made him a little sad. He wanted everyone to know she was his, but he'd play his part in keeping things a secret. For now.

So he'd already planned an excuse—one he hoped Grams wouldn't see through.

"I'm going out to dinner with Hanna and Tucker," he said.

Grams studied him, her eyes narrow with suspicion.

"Sure do look nice to go see two of your best friends," she said, putting her hands on her hips and jutting her jaw out.

"Hanna wanted to try some new, fancy place," Shawn said, his hands getting clammier by the second. "She called me and told me to wear this."

He forced the lies to roll off his tongue naturally, but Grams didn't budge.

"And what's it called?"

He should've seen this coming.

"The Krusty Krab," he said hurriedly, before he could overthink it.

Even if the name rang a bell for her, he doubted Grams would put together that it was from SpongeBob.

She scrunched her face up in thought. "Krusty Krab? Doesn't sound fancy."

"Well, it is. You know how seafood restaurants are. Their names never sound fancy."

"Where is it?"

"My map will tell me," he said with a grin, pulling his phone out of his pocket.

"Hmm."

He put his phone back in his pocket and grinned. "Can I go now? Is the inquisition over?"

"Can't blame me for hoping you were going on a date," she said with a frown. "Why didn't you invite Hanna and Tucker over here to see me?"

"I will next time, Grams," he said, giving her a hug and a kiss on the cheek. "But I gotta go. I'll tell them you said hi, okay?"

"Alright," she said, plopping down into her chair and lifting her feet. "I'll be watching *The Holiday* tonight if you need me. So don't need me."

Shawn chuckled. "I'll do my best. Love you."

"Love you, too, Scooby."

Grams wasn't the only reason he was nervous.

He had big plans for Willa tonight, and everything needed to be perfect. Keeping Grams off his scent was a small part of making sure tonight went smoothly. The rest of it—well, he'd spent most of the day getting everything ready.

Shawn wanted to earn Willa's trust. He wanted her to know that he believed in her, knew her, listened to her, and cared about her. And he wanted to show her how much she meant to him.

He climbed into his truck and drove a couple houses down, into her driveway, where she was waiting looking like an absolute goddess in that dress.

It was the seafoam green one she wore on the first day they met, when she showed up at his bait shop and turned his life upside down. He got out of the car, barely remembering the bouquet of flowers he'd bought earlier and kept in his truck to avoid any questions from Grams.

Willa beamed at him.

Shawn swallowed and held them out to her.

"Such a gentleman," she said with a wink, then stepped closer to him and kissed him on the cheek.

He froze, thrown off by the sudden display of affection.

Forget the fact that they'd been screwing each other senseless the past couple of months.

The light peck on the cheek made him feel like a giddy teenager again. Like they were taking it slow.

Like they were *really* in a relationship.

He couldn't remember the last time someone kissed him on the cheek like that.

"I'm going to put these in some water real quick," she said. "Want to come in?"

Shawn nodded.

He must've lost his ability to speak because he wanted to tell her how perfect she looked, but couldn't find his voice. So he trailed behind her into the kitchen, where they sat in one of those companionable silences they often shared on the wharf as she methodically cut the stems and put the flowers in a vase.

"I love sunflowers," Willa said. "How'd you know?"

He'd taken a wild guess. The flowers reminded him of her, and one of the locals grew the most beautiful sunflowers on their farm a few miles down the road. He drove down there to buy them earlier that afternoon.

When he had the idea to buy her some flowers today, the traditional, romantic bouquet isn't what came to mind. He wasn't about to drop $50 on the perfect selection of red roses. But sunflowers? The ones he could see growing in fields down the road from the Bay? For some reason, they reminded him of her—warm and inviting and a little bit wild.

"Nobody's ever bought me sunflowers before," she murmured, more to herself than to him.

He was going to buy her sunflowers every damn day they were in season.

"I'm glad you like them," Shawn responded, finally finding his voice.

She gave him a shy smile, and he felt the gravity of this first date.

For both of them, for different reasons, this was a big deal.

So he stepped toward her, grabbed her chin with his fingers, and delicately pecked her perfect lips.

"Thanks for letting me take you out tonight," he whispered against her mouth. "I know this must be scary for you. Just let me know what you need."

She released a big sigh and buried her face into his chest, wrapping her arms around him. He tugged her in and rested his chin against the top of her head.

"Thank you," she whispered, so quietly he almost didn't hear it.

"I've got some big plans for tonight," he said, nerves re-entering his system.

"Am I dressed okay for it?"

He pulled back and grinned at her. "You look perfect. Have I not said that yet?"

She shook her head, biting her lip.

Leaning into her hair, Shawn brought his lips against her ear and her breath caught as he whispered, "This is the dress you wore the first time I laid eyes on you. This is the perfect dress for any occasion. You look stunning."

He heard her intake of breath before making eye contact with her again. "Shall we?"

She nodded, and he led her to the car.

So far, so good. As she buckled into the seat, he turned the radio on and pulled out of the driveway. He hoped she liked what he had planned.

WILLA TWIDDLED HER THUMBS NERVOUSLY.

Shawn remembered this dress.

Of course he did.

But still. It meant the world to her.

She took a calming breath in a feeble attempt to get her heart rate to slow. Between the flowers and the whispering in her ear, she was more than a little turned on. But mostly, she was terrified.

It's Shawn, she'd been telling herself all day. *I trust Shawn.*

But how could she trust anyone after what she'd been through?

Her therapist told her that sometimes she just had to do it scared. That it sounded like Shawn held space for her to express when she was feeling insecure about their relationship, and that was a step in the right direction. That if she never put herself out there—never *tried*—she'd never learn to trust herself again.

It took her three tries to apply her eyeliner because her hand was shaking from nerves.

But she did it, and she'd do this, too.

Willa realized she hadn't been paying much attention to where Shawn was driving as he pulled into the church parking lot where Bingo was held.

Confusion mixed with amusement laced her tone as she said, "Are you taking me to Bingo for date night?"

He grinned at her. "Not quite."

Shawn got out of the car and jogged to the passenger side, where he opened the door for her. He grabbed her hand, fingers laced with hers, and gave her a kiss on the forehead.

"I have a few surprises for you tonight," he said. "This is one of them."

Willa felt the nervous anticipation of uncertainty and curiosity, but followed Shawn's lead through the front doors of the church. He walked through the hallways, past the sanctuary and into the room where Bingo was typically held. He turned on the light, then led her up to the front, onto the small, makeshift stage where Amos typically stood as he emceed for Bingo.

"Ta da," Shawn said.

"Ta da?" Willa asked, biting back a laugh.

"I talked to Amos about the possibility of you teaching some yoga classes here," Shawn said. "Not sure if you know this, but he doesn't just run Bingo. He's the community outreach manager for the church. Helps put on all sorts of events to engage with the neighborhood, but mostly to keep the seniors around here active. I told him how you teach yoga and how you worked with Grams, to see if he'd be interested in having you teach a few classes a week here at the church. He loved the idea."

Willa gasped. "You... wait, I—" she spluttered.

"I told him you needed a paying job, so he said you could discuss the particulars of how much you wanted to charge community members. But he said you could keep 100% of the profit from classes. The church has a lot of big donors locally. They just want to reach the community in more ways. And he thinks this'll be a big hit. Especially since Grams is such a big fan of yours already. He wants to announce it at Bingo every week."

"I can teach yoga here?"

"Only if you want," Shawn continued. "I told him you were just exploring your options right now, but he really wants you to do it. He thinks it might help get some young people showing up at the church, too."

Willa took a deep breath and tried to process what she just heard. Shawn found her a job. A real job. Where she could work with seniors, like she'd always wanted. People like Grams. Where she could make a real difference, and still be only a few minutes away from work.

"You... you found me a job," Willa said.

Shawn reached his hand behind his neck, his cheeks reddening. "If you want it. If you hate the idea, that's okay, too."

"Shawn," Willa said, her eyes misting. "You found me a yoga job teaching seniors."

"Are you mad?" he asked, his brows creasing. "I know it was a bit presumptuous—"

"Mad?" she laughed. "Shawn, how could I be mad? This is the nicest thing anyone has ever done for me."

She launched herself into his arms and giggled, her happiness bubbling over. He froze for a moment, then tugged her into his body.

"Thank you," she said. "I never would've thought of this. I can't thank you enough."

He beamed.

"Happy to help." She could tell he meant it. "I'll tell Amos you're interested and have him give you a call."

"Sounds perfect. Thank you."

"You're welcome."

Her nerves had softened amidst the excitement of this news, and now she couldn't wait to see what he had in store next.

"The first surprise was a success. What's next?" she asked him.

He kissed her on the nose. "Let's find out."

SHAWN HAD THOUGHT for a moment that he'd messed up. Been too heavy-handed. Tried too hard.

He hadn't had a girlfriend.

Ever.

But he wanted to spoil Willa. Wanted to be the one to solve all her problems, or at the very least, hold her hand through them all.

So he'd gotten on the phone with Amos. It was an easy call. He'd known Amos for years. Fixed his gutters after the tropical storm last summer. House-sat for him when he went on a two-week trip to Europe.

But as Willa stood in the multi-purpose room of the church in stunned silence, he thought maybe he'd gone too far.

Until her eyes had gone glassy and she laughed with such pure joy that he felt it deep in his bones.

His left hand rested at the top of the steering wheel and his right sat atop her leg, her fingers gently toying with his. He hoped this next surprise went just as well. After the last one, he was feeling a bit more confident.

He pulled into the marina—just a few minutes down the road from the church—and parked in his usual spot.

She glanced at him shyly, her eyes bright with curiosity.

Shawn got out of the truck and opened her door, holding a hand out to her.

She grabbed it and they walked toward the marina office together. Willa looked at him quizzically as he led her into the tiny office at the front of the pier. He grinned at her and led her inside, where Bo was sitting with a sudoku and a beer.

"This her?" Bo asked gruffly, his accent so thick that even Shawn noticed it.

"Bo, this is Willa," Shawn said. "Willa, this is Bo. He runs the marina."

Willa extended her hand to Bo and they shook.

"Firm handshake," Bo drawled. "I can see why you like her."

Then he winked at Willa.

"Hey, man, that's my girl," Shawn jested, wrapping a protective arm around Willa.

Bo lifted both his hands up in surrender.

Shawn had known Bo since he was a kid, much like the rest of the community around the Bay. When he was little, Bo used to let him sneak candy from his office before he went on boat rides. Now, Bo gave Shawn a hell of a deal on docking his boat and helped him out on the occasional tour.

Bo was a former veteran who was almost always clad in khakis and a polo. He'd bought the marina after getting out of the Navy, and Shawn was pretty certain he'd never retire. He'd hired people to help with the logistics and manual labor so he could be the face of the marina. He loved talking to people, and this job allowed him to meet all sorts of people.

Like Shawn.

And now Willa.

"Shawny tells me you're one hell of a yoga teacher," Bo said. "Done it a couple times myself. It's some tough shit."

Willa's eyes lit up with amusement as she responded. "It definitely can be."

Bo hummed, studying Willa carefully. "He seems to think offering yoga classes out on the marina's pavilion or beach might be a big hit."

Eyes wide, Willa looked over at Shawn. "He does?"

Shawn nodded. "I see you doing yoga out on your wharf every day. Thought other people might want to do the same."

Willa grinned. "I think people would love it. Locals and tourists."

"Exactly what Shawny here said," Bo responded. "And I trust him. If he says you're a good egg, then you're a good egg in my book."

"She is," Shawn said.

Willa bit her lip. "Thanks, Bo. So how do you want to go about doing this?"

Shawn pulled up a couple of chairs so they could sit down as Willa and Bo discussed the details, including class schedule and how she'd get paid. Bo offered to keep her on retainer, so long as she taught at least three classes per week. By the end of their conversation, she'd come up with a tentative class schedule starting the following week, talked through a plan to get the word out, and shook on their plan.

Shawn could tell Willa was thoroughly charmed with Bo, and he couldn't blame her. He had a way of making people feel seen and special.

He grinned to himself as they walked out of his tiny office, and Willa was buzzing with energy.

"So you found me two jobs," Willa said.

"I hope that's okay," Shawn said.

She stopped. "It's more than okay. It's..." She sighed. "Thank you, Shawn."

He lowered his head and kissed her forehead.

"No problem." Grabbing her hand, he led her toward the dock. "You ready for the last surprise of the night?"

29

Willa had accepted that her heart wouldn't slow. Everything Shawn had done overwhelmed her.

Sure, she'd received flowers before. But never her favorite, sunflowers. Even though she'd told Leo more than once they were her favorite flowers, he always bought her the most expensive ones he could find. He said sunflowers were a "common flower." That she should've appreciated the two dozen red roses he bought her more.

Again, she kicked herself for not seeing some of the red flags he waved.

And somehow, between this morning and tonight, Shawn had coordinated not one but two job offers for her.

She barely noticed they'd been walking toward his boat until suddenly, it was in view. And it had twinkling lights on it—along with a perfectly set table with a bottle of champagne in an icebox and two identical glasses next to it.

Willa stopped in her tracks.

"Shawn," she whispered.

"The first time I brought you on my boat, I kept wishing

it was a real date," he said, tugging a stray strand of hair behind her ear. "I wanted a do-over."

"Me too," she said.

He kissed her fingers, still cradled in his hand, and led her onto the boat. As she sat down, he popped the bottle of champagne and she let out a delighted squeal. He grinned at her and poured her a glass, and Willa just couldn't take it anymore.

As he set the glass of champagne in front of her, she grabbed his wrist, tugged him toward her, and pressed her mouth to his. He grunted in shock, then leaned into it, his calloused hands gently grabbing her neck, her cheeks, tangling in her hair. His tongue lapped against hers and he nipped her lip. Willa gasped, tugging him even closer, standing up so their bodies were closer, tighter.

His hands lazily grazed down her sides, grabbing her hips, pulling her against him so she could feel his hardness.

"Willa," he whispered against her lips.

She opened her eyes. His were black and half-lidded with desire, his chest rising and falling with deep pants of lust.

"Tonight has been..." Willa took a deep breath. "Amazing. Perfect. The best date I've ever been on."

He dropped his head so his forehead leaned against hers.

"For me, too," he said.

"And we haven't even gotten to the dinner part."

"Or the after dinner part," he said with a wink.

She laughed.

"Speaking of dinner," he said, "you have to be hungry."

As if on cue, her stomach rumbled. She hadn't eaten since the mullet she fried for lunch, and it was almost 8. Now that he mentioned it, she was starving.

"Yes, please," she grinned.

Shawn turned around and grabbed a couple of coolers. Out of one, he pulled out a shrimp cocktail, a pitcher of water, and a charcuterie board, setting them gently on the table he'd set.

"Don't worry, there's more," Shawn said with a grin. "But I thought you'd like to start with some apps."

She reached for a shrimp and dipped it in the sauce before taking a bite.

"How'd you pull all this off?" she asked.

"The shrimp cocktail?"

"Well, yes," she said, grabbing another one. "All of it. The jobs. The boat. The food. In one day."

"Ahh," he said, grabbing a shrimp of his own. "Well, the jobs were easy. I knew both of those guys. After I heard you talking the other night about your job, I gave them both a call. I was going to tell you about it last night, but…"

She smirked.

"So I called them this morning and asked if we could drop by today. They both agreed."

"I can't thank you enough, Shawn," Willa said, her voice growing thick.

It made her want to cry—how wonderful he had been, how sweet he was, how thoughtful and kind and generous. She'd never dated a man like him.

He was the definition of *If he wanted to, he would.*

"It's no problem, Willa," he said.

And she knew he meant it. This is what Shawn did. Helped people. Stuck his neck out for them. Cared for them.

But she appreciated it all the same.

More than he'd ever know.

"And the boat? The dinner?"

"Yes, that," Shawn said with a chuckle. "Well, I'm not

sure if you know this about me, but I run a pretty successful charter boat company."

She cackled. "Okay, duh, but still."

"So I have connections. I have supplies. This isn't the first time I've organized a romantic dinner on this boat, Greene. Certainly won't be the last."

He locked eye contact with her as he said that last sentence, and she blushed.

Willa continued to snack on the appetizers and sip her champagne as she sat with Shawn in a comfortable silence. That's what she loved most about him—how easy it was to just be with him in silence, not feeling like she had to be anything other than herself. She loved how easy it was to—

Willa startled. Sat up.

"You ok?" Shawn asked.

Yeah, it's just that I realized I'm in love with you, she thought.

No, she wasn't going to say that.

"Willa?"

She cleared her throat.

"Sorry," she said. "Just... I think I forgot to turn off my curling iron."

He chuckled. "Your hair is straight tonight, Greene. But whatever you say."

She blushed again.

Maybe that's what she loved most about him. He trusted her. It made it all the more easy for her to trust him.

"Ready for the main course?" he asked.

She nodded, and he cleared away the empty appetizer plates, then pulled two covered plates out of a different cooler.

"Crab cakes, asparagus, and mashed potatoes," he said. "And they should still be warm."

She grabbed her fork and took a bit of the crab cake.

"Holy shit, this is amazing," she said. "Where'd you get this?"

"One of my favorite restaurants on the water," Shawn said, refilling her champagne glass. "It's called Fish Food. I'll take you there next time."

"I'd love that," Willa responded.

Shawn beamed at her and tucked into his food. As they ate their dinner and chatted a bit about their weekend, they watched the sun set over the Bay. Willa couldn't help but feel like maybe this was a fairytale—a bit fairytale-ish, at least. The sunset was so picturesque she didn't want to look away, and her brain was just fuzzy enough from the slight buzz the champagne gave her.

And then there was Shawn—who was wearing an outfit she'd never seen him in, his hair styled just so, in a way, she could tell he'd put in the extra effort. Not to mention how he smelled. He always smelled good—like soap and the ocean and the salty air—but tonight there was something else. Cologne, probably. And even outside, sitting across from him at the table he'd set on the boat, she could smell him.

"Ready for dessert?" he asked her, interrupting her thoughts.

"Dessert?" she asked with a giggle.

He pulled out a small box from one of the coolers and opened it up. Inside was a decadent chocolate cake.

"I'm so full," Willa said. "But..."

She reached for a fork, took a bite, and groaned.

"Oh my god, please tell me this is from that same restaurant and I can have this again when we go on the actual date there," she said as she grabbed another bite with her fork.

Shawn chuckled. "It's all from the same place."

"Thank God," Willa said. "Give my regards to the chef."

"Will do," he responded, grabbing a bite of his own.

The cake was gone before they knew it, and the sun had set behind the Bay. Willa was full and sleepy, but mostly content, as she wandered over to Shawn's side of the table and sat in his lap, cuddling close to him.

"This was the perfect first date," she whispered into his ear. "Thank you."

He tipped his head down and gave her a gentle kiss on the lips. "Only for you."

SHAWN WAS ON CLOUD NINE.

Their date couldn't have gone any better. The day he'd spent prepping it was entirely worth it.

Anything for Willa was entirely worth it.

She rested her head against his shoulder, her fingers gently twiddling with his right hand. His left was on the steering wheel as he drove them home, ready to take her inside to bed. He didn't care if they had sex. They were both probably too full for that, anyway. He just knew he wanted to wake up next to her again.

As he pulled into her driveway, he gave her a quick kiss on the head and whispered, "We're here."

She sat up and grabbed his cheeks between her hands. "Come inside?"

"Of course."

She kissed him, gently, slowly. He got out of the car and walked around to her side, opening her door and helping her out. She leaned into him as he led her toward the house, and Shawn never thought he'd been so happy, never thought he'd find a girl like Willa, never thought she'd—

"Willa?" a deep, piercing voice came out from the front porch.

Willa stiffened, and Shawn looked up to where a man in a suit stood, arms crossed, a frown on his face. He glanced back at Willa. Her face was pale, and she clutched Shawn's arm so hard he could see the whites of her knuckles.

"Leo?" she asked, breathless.

30

"Leo?" Shawn heard himself ask.

He shoved his sleeves up his forearms and started walking toward him, his vision red with rage.

"Shawn, wait!" Willa suddenly stood in front of him, both hands against his chest. "Don't."

She looked panicked.

Panicked for this fucker?

"Please," she whispered. "He's not worth it."

Her eyes were wide with worry.

He searched her face, for something—anything—to tell him what the fuck was going on in her head. All he saw was a desperate plea for him to stop.

She could ask him to walk over a pile of coals and he'd do it.

So he nodded at her and stepped back.

She breathed a sigh of relief.

It hurt—that she was protecting the idiot who broke her heart.

"What the fuck are you doing here, Leo?" Willa asked.

Okay, so maybe she wasn't protecting him. Shawn was getting whiplash. What was going on in her head?

"Let's talk in private, babe," Leo responded curtly.

As if his word was final.

As if he had the right to call her babe.

As if he had the right to speak to her at all.

God, Shawn hated him.

"Babe?" Willa all but shrieked. "Don't fucking call me babe."

"Calm down, ba—Willa," Leo said. "I just want to talk. In private."

"Whatever you need to say to me, you can say in front of him," Willa said, crossing her arms as if taking a battle stance.

God, he was proud of her—for sticking up for herself, for being brave, for not putting up with this fucker's bullshit.

"I'm not leaving until I can talk to you alone, Willa," Leo's menacing voice came out like a man who was used to getting what he wanted. "I can play this game all night."

He looked at her meaningfully, and Shawn felt Willa deflate.

"Shawn," she said, turning around to face him. "I need you to go."

Fuck. "Willa—"

She shook her head. "Please, Shawn. I don't... I can't deal with all of this. I'll call you later. Promise."

Deal with all of this?

Deal with what?

Shawn?

Or Leo?

Shawn took a deep breath, leaning down to kiss her on the forehead.

"Call me later," he reiterated, and she nodded.

It was the hardest thing he ever did—turning around, getting into his truck, and driving away.

WILLA'S EYES misted as she watched Shawn drive back to his place, just a few houses down. She heard him put his car in park and shut the door with so much force she figured people a few miles away could hear it.

When he looked at her before he left, she tried to communicate with him silently: *If you punch him, he'll take you to court for all you're worth. Don't do it. Not for me.*

Shawn was angry and he had the right to be.

But she needed to get rid of Leo, and that'd be easier to do if she wasn't worried Shawn was two steps away from giving him a black eye.

"You moved on quick," Leo's voice pierced through the darkness.

"Fuck you," she said, crossing her arms. "What do you want, Leo?"

"So hostile," he said with a smirk. "Aren't you going to invite me inside?"

God, what had she ever seen in him? Had he always been this calculating?

The audacity.

He was handsome—in the bland, conventionally attractive way so many rich businessmen often were.

"No," she said. "This is going to be quick."

"Listen babe—"

"Don't. Call. Me. Babe."

"Willa," Leo said, and for the first time, he looked flustered. "I'm sorry. I never should've lied to you or led you on the way I did. But you have to know, I really did love you."

"Bullshit. How did you even find me?"

"I.. well, I remembered you had a place on the Gulf, but couldn't remember where. Tried to find you on social media or ask some of the instructors at your old yoga studio. Nobody would tell me."

Willa grinned at that. Her friends were awesome.

"So I took matters into my own hands," Leo said, standing up straighter, looking down his nose at Willa like someone would look at a petulant child.

Willa crossed her arms and looked at him expectantly.

Then, she put it together.

"You hired a fucking PI to find me?" she asked.

"You left me no choice."

SHAWN LAID down in his bed and ran a hand over his face.

He grabbed his phone and set it on the bed next to him, willing it to ring.

He wanted to talk to someone, anyone—but it was almost 11 p.m. Tucker and Hanna were most likely asleep, and they were the only ones who knew about Willa. He took a deep breath, and tried to tell himself Willa was probably punching Leo in the face right now. Maybe that's why she didn't want Shawn to do it. So she could do it herself.

He groaned and rolled over, then heard a small sound down the stairs.

"Grams?" he shouted.

He heard the sound again. It sounded like a whimper.

Heart hammering, he stood up suddenly.

"GRAMS?"

He ran downstairs, barely registering his surroundings until he was standing in the living room over Grams's limp body.

It was different than the last time he'd found her like this.

Worse. So much worse.

"Grams," he said, his voice cracking. "What happened?"

"Fell," she croaked, her face pale.

When had she fallen? Right after he left? He'd been gone all night—would've been gone longer if he'd stayed at Willa's, and then what? He wasn't paying attention when he walked into the house, so caught up in his own feelings he didn't even notice his grandmother had collapsed on the floor.

His eyes blurred, and he realized he was beginning to cry.

He grabbed his phone and called Willa.

It was an instinct.

But it went straight to voicemail, and then he remembered why.

"I'm going to take you to the hospital, Grams."

She nodded.

It was no use trying to call an ambulance. The hospitals were understaffed in this area, and he knew it'd be faster to take her himself.

He bent down and gently picked her up. She moaned, and he stiffened.

"What hurts, Grams?"

"Wrist," she wheezed. "Ribs."

Gently—even more gently—he continued picking her up, and she moaned.

"I'm sorry, Grams," he said. "I'm so sorry. I'm going to get you to the hospital."

He grabbed his keys from the kitchen, slowly with the hand holding her legs, and carried her outside to the car. Their front door swung open and he didn't bother closing it. He didn't care. Getting her into the front seat of his car was a challenge, but he sat her down and buckled her in as slowly as he could.

Shawn couldn't remember what happened between leaving the driveway and pulling into the hospital, but he was there. It was usually a 40-minute drive, but he must've gotten there in half the time, because it wasn't even midnight.

He rushed into the emergency room, carrying Grams as delicately as he could.

"Help," he shouted. "My grandmother fell. Please help!"

A few nurses rushed over to him, one carting an empty bed, and he gently laid her in it.

They asked him a few questions.

Name, age, blood type, medications, allergies.

All questions he'd known the answers to since he moved in and made it his mission to take care of her. A mission he failed.

And then he was alone in the waiting room, being told that they'd update him as soon as they could.

He sat down in one of the dozens of empty chairs and threw his head into his hands, tugging at his hair in an attempt to feel something other than utter despair.

"No choice?" Willa screamed, then laughed humorlessly. "You could've let me live my life! Could've taken care of your wife and child and let me go! You had a million choices, but

robbing me of more of my time was not the one you
should've chosen."

"Willa, I'm sorry."

"You're sorry?! And have you apologized to your wife
and daughter, as well?"

Leo shifted. "Lacey and Ella don't know about us."

"You've gotta be fucking kidding me." Willa closed her
eyes and groaned. "Why are you here, Leo?"

"I wanted to apologize, Willa. I messed up. My marriage
was in shambles and I was struggling when my wife was
pregnant. It wasn't right, what I did. But I owed you an apology, so—"

"Nope," Willa said, popping the p. "You hired what I'm
assuming is a really fucking expensive PI to find me so you
could *apologize?* I'm not buying it."

"It's true," Leo responded, eyes wide and clear. "I
didn't feel good about the way we left things. We were
together for two years, and even though it ended poorly,
it still meant something to me and I'm sorry about
tha—"

"Ended poorly?" Willa deadpanned. "Dude. I found you
at my favorite restaurant with your wife and child right after
you told me we could move in together. If you owe anyone
an apology, it's them."

"Willa, I—"

"No. Nope. I'm done. What do you want, Leo?"

"All I want is to apologize to—"

"I don't forgive you. You're an ass. Is that all?"

Leo sighed.

Pulled an envelope out of his jacket pocket.

"My wife can't find out."

Willa's rage boiled over. "Is that an NDA?"

"I'll give you $250,000 to sign it."

Willa laughed. "You're joking. Please tell me you're joking."

"I'm dead serious."

Willa searched his eyes for something—anything—that reminded her of the man she was with. Was he always this cutthroat, deceiving, and manipulative?

"You're not scared of your wife. Who are you afraid of finding out?"

Leo's eyes narrowed. "Just sign it, Willa. And I'll wire $250,000 to you tomorrow."

Willa sighed, rubbing her temples. "Leo, you really are an idiot and I don't know what I ever saw in you."

SHAWN PULLED his phone out of his pocket. Still no word from Willa. He tried calling. Straight to voicemail.

And again.

And again.

She'd probably put it on do not disturb during their date, but now?

What was she doing with Leo?

Finally, he left her a voicemail.

"Willa, Grams fell. It's bad. We're at the hospital if you can come. Please."

There was so much more he wanted to say: *I love you* and *I need you* chief among them. But he couldn't find it in him to say those words, not when she asked him to leave her house after her ex showed up. So after an awkward pause, he hung up the phone.

And threw it into the wall.

"FUCK!" he screamed, his rage bubbling over into something he couldn't control.

"Sir," a nurse said sternly, "control yourself or I'll have to ask you to leave."

Shit.

"Sorry," he said. "Won't happen again."

The nurse's eyes softened. She was a Black woman, probably in her forties or fifties, wearing blue scrubs and sneakers.

"Is there someone I can check on for you?"

Shawn sighed. "My grandmother. Ida Gray."

She nodded. "I'll see if I can find anything out."

"Thank you."

It was more than he deserved after the scene he'd caused in the waiting room. But he was grateful.

He just wished someone were here with him—someone who could hold him and share the burden of being afraid with him. It clearly wasn't going to be Willa. He tried not to hold it against her, but he wanted her here. Needed her here.

Tucker came to mind, and he felt stupid for not trying to call him sooner.

He walked over to where his phone had landed on the floor, and miraculously, it still worked. The screen was cracked, but it still lit up.

He clicked Tucker's contact and put the phone to his ear, begging him to pick up.

"'Shawny?'" Tucker's tired voice came over the phone.

"Tuck." Shawn's voice broke.

"What's wrong?" his voice cracked through, more alert this time. Shawn thought he heard Hanna mutter something in the background.

"Grams fell. Bad. We're at the hospital."

"Shit," Tucker said, then the phone crackled a bit with the sound of sudden movement. "We're on our way."

~

THEY'D BEEN TALKING in circles for a while now, and Willa was done with it.

"I'm not signing your fucking NDA," she said for what felt like the hundredth time. "Tell your wife you fucked up and get away from me."

She walked up to the door and went to unlock it, turning her back to Leo.

"I'll give you $500,000 to sign it."

Willa stopped in her tracks.

"What the fuck?" she whispered.

Something bigger was at play here—something she might have had the energy to try and figure out if she didn't already feel a headache coming on. Why was he willing to give her half a million dollars to keep his secret?

He put his hands in his pockets and leaned against one of the pillars on the front porch. "That's as high as I'll go. Sign it now and it's yours."

"Leo, no. I don't care about the money." She bit her lip, then added quietly, "Why are you doing this?"

His eyes blazed. "Last chance."

She stiffened. "I don't give a fuck, Leo. Leave me alone. If I ever hear from you again, it'll be too soon."

She unlocked the door and stepped inside.

Took a deep breath.

Listened carefully as he got into his car and drove away.

Thank God that was over with. Hopefully, he'd give up now. Willa wasn't so sure. The champagne that had lulled her into a comfortable buzz earlier that night suddenly felt like she drank it days ago, so she went to the kitchen and poured herself a glass of wine. Checked her phone.

"Shit," she said upon seeing the six missed calls from Shawn.

One was right after he left, and the others were back-to-back about thirty minutes later. Had that much time passed since Leo had showed up at her doorstep?

"Shit," she said again.

That fucker really loved to ruin things for her.

She listened to her voicemail.

And her heart shattered.

31

S hawn felt a hand gently clasp his shoulder, and he looked up from where he'd buried his head in his palms to see Hanna standing over him with misty eyes.

"Shawn," she whispered.

Shawn stood up, and Hanna tugged him into a hug. He buried his face onto her shoulder, even though she was much shorter than him, and let his tears flow freely. Seeing them here—his best friends—made him breathe a sigh of relief.

He didn't know if Grams would be okay.

He didn't know what was next.

He felt like a failure of a grandson.

But he wasn't alone in this bright white, clorox-smelling waiting room anymore.

Tucker tugged them both into a hug, and the three of them held each other in silence for a few moments.

"It's my fault," Shawn said, uttering the words out loud that had been echoing in his head for the past hour.

"Don't say that, Shawn," Hanna replied. "That's not true."

"I should've been with her," he said, stepping back and wiping his eyes. "If I was with her, it might not have been so bad. I don't even know how long she was laying on the floor before I found her."

"Shawn," Tucker said. "You can't be with her all the time."

"I could be with her more," he said. "Instead of being with—"

"Nope," Hanna said, cutting him off. "We're not doing that. You aren't going to rob yourself of happiness so you can constantly watch over Ida. She wouldn't want that. She wants you to be happy. Plus, if you were constantly keeping an eye on her, I'm pretty sure it'd drive her crazy."

Hanna gave him a weak smile, and he blew out a breath. Somewhere, in the depths of his mind, he knew she was right. But he couldn't stop feeling guilty.

"I didn't find her right away," he told them. "I was too wrapped up in my own shit. Then I heard her moan."

"You got her here," Tucker said. "That's what matters."

Shawn sat back down and buried his hands in his head, trying not to play through every single what-if that was running through his mind.

It was torture.

What if he'd been there?

What if he'd found her sooner?

What if he'd never been out with Willa at all?

Hanna sat next to him and threw her arm around him.

"Where's Willa?" she asked. "How'd the date go?"

He instantly deflated.

"Don't tell me it went bad. Tuck made some of his best food for that date."

Shawn chuckled humorlessly.

He'd meant it when he told Willa he'd give her regards to the chef.

That chef was Tucker. He'd had his own restaurant for a few years, and his seafood was the best in the entire county. When he called Tuck that morning to see if he could whip up some food for their date, he enthusiastically agreed.

"The date went great," Shawn said. "Perfect, actually. Better than I could've dreamed. And she loved your food, Tuck."

"'Course she did," he responded with a smirk.

"But then we got back to her house and her ex was there. And she asked me to leave so she could talk to him."

Hanna frowned. "And you haven't heard from her since then?"

Shawn shook his head. "Called her a bunch. Left a voicemail."

"Well, we're here, bud," Tucker said. "All night and all day tomorrow if you need us."

"Thanks, man," Shawn said, only now realizing Hanna and Tucker were still in their pajamas.

"Why don't you go find a vending machine and get us some snacks, babe?" Hanna said, her hand gently rubbing Shawn's back as she directed her question toward Tucker.

"Sure thing."

WILLA DIDN'T BOTHER CALLING Shawn back.

Not when it would take time away from her actually getting to him.

She plugged the hospital into her phone's map, hopped in the car, and gunned it.

Shawn didn't need empty words. He needed her there. And she felt like the absolute worst girlfriend for not being there. For missing this.

If he'd still have her, that is.

She tried to bury that worry and focus on finding Shawn. Luckily, small town hospitals were more compact and easier to navigate. She asked someone about Ida Gray immediately upon walking in and was directed to the ER waiting room.

She bustled down a long hallway until she saw the waiting room come into view.

And she came to a stop.

Shawn—still clad in his outfit from their date—was laying his head on the shoulder of a short brunette. One of her arms was stretched around his back, and her other hand was in his. His eyes were closed, but she could tell he'd been crying.

Willa wanted nothing more than to pull him into her arms and hold him.

To tell him she was sorry.

To explain why she had to ask him to leave.

To promise him that she was here—that she was *his*.

And yet, her eyes settled on where their hands were connected.

Willa's heart was pounding so loud she could hear it.

Her stomach dropped, thinking back to that treacherous day when she saw Leo out with his wife.

But what she felt now—instead of clarity of thought and the desire for revenge—was utter despair.

Sadness, unlike anything she'd ever felt before.

Anxiety and fear, manifesting in the form of nausea and light-headedness.

And hope.

Hope that maybe there was some sort of explanation. Some reason why a woman she didn't know was comforting a man she'd fallen in love with.

But then, the brunette looked up at her.

Smirked.

Squeezed Shawn's hand.

Whispered in his ear.

Willa's breath caught.

Shawn looked up, eyes bloodshot.

And she couldn't take it anymore.

Turning on her heel, she ran back down the hallway where she came. It felt like she was standing in front of Chadwick's all over again, watching a man she trusted share an intimate moment with someone who wasn't her.

"Willa, wait!"

The tears were pouring now.

She wanted to throw up.

Willa knew—most of her really *knew*—that Shawn wasn't Leo.

But she couldn't stop running.

Not when it *felt* the same.

Not when it felt even worse.

"WILLA," Shawn was shouting now. "STOP, PLEASE!"

She choked on a sob and kept running.

Shawn had no other thoughts besides explaining himself to Willa.

When Hanna whispered in his ear, "I think your girl's here," part of him couldn't believe it.

He looked up, and there she was.

Utter perfection.

Then, he saw her face crumple a split second before she turned around and ran. And he realized what she was looking at—him with another woman. A woman she didn't know, in a scene that probably threw her back to those months ago when she found that scumbag of a boyfriend with his wife.

He muttered an expletive under his breath before chasing after her.

They were causing a scene, but he didn't care.

He needed Willa.

And he needed her to understand.

He was on her heels now, so he shouted her name again, then added," That's my best friend's wife!"

She slowed.

"Hanna," Shawn said as he caught up to her. "That's her name. She married my best friend, Tucker, a couple years back."

Willa turned around, her face wet with tears.

"She's not... She's just a friend," Shawn said, approaching her slowly. "A good friend. Basically a sister. That's it. I promise."

Willa took a deep breath, closed her eyes, and tipped her head back.

"You can talk to her, look at my phone, whatever you need to believe me," he said. "I promise, she's just a friend."

She opened her eyes, a hint of shame and sorrow radiating from her.

"I'm sorry," she said. "For thinking you'd..."

"It's okay," Shawn said, wiping her tears away and tugging her into a hug. "It's okay."

She wrapped her arms around him and he laid his cheek on top of her head.

This was what he wanted all night—to hold her, feel her

in his arms, to sit with her while he waited for an update on Grams.

"Shawn," Hanna's voice pierced through the silence. "The doctor says you can see Ida now."

He pulled back and laid his forehead against Willa's. "Come with me?"

She nodded.

He grabbed her hand and pulled her toward where Hanna was standing, waiting for them.

"Hanna, this is Willa," Shawn said. "Willa, this is Hanna. One of my best friends."

Hanna beamed at Willa. "It's so nice to meet you. I mean, shitty circumstances. But he won't shut up about you. We've been begging him to bring you over for dinner."

"Her husband, Tucker, was the one who made our dinner tonight," Shawn said. "He owns the restaurant I told you about."

"Well, then count me in for dinner anytime," Willa said. "Nice to meet you, Hanna."

"Let's chat more later. I want to know all the things. But first, let's get back to Ida."

Hanna led the way, and Shawn and Willa followed, hand-in-hand, until they were back in the room where the doctor was waiting for them.

"Wyatt?" Willa asked as they approached.

Shawn grinned, realizing it was Mary's grandson, from Ida's Bingo group. "I think it's Dr. Wetherington around here."

"Y'all can call me Wyatt," he grinned. "Nice to see you again, Willa. How's your friend, Charlie?"

"Why don't we start with you telling us how Ida's doing?" Willa responded.

"Fair enough," Wyatt said. "All things considered, she'll

be alright. She has a broken wrist—probably from trying to catch herself when she fell. I won't lie: that'll be a bit of a tough recovery for someone her age. But we've put her in a cast, and we can explore rehab, if needed, once we take it off in about eight weeks. And she has a couple of bruised ribs, which should be fine in a few weeks. She was also pretty dehydrated when she came in. She's not drinking nearly enough water, and my guess is, she'd been down for a while by the time you brought her in. I'd like to keep her overnight to monitor her, but she'll be discharged in the morning."

Shawn breathed a sigh of relief. "She's okay?"

"She's okay," Wyatt said. "But it might be time to talk to her about using a walker."

"She'll never do it," Shawn said immediately.

"It'll help her get around. She doesn't have to have it all the time. But it might be helpful for those moments when you're not there."

Shawn sighed. "I'll try to talk her into it."

Wyatt nodded. "Ready to see her?"

"Let's do it," Shawn responded, squeezing Willa's hand.

"Perfect. Right this way."

They followed Wyatt into a room where Grams was asleep in a hospital bed, her right hand in a cast. Shawn quickly moved over to the side of the bed and grabbed her left hand, then pushed some hair out of her face.

"She must've fallen asleep," Wyatt said. "She was pretty exhausted when you brought her in, and the pain meds might have made her a bit drowsy. You can wait in here with her until she wakes up."

Shawn grabbed two chairs and pulled them up to her bed, gesturing for Willa to take a seat before shaking Wyatt's hand.

"Thanks, doc."

32

S ilence was their thing, Willa decided.

Even though they had a million things to talk about—even back when they barely knew each other—they could sit in comfortable silence for hours at a time.

But she needed to break it.

"Shawn?" she whispered.

He'd leaned back in his chair to lounge more comfortably, and he tipped his head toward her and grinned.

How could he be grinning at her when she'd caused a scene in the hospital and asked him to leave when her ex showed up?

"Thanks for being here," he said, grabbing her hand and squeezing it. "For showing up."

"I'm sorry I wasn't here sooner."

"S'okay," he said, his voice going deeper, more sullen.

"I know this isn't the best time to talk."

"Or maybe it is the best time. What else are we gonna do?"

She pulled her legs up underneath her on the chair and

squeezed Shawn's hand. "I'm sorry I asked you to leave. Leo is..."

Shawn's face hardened.

"I won't bury the lead. He asked me to sign an NDA, and I threw him out on his ass." Shawn's lips tipped up in a small, exasperated smile as she told him this. "Leo is a powerful man. A prideful one, too. If you'd done something —anything—to make him feel threatened, his attorneys would've taken you for all you were worth. I couldn't let that happen."

Shawn ran his hands through his hair, lips pressed together in thought.

"Every second he was there, I was wishing it was just the two of us again," Willa whispered. "We had the perfect night, and then he showed up and ruined it, and it was all my fault, and then when I got here and saw you—"

"Willa," Shawn said. "Slow down, baby. Nothing here is your fault."

He blew out a deep breath.

"I won't lie. It hurt when you asked me to leave. But now I understand why you did it."

Willa wrung her hands together. "I could tell you were going to follow through on your plan to punch him in the face."

Shawn smirked. "I hadn't gotten that far yet."

"He's gone now. I wish I could promise he was gone for good, but I don't know. He might show up again."

"If he shows up again, please let me stay with you," he said, leveling his eyes with hers. "I'll control my temper. But you don't have to deal with him alone."

"You're not... mad at me?"

"Of course not, Willa. He took us both by surprise. And I understand what was going through your head, now."

"What about... earlier?" Willa asked. "I'm sorry I assumed you and Hanna—"

"Consider it forgotten," he cut her off. "I meant what I said when I told you I'm all in. I'll do anything I can to earn your trust. And your trauma will show up sometimes. We have to work through it together."

Willa's heart melted.

Maybe that's what compelled her to say what she said next.

"I love you," she blurted out, then bit her lip and looked away.

She heard Shawn gasp and looked back at him. His mouth was agape. His eyes filled with wonder.

"I love you, too."

Willa's heart soared. "You love me?"

"Baby, I've loved you for weeks now. Just didn't want to scare you away. You are... everything. All I've ever wanted. All I've ever searched for. You're it for me."

"You love me." Willa said it again, as if she was trying to make it sink in.

She'd hoped, of course. Thought perhaps he shared her feelings. But she wasn't sure.

"I love you so much, Willa. I'll find you ten more jobs if you want. I'll bring you bait every night for the rest of our lives. I'll sneak Grams' brownies for you every time she makes them. I'll come to your yoga classes and take you on boat rides and carry you in from the car every time you get drunk and fall asleep on the drive home."

She chuckled, her eyes misting.

"Shawn," she breathed. "I'm still scared. But you make me less scared. You make me feel like everything is going to be okay. I love you. So much."

He tugged her into his lap. "Say it again."

"I love you," she whispered against his lips.

He claimed her mouth, pulling her in closer. The kiss didn't start off soft or uncertain—it was steady and sure. He pressed his lips against her, the feeling and power and gravity of the words they'd just exchanged behind every touch. His tongue tangled with hers, and she nipped at his lip. His hands wandered up her thigh, and she grabbed his cheeks with her hand, tugging his mouth, his face closer. She wove her fingers in his hair, taking the kiss deeper, and heat pooled in her core as she whimpered. She shifted in his lap, and he moaned, pressing into her.

Oh.

Oh.

He was fully erect against her, and they were barely 30 seconds into making out.

She *needed* him. Wanted to go find the nearest broom closet and drop to her knees, tug his pants down, and suck him so hard he still felt the force of her a week from now. Wanted to feel him press his fingers against her throbbing clit. Wanted to straddle him until she felt that growing bulge against her center.

His hand kept coming up higher, higher, higher...

Closer to where she needed him.

She whimpered.

"Shawn," she whispered against his lips. "We shouldn't... What if Grams wakes up?"

"I'm already awake."

Willa scrambled off of Shawn's lap and looked at Grams.

She was sitting alert in the bed, grinning from ear to ear, eyes ping-ponging between Willa and Shawn with deep satisfaction.

"You... how long—are you okay?" Willa spluttered.

"Damn it, Grams," Shawn said, grabbing her hand. "You scared the shit out of me."

"Watch your language, Scooby."

"Well, she's definitely alright," Shawn muttered under his breath as he locked eyes with Willa.

"I heard that," Grams said, then slid her eyes over to Willa. "So can I stop pretending I don't know about this now?"

Willa felt her cheeks redden. "Um..."

"What are you talking about, Grams?" Shawn said with a grin, crossing his arms.

"You two lovebirds is what I'm talking about!"

Shawn lifted a hand to her forehead. "Did you hit your head in the fall, too? Maybe I should call Dr. Wetherington back in here."

Willa covered her hand with her mouth and bit back a laugh as Grams swatted his hand away.

"Don't treat me like a senile old lady," she drawled. "I heard everything! You're in love with her and it's all thanks to me."

"And how do you figure that?" Shawn asked.

"I sent you over with those brownies," Grams said, crossing her arms. "I knew she'd never be able to say no to you after that."

"We're just friends, Grams. You know that. This fall really is making you see things."

Willa knew she needed to intervene.

But it was just too entertaining.

And she was still reeling from Grams waking up while she and Shawn were tangled up in each other like a couple of horny teenagers.

In the middle of a hospital, no less.

She might never recover from the embarrassment.

"Friends, my ass!"

"Language, Grams," Shawn said, looking stern but amused. "Can I get you some water?"

"I've been watching you two through my binoculars all summer. There's been some funny business going on!"

"Whatever you say, Grams."

"Now, listen here, Scoob—"

"It's true," Willa said softly, her face going hot. "We're together."

"Aha!" Grams said, pointing her hand with the broken wrist toward Willa in triumph, then grunting in pain.

"Dammit, Grams," Shawn said. "Are you okay?"

"That's what you get for lying to an old lady," she said between labored breaths. "I'll be fine. Just got too excited is all."

Willa slumped down in her chair and took a deep breath.

Grams knew.

Grams had known all along.

Because of course she had.

Willa wasn't all that surprised, but she knew it was time for Grams to know. For real. After she and Shawn had talked through everything tonight, she knew he really was all in. And she was, too.

"I'll take that water now, Scooby," Grams said weakly.

Shawn nodded, then glanced at Willa before speed walking out of the room.

"You can trust him, you know," Grams said softly to Willa after a moment.

Willa nodded with a sigh. "I know. Easier said than done. But I know."

"I've never seen that boy look at anything the way he

looks at you," Grams said, and Willa's lips tipped up in a shy smile. "Thank you, sweetie."

Willa felt her brow furrow. "For what?"

"For giving this old lady the gift of watching her grandson fall in love."

Willa grabbed Grams' hand. "Thanks for being the mastermind behind the whole thing."

Grams chuckled and sighed. "I don't know what I'm going to do with all the time on my hands now."

LIKE WYATT PROMISED, Grams was discharged the next morning with a prescription for some pain medication and the recommendation for her to get a walker.

She flat-out refused.

Shawn rolled his eyes as Grams refuted every one of Wyatt's arguments.

But he stopped at a Walmart on the way home and bought her the nicest walker he could find after treating her to lunch. She balked when she saw it, but he put his foot down.

"I love you, Grams, and I'll never regret moving in with you. It's been one of the best parts of my life. But I'll be damned if I come home and find you like that again. You don't have to use it all the time, but at the very least, use it when I'm gone. Give me some peace of mind. Please."

His voice broke at the tail-end of his practiced speech, and he could tell that's what pushed her over the edge.

She was reluctantly pushing it around the kitchen, putting on a show for him—a promise that she would use it if she needed to.

"The girls will be here soon," Willa said, and Shawn grinned.

Tucker offered to cook dinner for the family tonight. Grams was still recovering from her fall, but she insisted on inviting everyone over for what she called a "family dinner."

"I'm not dead yet, and your friends keep me young," she said, and that was that.

Willa invited Layla and Amanda, and Hanna and Tucker had showed up a half hour earlier with boxes of food Tucker had spent the day preparing. Willa was setting the table with Hanna, going back and forth about each other's jobs and how they ended up in Alabama.

The doorbell rang, and Amanda bustled in before anyone had the chance to answer it, with Layla right on her tail.

"Willaaaaa," she said as she walked in, dragging out the end of her name. "Where's your sexy neighbor? I need to ask him about his intentions."

Shawn chuckled to himself as he heard Willa mutter something about "nosy friends," before she engulfed the two of them in a hug.

"Alright, now, I made lemon bars and brownies," Grams said, wiping her hands on the apron. "They'll be done in about 20 minutes, so let's eat!"

Shawn led her to the table and pulled out her chair, everyone else following, conversations weaving throughout the group as everyone settled in. The table was set to perfection and littered with crab cakes, shrimp cocktail, fried grouper, a salad, and some of Tucker's famous french fries, among other things. It was all meant to be served family style, and Shawn's mouth watered at the thought of everything Tucker had carefully prepared.

As they started passing around plates, Shawn took in a deep breath and smiled to himself.

This.

This is the thing that had been missing for the past couple of years.

His community.

His friends.

His people.

His *girl.*

"You alright, baby?" Willa asked, resting a hand on his cheek.

He grabbed her hand and kissed her knuckles. "I'm perfect, love."

EPILOGUE
THREE MONTHS LATER

S hawn smelled the brownies before he even walked in the door. Pocketing his keys, he thumbed the house key to the Greene's place—the key Willa had given him shortly after they brought Grams home from the hospital.

"Honey, I'm home!" Shawn shouted as he toed off his boots in the foyer.

"'Bout time," Grams muttered from the kitchen, just loud enough for Shawn to hear her.

Willa's chuckle carried over to him as he followed the sound of their voices, and he leaned against the doorway. Willa was cleaning up the kitchen, a bit of flour smudged on her cheek as she wiped up the countertop. Grams was sitting on her walker, contentedly chatting with Willa about the latest drama in her knitting circle.

"So she brought this big, beautiful scarf to show off, but she forgot to take the tag off it," Grams said conspiratorially. "I called her out on it, of course. She can't knit worth a damn. And we're not going to let her pretend otherwise."

"Grams, why is Nancy Siders in your knitting circle to begin with?" Willa asked, biting back a laugh.

Shawn felt his lips stretch into a smile. His two girls, together—his heart could barely stand it.

"We don't say her name, and you know that," Grams said, heatedly. "And besides, we let the She-Devil in our knitting group because it's the nice thing to do. Plus, it provides us with entertainment."

"Is that so, Grams?" Shawn said, coming up behind Willa and wrapping his arms around her waist. "Hi, baby."

He kissed her on the cheek, and she leaned back into him. "Hi."

He reached over her shoulder for a brownie, which was sitting on a cooling rack. She swatted his hand.

"Um, that's not for you," Willa said sternly.

Shawn's jaw dropped. "Seriously?"

She pressed her lips together, holding back a laugh. "Seriously. They're for Layla. She's engaged."

"Engaged?" Shawn said. "I didn't even know she had a boyfriend."

"She didn't." Willa continued wiping down the counter, unbothered by Shawn's clear desire for more information.

"If you were home on time, you would've gotten the full story," Grams added, turning her nose up.

"I had to stop by Amos's to help him move a big branch that fell in his yard during the last storm!" Amos called him as soon as the shop closed to see if Shawn had a few minutes to spare to help him out.

"And that was very sweet of you, honey," Willa said. "But you still can't have a brownie."

"Layla won't even know I had one."

"But we will."

"I've trained you well, sweetie," Grams said, a smug smirk tugging at her lips as she stood up. "And now it's time for my nap. I trust you to guard the brownies."

Willa laughed and untied her apron. After putting it away, she wrapped her arms around Shawn's neck and tugged him in for a kiss.

"Did you have a good day?" she asked.

He nipped at her bottom lip. "It was a great day until my girl denied me a brownie."

Willa chuckled. "You have such little faith in me?"

She picked up a pile of washcloths, and underneath them sat a tupperware with a brownie inside. "I set this aside for you when Grams went to the bathroom."

"Oh my god, I love you," he laughed, then grabbed the tupperware from her hand, opened it, and shoved the brownie in his mouth. "Holy fuck, that's good."

"Glad you like it. It only took me asking her every day for the past two months for her to finally teach me the recipe."

"You should be honored," Shawn responded before swallowing his brownie. "She barely even shares that with family."

But Willa had become family over the last few months. They stayed at Grams' place most nights, ate dinner together every night, and fished off the wharf when the weather was nice. She and Grams still went on walks every morning, and Willa even started offering a few classes for seniors at the church. Grams, Mary, and even Nancy Siders were regulars.

"I'm honored," Willa said, leaning into him as he wrapped his arms around her lower back and tugged her closer.

He could get used to this—*wanted* to get used to this. He

knew Willa was his forever—and so did Grams. She'd pulled him aside a few weeks ago and given him her wedding ring.

"Grams," he'd told her, "we've barely been dating for six months. I can't—"

"When you know, you know, Scoob," she said. "Take your time, but don't take too long. I love that girl. I can't imagine anyone more perfect for you, and I'd like to see you get married in my lifetime."

"Grams, don't guilt-trip me."

"Why not? It works."

Shawn chuckled as he remembered the way she shoved the ring in his hand, and wondered if she'd be checking back in on him to see if he'd be popping the question anytime soon. He knew they both had things they needed to work on before they'd be ready to say "I do"—but Willa was his.

Forever.

One way or another.

THE END

$\backsim$

WANT MORE **of Shawn and Willa?** Get a bonus scene of Grams spying on them! She's up to her usual shenanigans and masterminding their entire relationship.

Download it here: https://www.vanessawilder.com/catch-and-release-bonus-scene

. . .

THANK you so much for reading Shawn and Willa's story! If you enjoyed it, I hope you'll consider leaving a review for *Catch and Release* on Amazon or Goodreads. Even just a short sentence can make a *huge* difference! Reviews help authors find new readers, and help other readers find new books to love!

ACKNOWLEDGMENTS

This is my debut novel, and it takes a village—so bear with me.

First and foremost, thank you, reader, for taking a chance on my book. It means more than I can ever adequately communicate that you made it this far.

To my editor, Sara. Thank you for enthusiastically offering to help me get this book edited and published. Thank you for your thoughtful feedback, for texting back and forth randomly for months, for brainstorming scenes, for thinking through the rest of the series, and for believing in me. Most importantly, thank you for encouraging me when I had to delay publishing to prioritize my health. I could not have done this without you, and I wouldn't want anyone else to be my editor. You helped me take this book from good to fucking awesome. You are a Godsend. A million times over, thank you.

To my amazing proofreaders, Krysten C. and Lee K.: Thank you for happily agreeing when I asked this of you, and for your kind, thoughtful feedback that made this book infinitely better.

To my beta team, Alexandria D., Andi E., Elizah C., Evan L., and Maggie Y.: Thank you for your time and your feedback.

Each of you brought unique insights, and I'm so grateful for how you helped shape this book.

To authors who generously answered my questions and helped me figure out what the heck I was doing: Andrea Anderson, Julie Olivia, and Neva Altaj. Thank you for being so generous with your time and expertise! (Go read their books!)

To the friends who encouraged and believed in me no matter what: Anna M., Bryan G., Jill H., Kimberly B., Lauren L., Maddie C., Nana A., Sami W., Sara S., Shuler S., Uraidah H. Thank you.

To the family who supported me: my mom, my brother, my cousins, my aunt Posey, and my grandparents. Thank you.

Nana and Papa: Thank you for always believing in me and asking how my writing is going. Thank you for reading this book and loving it, even though it had explicit sex scenes written by your granddaughter. Thank you for the memories I have on Perdido Bay and the home you cultivated there. I've lived in eight states and at least 15 homes, but yours has always been a constant—and it inspired the location of this novel. I love you both.

Wongani M.: Thank you for being my biggest supporter and encourager. You are my best friend and my platonic soulmate. I couldn't have done this without you. I love you dearly.

Andi E.: Thank you for encouraging me every step of the way, for reading my books and giving thoughtful feedback, and for holding space for me. You read my first book—one that will probably never see the light of day—and your notes helped me write an even better story this time around.

Alexandria D.: Thank you for being my cheerleader through every phase of my adulthood. Thank you for being patient and kind and gentle. Thank you for helping me fall in love with reading again, which ultimately led to me writing this book.

Chris H.: You are the older brother I never thought I needed. Thank you for encouraging me to write since I was 15 years old. Thank you for believing in me, for teaching me what it means to be a good storyteller, and for supporting me in every turn my life has taken.

Molly H.: For believing in me, for loving me, for your kindness and gentleness, and for challenging me in ways other people wouldn't. Thank you. I'll send you a version of this book with all the sex scenes blacked out.

Evan L.: What started as bonding over a shared love of reading has turned into one of my most meaningful, joyful friendships. Thank you for being nothing but thrilled for me when I told you I dreamed of being a writer. Thank you for letting me bounce ideas off you, for being a sounding board through this whole process, for reviewing silly little TikToks I made to promote this book, and most importantly, for believing in me before you'd even read a word I'd written. God knew what She was doing when She brought you into my life.

To my dad: I miss you every day. I wish you were here to see me pursue this dream. Thank you for reading Shakespeare to me when I was kid and nurturing a love for literature. I think you might be rolling in your grave at the spicy scenes in this book, but I know you'd also be proud.

Toto, Swiftie, and Alfred (my dog and cats, respectively): You can't read but I love you and I only work so you can have a better life. Thanks for hanging out with me when I was laboring away at my laptop.

Lastly, to my partner, Jon. For the late nights writing when you brought me tea, for the times I wanted to give up and you didn't let me, for the moments when I was afraid and you encouraged me, for the laborious journey you carried me through to get here—thank you. When I got so wrapped up in writing that I forgot to eat or shower or use the bathroom or step outside, you made sure I was taking care of myself. Thank you for reading this book and loving it so much that you immediately gave it a 5-star review on Goodreads and made a series of TikToks about it. I love romance novels because they are joyful and escapist, but also because I know a passionate, all-consuming love is possible. You show me that everyday. Thank you for choosing me. Thank you for all you sacrificed to support me getting here. Thank you for being you. Thank you for being mine. I love you.

ABOUT THE AUTHOR

Vanessa Wilder is a contemporary romance author who writes cozy love stories with R-rated spicy scenes and laugh-out-loud moments. When she's not writing, Vanessa is probably throwing elaborate parties, reading a book in one sitting, or sweet-talking her husband into watching The Vampire Diaries with her. She lives in Virginia with her pastor husband (the cool kind!), a dog, and two cats. Vanessa loves to hear from readers, so feel free to connect and reach out!

https://www.vanessawilder.com/

facebook.com/authorvanessawilder

instagram.com/authorvanessawilder

tiktok.com/@authorvanessawilder

Made in the USA
Middletown, DE
26 April 2024

53478547R00188